A NOVEL SET IN THE BACKDROP OF THE AUDIT PROFESSION

TICKING TIMES

An Accountant and a Gentleman

notionpress.com

A NOVEL SET IN THE BACKDROP OF THE AUDIT PROFESSION

TICKING TIMES

An Accountant and a Gentleman

V PATTABHI RAM

notionpress.com

Notion Press

Old No. 38, New No. 6

McNichols Road, Chetpet

Chennai - 600 031

First Published by Notion Press 2016

ISBN 978-93-5206-495-3

This is a work of fiction. Any resemblances to characters or situations is purely coincidental.

The Chartered Accounting Profession

In audit, a 'tick' is an abbreviated notation used on audit work papers to denote auditing actions taken.

Contents

Praise for Ticking Times

V Pattabhi Ram, known for his mesmerizing narrative skills, has rightly embarked upon fiction writing through this novel. With his inimitable story telling style he keeps the interest of the readers undiminished all through, till the finish. Keeping the chartered accountancy profession as the base in which his characters operate, he makes it meaningful even for lay readers to familiarize with certain essential but fundamental aspects unique to that field.

T.N. Manoharan, Non-Executive Chairman of Canara Bank & Past President of ICAI

A rags-to-riches story: a corporate saga; the life of Mike Mahi unfolds in this taut thriller in an unputdownable fashion. The story is set within the setting of the accounting and auditing profession, something which the author knows intimately. A great novel that keeps you hooked from start to finish.

Dinesh Gopalan, IIM-A; Finance Consultant, formerly CFO of Advinus Therapeutics, a Tata Company

A gripping novel with the accounting profession as a background: possibly, a first of its kind in the Indian scenario. A roller coaster ride that takes you along the journey of two ambitious CAs – detailing their journey through college, the inane but interesting world of internship, and also the various conflicts that life throws at them. There will be a lot of "Hey, I have experienced that" moments in the book. A must read for all CAs!!

Srinivasan Natarajan, CA Coach, Mumbai

There is a solid kernel of a story in the novel -- the story of two contrasting characters toughing it out in a very real world, their brushes against each other, and with 'law and morality', is a gripping tale. Choosing the profession of accounting as the field for the story is refreshing, offbeat, and engaging. The style of writing – crisp, short sentences and paragraphs makes for a racy reading.

Srikanth Meenakshi, Founder and Director at FundsIndia.com

Thanks to

Rahul Soni in New Delhi, for the initial manuscript critique.

Kanishka Gupta in New Delhi, for his sage pieces of advice.

Anuradha Ramani in the UAE and **Usha Ganapathy Subramanian** in Bengaluru for adding flesh and blood to the plot.

Achala Upendran in Hyderabad, for substantive editing.

Jana Pillay for copy editing.

Amrutha Lakshmi Sunku, Nithya Sharma, and Ramya Venkat in Chennai, **Lavanya Venkatesh** in Cochin, **Archana Sarat** in Mumbai, **Abraham C Mathews** in New Delhi, **Yeshwanth Ram and Adithya Sudharshan** in Coimbatore for their suggestions. **Hari Kumar and N Malaiselvan** for the constant support.

The whole team at Notion Press for their tireless efforts.

And of course, many more who would possibly be too embarrassed if I were to acknowledge them here!

Key Cast

PEOPLE:

- Mike Mahi: The son of a colliery worker rises to become the poster-boy and later the President of NICPA, the country's accounting regulator.
- Tejas Arya: India's top television anchor has a love-hate relationship with Mike Mahi.
- Tanya Roy: A psychologist with a heart of gold who understands the psyche of young students.
- Alka Varma: A partner in a Big Six firm, and later the star-witness.
- Cranco Doc: Mahi's man-Friday.
- Prof Muscles: The classy professor isn't beyond playing a subterfuge or two.
- Uncle Krishna: Retired criminal lawyer, now mentor.
- Jia Sharma: Once model, now Arya's wife.
- Kashyap Woraiyur: Prosecuting Attorney.
- Ramnath Parkar: Defense Attorney.
- Sheila Nair Talwar: A former actress with a strong intellect. Now a judge.
- David Kochar: Mahi's friend and campaign mate.
- Dina Iyengar: Intern.

FIRMS:

- Mike, Mahi & Associates: The CA firm with a queer comma that Mahi forms.
- Hunt & Smith: A 'Big Six' public accounting firm.

PART 1: NOW 2014

1. Prologue

YEAR: 2014
DATE: June 21
Saturday 10:30 p.m.
Mumbai

Seated in his glass-paneled corner office on the 24th floor of Express Towers, Mike Mahi reflected on the busy week ahead. He had read and reread, at least a hundred times, the contents of the slim folder that was now before him and he knew each word and every punctuation mark that appeared in it. Besides the national partners, whom he had briefly taken into confidence, only his two trusted lieutenants, Doc and Dina, knew the details.

A small but high profile team had worked on the document non-stop for the last fifteen days. They had been populating the spreadsheets, modifying the PowerPoint, and re-examining the big ideas. There had been no breaks, except for the occasional coffee. No sleep, except for catnaps. The team from the US was to arrive on Monday and Mahi would lead the discussion himself. There was no margin for error as there would be no second opportunity. It would be the most crucial meeting of his life.

Also on his "must-do" list for the week was the television interview that he had promised the *New Delhi Times* anchor; the guy had been shadowing him for months now. It was downright stupid of Mahi to have agreed to do it this week, but then he couldn't afford to get on the wrong side of the media. These guys could hurt you at unexpected times and it was good to humor them occasionally. Mahi's status as the czar of the accounting profession meant that he had to be doubly careful.

The last five years had been tumultuous for Mike Mahi. Breakfast in Chennai, lunch in Mumbai and dinner in Delhi had become a ritual when in India. Two days in London, two in Los

Angeles and three in Paris – that was how the weeks went by. These five years he had hardly met his wife. He had almost never seen his kids. On the few days that he came home, he would come in late in the night when the kids were asleep and leave early to catch the morning flight while they were still sleeping. Next Monday, he believed, should see the fulfillment of all those sacrifices.

He prayed, perhaps only for the second time in his life, that nothing go wrong. Once the week was out and this meet with the US Team went well, things would change dramatically over the coming year. After that, he could cut down on international travels and lobbying and focus on television appearances and speaking engagements. Life could cool down.

It was then that his private line, the one with the unlisted number, crackled to life, shattering the silence of the night. Only his executive assistant (EA), a couple of national partners and his wife had access to this number. It couldn't be his EA; she had taken the day off after having worked round the clock the last fifteen days. His wife had once called while he was in a meeting to tell him that their son was unwell. He had snapped, "You take him to the hospital; I will come later." After that, she had made it a point to never reach him in the office. It was too late in the night for any of the national partners to call. Who could it be?

Doc, widely regarded as Mahi's Man Friday, took the call in the anteroom. A perfectionist, he documented every scrap of conversation and every piece of evidence. The world therefore called him Doc.

"Mahi, a lady is insisting that she speak to you immediately."

Mahi was in no mood to talk to anyone. He said, "Not now, Doc."

"That's exactly what I told her. But she says if you knew who she was and if I didn't connect her, you would never forgive me. Her voice sounds familiar, but I can't place it, and she isn't giving me her name."

Mike blanched. Only one woman would speak like that. And that woman was not someone he wanted to talk to this week. What could she want at this time of the night? She must surely have a strong reason.

Mike Mahi could not have been more right. Alka Varma, Partner, Hunt & Smith, a Big Six public accounting firm, wouldn't call him at 10:30 p.m. merely to say hi to him.

Mahi's sixth sense, the one that could alert him to a crisis a mile away, had woken up. His heart raced and in every nerve he felt that this was going to be real, real bad news.

"Good evening, Alka." Mahi tried his best to keep the edge out of his voice. He wanted to stay focused for Monday's meeting and this was a painful distraction.

There were no preliminaries from the other side. No greeting. No "sorry for the late call." That was typical of Alka. She had no time for such pleasantries.

"Mahi, have you heard the news?"

"What news?"

"Boss, switch on *New Delhi Times*." Every public accounting firm of some size had television screens placed in the rooms of its honchos. And Mike Mahi ran one of India's largest public accounting firms, spanning countries and continents.

"What? *New Delhi Times*?"

"Yeah."

By then, Doc had punched 59 on the remote control, and the late night edition was just coming up. The words **BREAKING NEWS**, in big, bold red letters, flashed continuously.

Mike Mahi looked up, and his blood ran cold. **"Financial scandal hits Hindustan Bank."** Flash. Flash. **"Mike Mahi under the scanner."** The television anchor's face had come up on the radar. He was screaming in the way only he could, as though his bottom was on fire.

"A Rs 5,000 crore scandal has hit Hindustan Bank. CEO Rahul Mazumdar has stepped down. More heads are sure to roll. Reliable sources tell us that the bank's external auditors Mike, Mahi & Associates will be sacked. And this can knock the bottom out of the firm."

Mahi cursed.

He didn't give a fig about what the anchor was saying about his firm. If the guy had the details, and journalists invariably never did, the guy wouldn't be saying all this. Even if Mike Mahi lost Hindustan Bank, it wouldn't hurt the firm very much. It would shave off five percent of the top line, but the firm could manage it. But this story was sure to affect the outcome of Monday's meeting. It could harm the firm's reputation too and could not have come up at a worse time.

"Thanks a lot, Alka. I will not forget your call. I owe you one."

"Mike, just a minute. While the details aren't out in the public domain, they will soon be. Someone is singing to the press. I am told the cops are going to pick you up for questioning. Should you need any help, please let me know."

The warmth was genuine.

Mahi was touched. Alka didn't have to do all this. After all, both of them were running fiercely competing firms, insanely fighting for clients and for resources. Someone else in Alka's position might have rejoiced at Mahi's discomfort. Mahi wasn't even sure he would have acted the way Alka had acted if she was in his position.

"Thanks, Alka. I will remember that."

"Mike, I am sorry for getting your unlisted number from Tanya. Don't get upset with her. She actually refused. But I pushed her into it, telling her it was frighteningly important."

Tanya was Mahi's wife.

"No issues, Alka. Thanks for everything."

There was some consolation. At least the news would not be exploding at him via the morning paper. But first, he must reach out to that blessed anchor. Not the one who had been on television today, but the other guy, the one people called the 'award-winning' journalist. The man had promised that he wouldn't break the news until the meet with the US team was over. This was a breach of trust.

If the meeting went well, Mike Mahi would have an international affiliation with one of the top three audit firms globally, which would catapult his firm to prime position in India. It would take him ahead of Hunt & Smith, the firm where he had interned and where Alka Varma was now a partner. It would be a significant step forward in his ambition to make Mike, Mahi & Associates the world's number one player.

"Get me Tejas Arya," he told Dina.

Mahi's mind was racing. He knew about these so-called financial scandals. They either blew away or they could rapidly snowball into major catastrophes. Until he saw the morning paper or spoke to Tejas Arya, he wouldn't know what kind of press he would receive.

"Mahi, his mobile is switched off. He isn't in his office. Nor is he at his residence. No one seems to know where he is." Dina could anticipate his every need.

"Great," sighed Mahi.

OOO

YEAR: 2014
DATE: June 21
Saturday 10:30 p.m.
Mumbai

It was her second straight night at the Breach Candy Hospital.

Tanya Roy was of medium height and slight in build, with what some would call an angelic face that gave her a child-woman look. A psychologist by profession, she appeared a lot younger than her actual age of thirty-six. Dressed in a black cotton sari, her long luxurious hair thrown back, she sat in the lobby lost in Arthur Hailey's novel, *The Final Diagnosis*. She was amazed at the research that had gone into writing the book. "I should thank Rupa for asking me to read this!" she thought. Rupa was Mike Mahi's Executive Assistant, and was widely known as his 'shadow'.

At that very moment, a car came to a sudden halt. It had entered the hospital from the wrong gate. The security guard rushed forward saying, "Not this way. Not this way." A bald elderly man, seemingly in his late fifties, snapped, "EMERGENCY." Tanya decided she did not like the man. It may have been an emergency, but did he have to enter a building through its exit?

It was raining and the lights were dim. Another man, familiar looking, got down from the car. He was wearing a shawl and his face was partially covered. She wondered where she had seen him before. Despite trying hard, she could not place him. She was annoyed.

The security guard was still talking. "You can't park here. Take it to the parking slot please." The bald elderly man retorted, "I am a doctor. This is my car. It will stay parked here." Tanya's dislike increased. So what if he was a doctor? Shouldn't doctors respect rules, more so those framed by hospitals? She felt her anger rising.

It was then that she noticed her chief standing at the entrance. Hair disheveled, sloppily dressed, and wearing Kolhapuri slippers, he hardly looked like the much-worshipped genius he was. It took her breath away. Gosh! The Chief? The man hardly ever stirred out of the operation theater; and now he was waiting in attendance. It had to be a VIP encounter. And if so, who was the VIP? Was it the doctor? Or was it the familiar looking younger man?

"Damn it. Who is he?" She was now sure that she knew him. Suddenly, it hit her. "Goodness gracious. How could I have forgotten him?" She panicked. Clad in faded blue jeans and a sparkling white t-shirt, he was smiling. Not at her but at the Chief. There were only traces of his boyish looks of yore. But the smile was the same bewitching one she had seen years ago.

Yes! It was him. There was no doubt about it. But what was he doing in a hospital at this ungodly hour with a doctor in tow?

Tanya Roy did not know what to do. She just stood there like a statue as realization sank in.

He was Tejas Arya. The Tejas Arya.

OOO

PART 2: GROWING UP
1971–1994

2. Genesis of a Relationship

If Mike Mahi had decided to follow in the footsteps of his forefathers, he would have become another nameless worker with another identity number, working in another colliery, reporting for work at the sound of a siren, and returning home to the sound of the horn.

Ever since he could remember, Mahi would accompany his father to the workplace on the colliery's weekly payday. There he would stand glued at the sight of the foreman counting cash, handing it out to the workers, recording it in a notebook and getting their signatures.

Mahi's was a small family: Papa, Mamma and him. The house was smaller: a living room with space for just a worn-out sofa-cum-bed; a bedroom with an iron cot, and a few pillows carelessly strewn over it and a couple of trunks pushed under! The kitchen was tiny and Mamma spent most of her time cooking simple but tasty meals for her husband and for her son. Mahi's school was definitely beyond their means, but Senior wanted to give Junior a good education. Had Mamma gone to work, it would have helped. But Papa was too proud to allow that. Soon the family grew bigger when Mamma delivered twins, but they continued to live in the same house.

In school, Mahi scored in the range of seventy-to-eighty in most subjects. Not out of 100; out of 200! The science lab gave him the creeps. In the History class, he wondered why one should learn about Otto Von Bismarck and Count Cavour. Geography's focus on capitals, countries, continents, crops and oceans wasn't his idea of fun. Math was an exception. Here he scored centum, always. The teacher would write arithmetic puzzles on the reverse of the blackboard, swirl it around, and the students would have to call out the answer. Mahi was always the first to answer, and he was always right.

But it was sports that made Mahi's eyes dance.

Hockey was his first love. When he scored that incredible goal, dribbling solo from the center and won his school the state hockey title, the girls cheered in joy at his sheer elegance. His friends thought he would play for India one day. He was that good.

ooo

Mahi's father often worked long hours in the colliery, well beyond closing bell. Such extra hours counted as overtime and helped him bring home more money. Mahi knew which weeks were overtime because at the end of such weeks, Senior got sweets for the wife and kids.

Once in two months or so the family would go to the nearby theatre, occupy the less expensive seats, and watch movies. Mahi was seven years old when he saw *Sholay* and fell instantly in love with the blockbuster. He fancied himself as Gabbar Singh and would recite every dialogue, word for word. At the theatres Mahi learnt about social distinction: the rich on one side and the lower middle class on the other. Most of his friends bought high cost tickets. There were some sly remarks made by a few parents, but Mahi was too young to let it bother him.

On his tenth birthday, Mamma decided they should dine at the *Mama-Mia* restaurant. Senior was shocked. His legs wobbled and he stared at his wife. The Udupi restaurant, where they went occasionally, made a hole in his pocket; *Mama-Mia* would be a rip off. But Mahi was excited.

There Mamma ordered her usual one plate of idly, Papa had dosa and Mahi had his stomach's fill. After that Mahi said, "I will have an ice-cream."

Papa's heart sank. An ice cream would cost 20 percent of their bill. "Mahi, we will pick it up from the guy in the streets who pushes the ice cream cart."

"No Papa, let's eat here."

Mamma stared at Senior and then turning towards Mahi she said, "Okay Mahi, go ahead."

"Waiter, three ice-creams."

Now Mamma's nostrils flared up; she managed to control it and said under her breath, "Don't they teach you manners at school? Were you not told to say, 'please'? You should also say 'uncle', not 'waiter'. Understood?"

"Sorry, uncle. Sorry, three cups of ice-cream please." The waiter smiled. It was rare to see nice parents with a nice kid.

Senior told the waiter, "Sir, make it one ice-cream only." The waiter smiled again; their wardrobe told all, and he loved parents who sacrificed their comforts to provide luxuries for their kid. Mamma wouldn't eat the next two days. Cost reduction.

Soon the evening at *Mama Mia* almost turned out ugly.

A friend's mother walked away from the nearby table saying, "We can't occupy seats near that of a coolie." Senior was in work dress, he wasn't a coolie; but the office uniform and talking style indicated their strata in society. Mahi seethed but Mamma silenced him. His friend argued with his mother, with tears in his eyes. "Ma, he studies in my class." She had retorted, "Then you need to change Sections."

That night Mahi decided he would some day become rich and famous.

Soon one day the school announced they would be going on an excursion. "Mamma, I want to go. Each student is to contribute Rs 75." So saying, Mahi ran out to play. That week, Senior maneuvered to work two shifts on all seven days to fund the trip. A few months later, when the school decided to take kids for the New Delhi Asian Games, Mamma sold her only gold bangle to ensure Mahi didn't feel left out and that he too went.

ooo

At school, during the evenings, they played hockey; during lunch breaks and during monsoon, they played marbles.

If your marble fell within a palm's distance of your opponents' marble, you pocketed his marble. If it hit his marble, you picked an additional marble from him. There were other rules. If you joined a game, you couldn't leave while you were winning. You could leave if you were losing, or at the end of fifteen minutes, which was the duration of the game.

Slowly, an idea started forming in Mahi's mind.

Mamma would give him money to take the bus to school and back. Mahi would walk the four kilometers on the return and save the amount. Of course, he wouldn't return it to her. Over the weekend, he used the savings to buy marbles. Soon he started playing the game.

Some days he won, some days he lost: by the end of the first month, his initial capital of twenty marbles had grown to a hundred. In a pink colored book, he recorded these as "gains from playing". He kept a tally of his purchases, his wins, and his losses. It was his first exercise in bookkeeping.

Then he began lending marbles to those who had lost or who couldn't quickly buy new ones. He would loan them five marbles, and by sunset collect six. Each day's delay would entail payment of an extra marble. In his pink book, he recorded on the left the marbles given and on the right the marbles received. The additional marbles that he received for having loaned he called "gains from lending." To some, he loaned without seeking a "gain". Thus he built a reservoir of goodwill with people.

On weekends, he would make a summary of his gains and a list of the persons who still owed him marbles. When a borrower defaulted, Mahi would persevere to collect. He would even negotiate the quantum of "gain". And if the defaulter still dodged, Mahi put him on a blacklist in his notebook. Anyone on that list would receive no further marbles.

After some weeks, a few friends asked him whether he would lend and collect on their behalf, keeping their identity a secret. Mahi agreed on the condition that the gains would be shared equally. In his notebook, these were recorded as "gains from partnership." By the end of the term, his initial capital of twenty marbles had grown to 1147 through a combination of personally playing, lending, and partnering. It was his first exercise in entrepreneurship.

One day, it all came tumbling down.

ooo

Tejas Arya went to Stewart School, one of India's finest schools. At home, money was never an issue. His dad held a senior management position in a multinational corporation that paid him a salary, which you couldn't count but had to weigh. The Aryas were clear that their son must get the best education.

His teachers found him bright and hardworking, and at times a bit arrogant. He devoured history books like a hungry wolf. He was particularly fond of English. When the school announced its monthly magazine, he decided to write for it. He wrote a crisp piece on the ongoing Wimbledon championship and gave it for publication. The Editor, an Anglo-Indian, took one look at it and dismissively said, "We can't take it because it is not original."

Tejas was deeply hurt. He was a tennis buff. He knew the ranking of the top 100 players on the ATP circuit by heart. He could reel out the names of the champions at the All-England Lawn Tennis Championship from the year 1901. He could effortlessly pronounce the names of the Swiss and the Czech players.

He met the Editor and wanted to know how she could say he had copied the article. She told him that was not what she had meant. She said that Wimbledon was an event already well covered in the newspapers, and writing about it didn't add value to the readers. "Go find a story that has not been reported and write about it," she suggested.

The young Arya took it seriously.

ooo

It was around that time Tejas Arya heard about 'marbles'. He had scant respect for the silly game. In his home, playing marbles of the lose-and-pay variety was taboo. It was like playing cards for money: scandalous. He collected details about marble games in schools and wrote on how the game amounted to gambling, and about how some were lending and enticing others to become involved in it.

He wrote on how the addiction could affect studies and how when children grew up it could make them casino gamblers. He gave indications of the schools where this was happening. The article was well-written. The Editor approved the piece and had it published.

The State's Education Minister received a copy of the magazine in due course. He read the article on marbles. He spoke disapprovingly to the Collectors and asked them to confiscate marbles and stop the game in all schools.

Following the Minister's directive, Mahi's school reprimanded him and formally banned the game. His class teacher was particularly angry because Mahi was her ward. One day in the Geography class, she asked him, "What is the capital of Ghana?" Mahi was silent. Jia Sharma, a tall girl, who was two rows behind, hissed an answer. Promptly, Mahi said, "Miss, Adis Ababa." The teacher was livid. "You fool. You good-for-nothing-lad. You play marbles. You bring shame to the school. You are fit only to play that stupid game. Now get up on the chair."

The teacher turned towards the map to explain the capitals of other countries. A hurt Mahi threw the only marble he had at Jia. She saw it coming, stretched her hand to stop it from crashing into her face. In the process, she caught the marble and dropped it. As she bent to pick it, the teacher turned, and saw her with the marble. Furious that marbles were still around, the teacher walked to the girl and tweaked her ear hard.

As Jia brought her hand to her ear in defense, the teacher dragged the girl to the front of the class and made her kneel.

Tears started pouring down Jia's face as she rubbed her throbbing ear. The teacher tweaked and shook her other ear. Mahi looked at the girl in contempt. As he watched her kneel, a strange feeling overcame him. He didn't like the feeling. That night he dreamt of the teacher and of the tall girl. The following day when he narrated it to his cousin, his cousin told him that he had now graduated from being a boy to being a man.

Three days later, Tejas Arya was all over Page 1 of the local newspaper.

Mike Mahi had been the biggest loser. He lived some 350 kilometers away from Tejas Arya. He didn't read the papers. But word had spread about why the school had called off the game. His first business had gone down, and like any other businessman, he felt shattered. He promptly started to dislike Tejas Arya, although the two had never met and were unlikely to meet any time soon. He told himself that one day he would extract his pound of marbles from Arya.

Tejas 1: Mahi 0

That night Mahi cried and prayed that Tejas should roast in hell.

ooo

When the Class XII results were announced and Mahi had scored an average grade, Papa asked, "So when are you going to join the colliery?" Mahi responded, "Papa, I want to pursue a college degree." His father paused for what appeared to be an eternity and then said, "But I thought you had always wanted to work in the colliery."

"No Papa, it was you who always thought that I would work there," said Mahi perfunctorily.

"What will you gain with a college degree?" asked Papa, stumped at his son's hidden aspiration.

"I want to become a CA. There are no entrance tests. The course doesn't cost much. They also pay a stipend." There was a certain sense of finality to Mahi's decision.

"And where do you intend to pursue your graduation and later CA?"

"I will study at St. Anne's and will do my internship with Hunt & Smith, Papa."

There was a creaking sound as Papa slumped on his chair. St. Anne's was a top college of commerce and with his grades Mahi did not even have a chance of taking a peep inside the college. And Hunt & Smith was a top public accounting firm that audited the colliery. His father couldn't understand how his son would make it. Only the big people, the sahibs, worked there. But the very thought of Mahi wanting to intern there brought a smile to his father's face. He knew that if his son set his mind to something, he would achieve that something.

Surely his son was destined for better things than to work with him at Rampur Collieries. After all, he was born on December 16, 1971, the day the Pakistan forces surrendered to the Indian Army after their defeat in the Liberation war.

3. Mahi gets into St. Anne's

Mahi arrived at St. Anne's in New Delhi at a time when admissions were closing. The last date for applications was over. He hadn't applied because he hadn't heard about the college at all. Just recently someone had hinted to him how St. Anne's was the 'happening' place for anyone who wanted to do CA. That very day he had spoken to his father and two days later he was on the train to New Delhi.

He knew he was late, but there was still a chance, an incredibly long shot that he might get in. It was risky but Mahi was more than willing to take that risk.

He walked into college in outsized trousers that could accommodate another Mahi. They ended well above his ankles, as though he was getting ready to walk through floodwater. Rose petals were printed on his full-sleeved terylene shirt. The golf cap on his head was pointed in the northwestern direction and his dark glasses completed his *tapori* look. A large bag hung from his shoulders.

Mahi asked for Dr. Mukherjee, the Sports coach, and was directed to his crowded office. Mukherjee was interacting with two or three boys at a time. Mahi stood unobtrusively in one corner, waiting for the numbers to subside so that he could get the uninterrupted attention of the coach.

Ninety minutes later, he caught Mukherjee's attention. The coach said, "I notice that you have been here for a long time. What do you want?"

"Sir, I want to play hockey for the college."

"Well, if you have played hockey before, and if you want to play hockey for the college, please turn up at the ground next week when the trials for the seniors will be held. If you are a fresher, turn up a fortnight later." The coach seemed miffed at the young man not having seen the announcements on the notice board outside. "These young ones dress like clowns and don't apply their brains," he muttered.

"Sir, I have a problem: I have not been admitted to the college yet. And I have not filled in my application form."

The coach was now fuming. How could someone who had not even sent in his application want to play for the college? In clear, unequivocal terms, in a language Mahi understood, he asked him to, "Get lost." Mahi tried his very best, even suggesting that he could perhaps be considered in the sports quota against someone who had opted out.

"No one in his right mind would opt out of this college," thundered Mukherjee, banging his fist on the table. Cooling himself, he muttered, "One blow and this loafer will be thrown ten feet away, and out of the office."

"But, Sir, there must be, there must be, some way out."

"That's the way out," said Mukherjee, pointing to the exit, his hands quivering.

ooo

A day later, the college alumni played a friendly match against the college's hockey team. A biannual feature meant to celebrate bonhomie, the players and spectators of this match, nevertheless, took the game seriously. While the college boys were mostly in their teens, the average age of the alumni would be the late thirties. In the last two decades, the alumni had never won a match even when the collegians played a relaxed game. It was not for want of trying; it was because St. Anne's boasted of some outstanding players.

The packed stadium had just settled down when, in the fourth minute, the alumni went into the lead. Three minutes later they went two up. Soon all hell broke loose. In the tenth minute, a pale, poker-faced lad, playing right wing, picked a long pass from the center forward, ran solo dribbling his way past onrushing defenders, and upon entering the opponents' D majestically scooped the ball to the center forward who slammed it in, 3-0.

The audience was stunned not just at the sheer magic of the boy's game, but also his total selflessness in passing the ball when he could have himself taken a shot at the goal. The college team now realized that they were up against tough opposition.

In the fourteenth minute, a harsh tackle meant the alumni would take a penalty shot. The captain tossed the ball to the lad. Given the posture that he took, and the way he whisked his stick, everyone, including the goalkeeper, knew the ball would swish to the right of the shooter. So, the goalkeeper dived to his left and the ball banged the board to his far right! The ball had in the very last second made a beautiful swirl.

There was delirium in the stands. The crowd had seen nothing of this kind before. They were whistling wildly, very sure an upset was on the cards. They weren't wrong. By the time the hooter went for halftime, the alumni were leading 6-3 with the lad having scored a hat trick.

The second half was tantalizing. The packed stadium sat on the edge of its seat as the boy wonder was seen all over the field. Now attacking, occasionally defending, but always playing total hockey. It seemed as though the ball followed him everywhere. And at times, it looked like it was glued to his stick. By the time the seventy-minute game was over, the alumni had pumped in eleven goals and conceded five. Yes, 11-5 is what the score-line read. No one had ever seen such a massacre of the college team. The boy became an instant hero.

ooo

Watching the game, Coach Mukherjee was disturbed. The current team being drubbed by the oldies was a serious cause for concern. More disturbing was his inability to place the champion player. He couldn't remember when this boy had graduated from St. Anne's. He was sure he had never represented the college hockey team. And the portly Mukherjee had been the coach for the last twenty-five years and knew every player by his first name. How could St. Anne's have missed out on such prodigious talent? To make things worse, the boy's face looked so familiar.

The game over, Mukherjee walked up to him. The captain was beside the lad.

The captain dropped a bomb: "Sir, I must apologize to you. This is Mike Mahi. You have seen him play. He is not our alumnus. He hasn't also applied to the college. I understand he met you yesterday. We must get him into our college. And we must get him into the team." Mukherjee was scandalized. His face was red hot. How, how, how could someone do this? How could he play in the alumni team when he had never studied here? How could the captain allow it? He was angry both with Mahi and with the captain. Controlling himself he asked, "How could you allow this?"

The captain patiently explained: "Sir, one of our players couldn't reach on time because his bike got a flat tyre. Another player began vomiting as soon as he reached the venue. A third said he could play only the first half. Here was this boy with a hockey stick in his hand and who said he could, if we wanted, play for us. Since, this was a friendly tie, I thought he could."

Mukherjee sobered down. He realized Mahi would be star material. "But this has never happened before. Our admissions are closed. The Principal will not allow this."

"Dr. Mukherjee, what if there is no precedent? Let's create a precedent. If you really like this boy's game, you should speak to the Principal. Trust me, and I don't have to tell you this, Mike Mahi will play for India one day."

The coach had no doubt about that. He promised he would do his very best.

That was how Mike Mahi, the man who later aspired to become the president of NICPA, the country's accounting regulator, got into St. Anne's. Through the sports quota, because someone somewhere had a flat tyre. The year was 1988. A year later, a milky faced, curly haired sixteen-year-old, would hit the reigning king of leg spin for four sixes in an over, to announce his arrival in the world of international cricket.

4. Tejas Decides

YEAR: 2014
DATE: June 22
Sunday 0630 hours
Mumbai

The hurried discussion with the doctor the previous night was not what was uppermost in his mind as Tejas Arya collected his boarding card at the Chhatrapati Shivaji International Airport, walked past immigration, and awaited the departure call. Something equally disappointing had happened.

It was there on Page 1 of today's *New Delhi Times*, screaming in bold banner headlines. **"Financial scandal hits Hindustan Bank. Mike Mahi under the scanner."**

"A Rs 5,000 crore scandal has hit Hindustan Bank. CEO Rahul Mazumdar has stepped down. More heads are sure to roll. Reliable sources tell us that the bank's external auditors Mike, Mahi & Associates will be sacked."

Reports on scandalous deals and subterfuges at Hindustan Bank followed. The bank had grown huge in the last few years. True, it was so large and so interconnected that its failure could be disastrous to the economy, but there were too many of scams happening at the bank that it needed to be exposed.

New Delhi Times was India's largest circulated newspaper and part of the media group to which the television channel by the same name *New Delhi Times* belonged.

Tejas Arya was worried that his college classmate, Mike Mahi, who had done his CA internship in the same firm as him, was in trouble. Whether Mahi would be the center of the storm or would only suffer collateral damage did not matter. In either case, the bottom would fall from the accounting profession of which Mike Mahi was the undisputed poster boy.

As he boarded the flight, Arya's mind went back in time. He remembered his joining St. Anne's, and how Mahi and he shared different visions of the world, which meant they would always have a love-hate relationship. But he believed that in the balance sheet of life, Mahi had more assets than liabilities, at least when he was in college.

ooo

It wasn't that Tejas Arya had always wanted to be a CA.

As a kid, he had wanted to become a traffic policeman. He had once watched a policeman put up his hand to stop the Prime Minister's convoy. If a cop could be that influential, Tejas told himself, he would like to be one. But that desire didn't last long and soon he changed his mind.

The change had to do with his visiting Bombay on an annual holiday. There he saw skyscrapers dotting Marine drive, and that's when he started dreaming of constructing posh and plush hundred-storey buildings. In those dreams, builders, like factory workers, would work in three shifts. He would employ hundreds of top professionals to man key slots such as structural designing, interior decoration, liaison, etc. For the next year, whenever and wherever he saw old buildings, he thought about how to raze them and replace them with skyscrapers. He started reading about legendary architects like Charles Correa and Jack Masters.

Later, when he went into Class VIII, Tejas visited Uncle Krishna, a criminal lawyer and a family friend. A veteran lawyer, Krishna Iyer, B.A LLB, had once successfully defended a top cabinet minister in a murder case that had sex and sleaze written all over it. In another instance, he had saved a paramour from what the public thought would be a definitive sentence of "hanged until dead." Even today, top lawyers flocked to him for advice.

Tejas ransacked Uncle Krishna's library and poured himself into Erle Stanley Gardner's stories about Perry Mason. Mason's courtroom pyrotechnics touched a chord. Tejas told himself that when he grew up he would become a crack lawyer with a smart secretary like Della Street. An ace debater in school, he thought courtroom drama would be like another inter-school debate! Krishna narrated many a courtroom story from legal folklore. Tejas loved them.

The dream of becoming a civil engineer vanished into thin air.

When he came to Class X, Tejas read *The Citadel* and instantly wanted to become a doctor. A J Cronin's poignant story of a young doctor, fresh out of medical school, going out to a distant land wanting to play God, but slowly realizing how the profession had its feet of clay, made his eyes grow moist. As a doctor, he would change the medical fraternity, he told himself with childlike self-belief.

From traffic constable to civil engineer to lawyer to doctor, his dreams had been volatile. Then one fine day, he decided that his heart lay in the world of finance and so decided to join CA. His mother was aghast. She felt let down. Why on God's earth should her son want to be a lowly *munimji*? Oh, what a waste of extraordinary talent!

"Mom, the world of investment banking is very different from the world of accounting. Financial analysis appeals to me."

She didn't bother to ask how he had discovered that appeal. Instead, she said, "Thank God Mario Puzo's *Godfather* hasn't made an impression on you." Tejas did not miss the subtle humor. "Well Mom, the accounting world's gain is the underworld's loss."

ooo

The pilot was speaking in the clipped garbled accent that his breed had so wonderfully patented. "Ladies and gentlemen, boys and girls, this is your captain speaking. We are now flying at an altitude of 30,000 feet above sea level, the weather outside is ..."

Tejas Arya's mind drifted to his Class XII exams. That was the gateway to a prestigious college and later to a leading audit firm.

The pressure was immense. An outstanding student, Tejas was expected to score high. Worse still, his elder brother had finished all-India first three summers ago and everyone thought that it was in the natural scheme of things that Tejas would emulate his brother. His headmaster increased his misery by remarking, "The world recognizes only the winners."

Tejas knew he had to do very well if he were to get into St. Anne's College, the country's top college for Commerce. He studied hard, sometimes working long into the night. Once his mother remarked that it was okay if he didn't get into St. Anne's. Tejas had nonchalantly replied, "Mom, India's top class anchors do not come from any other college."

It was the first time the family realized their son harbored ambitions of being a journalist. Dad and Mom abhorred the media, albeit for different reasons. They knew their son would outgrow this infatuation like he had his earlier desires to be a civil engineer, later a lawyer, then a doctor, and finally an investment manager.

The Board exams came and went. Tejas believed he had given them his best shot. He felt thankful to his school for the dummy tests they had held.

Waiting for the results was like a prolonged nightmare. He saw himself solving accounting problems in his dreams. Sometimes, he imagined that he had missed the college cut off by one mark. He woke up sweating most of the time.

There was also the matter of his parents' prestige. Wouldn't they be embarrassed if he didn't make it to St. Anne's?

That was the time mom put him into a typewriting class, and he learned how the QWERTY keyboard was used. In later years, he would thank her because his knowledge of typewriting helped him immensely in his profession.

Soon the D-day came. There was both jubilation and disappointment. Jubilation, because he topped the school, disappointment because his marks would not fetch him national honors; they wouldn't get him an All-India rank. Such a rank would have given him direct entry into St. Anne's. Now he would have to go through the qualifying examinations. Unlike Wimbledon, there was no provision for a wild-card entry.

For the first time in his life, tears trickled down his cheeks. No, he wasn't crying copiously. Many years ago his dad had told him that men don't make a public display of their private feelings. That day, he resolved that he would set the matter of missing a national rank right by bagging one in his CA.

His parents were thrilled with their son's performance. They took him to dinner in a restaurant at a five-star hotel. They were greeted at the entrance and guided into the hotel. Tejas was bowled over. Pretty women were sitting at the reception, continuously answering calls and attending to the guests. What a lobby. "604," the dining room, was grander. Wow, what an eye-popping spread. Tejas had not seen so many dishes in one shot, cooked for one meal. It was an unforgettable night. Despite their wealth, the Aryas never believed in being ostentatious. "One day, I will frequent these hotels," he resolved.

Ten days later came the news that the entrance test for St. Anne's had been advanced by a fortnight. It upset Tejas. He wouldn't get a confirmed train ticket. And he had never traveled unreserved. He couldn't have taken a flight because, in the late eighties, Indian cities weren't well connected.

When he left home that day, his mom was very emotional. "Try to be a nice guy in college. Help others with their academics. Don't slack off. If there is competition, fight it. If you are your own competition, so be it." She had taken it for granted that he would be accepted into St. Anne's.

His dad and his dad's friend came to the station to put him on the train.

The train would halt for ten minutes. In that time, they would have to convince the ticket examiner (TTE) and get a confirmed ticket. When the train arrived, his dad's friend rushed up to the TTE and said, "Sir, I need a reserved seat."

The ticket examiner looked over his spectacles. "Does it look like you can get a ticket here? The train's overflowing."

"I'll pay you triple the ticket price. Please."

The TTE was saying, "Look at my shirt pocket. It's full of money. Even if I wanted to I couldn't accommodate all of these people. So don't waste your efforts and money."

Tejas got into a jam-packed unreserved coach. He sat on his baggage at the entrance to the compartment, adjacent to the loo. He looked at his dad, the unasked question being, "Dad, do I have to travel this way?"

His father remarked, "Top journalists have to undergo any hardship to meet their goals." Shakti Arya never gave a straight answer. Tejas loved him for that. He got the message: he had to travel, come hell or high water. To Tejas, it was an important realization. He realized that in the eyes of his father, he had grown up.

Soon the train was merrily chugging along at 70 kilometers per hour. The door of the compartment was ajar. The chill breeze caressed his face a bit too strongly. But the darkness of the night had its own charm. He hoped that halfway into the journey he would be able to sit in a more comfortable place. How wrong he was. He traveled the full distance to New Delhi sitting on his baggage at the entrance to the compartment. He didn't budge one inch for fear of losing that seat. When he reached Delhi, he was thoroughly drained.

Uncle Krishna was at the station to receive him. "Hey, so you have finally decided not to take up a career in criminal law," he said.

"A small correction, Uncle. I have decided not to take up a career in crime."

Krishna smiled.

Once they reached the house, Tejas jumped out of the car, leaving the chauffeur to manage the luggage. He ran from the gate to the entrance and began climbing the steps two at a time, screaming, "Seetha Aunty, I have come, Seetha Aunty I have come!" As the cherubic lady smiled at the sight of her friend's child, she realized how much he had grown. He rushed to hug her, and she ducked, "Idiot, you are stinking like a pig. Go take a bath."

Fifteen minutes later Tejas emerged from the bathtub, properly toweled, spick and span. In brand new shorts and a clean shirt, he yelled, "Aunty, I am hungry." He dived into the food bowl, helped himself to rice and fish curry. Tears of joy flooded her eyes as the matronly Seetha watched the little one she called 'my nephew' attack his food, screaming "Yummy, Aunty, Yummy."

That done, Tejas announced he was going to sleep. After a good bath and an excellent dinner came the comfort of a soft mattress. Ah, the smell of fresh linen, the chill of an air-conditioner, the comfort of a soft mattress and the pleasure of a blanket!

He slept like a new-born for the next twelve hours.

5. Getting into St. Anne's

YEAR: 1988
MONTH: May
New Delhi

On the morning of the entrance test, Tejas took an early bus to St. Anne's. He arrived well ahead of time, stretched, talked to no one and then took his seat in the exam hall fifteen minutes before time.

He closed his eyes, silently recited his school prayer, and when the invigilator tapped and handed the booklet to him, he carefully slit it open with a paper knife. Lovely questions in Economics stared at him.

If you are the tenth person to get a house for rent in a new town, will you be paying more, or less, or same rent as the ninth person? Name the economic principle involved.

I give you a pair of scissors. Which economist's name comes to your mind, and what was the relevant principle he propounded?

There were strong accounting problems, including those that involved the celebrated case of *Garner vs. Murray* followed by some math quickies that needed knowledge of algebra. A series of questions on English comprehension and a quiz on national affairs completed the test. After answering the mandatory 150 questions, Tejas walked out happy. He now had four hours to kill before the results.

A kilometer or so away, *Qayamat Se Qayamat Tak*, a new movie starring a promising debutant actor, Aamir Khan, and a former Miss India, Juhi Chawla, was playing. Tejas had never been to a movie alone, but this time he made an exception. There was no point going home and then coming back for the results. He enjoyed the film and told himself that this new actor would go a long way in Bollywood!

It was 5 p.m. when he re-entered the 100-acre campus. In the morning, he had been too tense to really pay attention to it. But now it was different. The building had a historic feel to it. There were separate playgrounds for cricket, hockey, and football. There were signposts pointing towards indoor stadiums for squash, basketball, badminton and table tennis. As he ambled forward, kicking an imaginary can of Coke, he noticed the giant church to his right. Tejas knew, deep down, that he would study here. Suddenly people were screaming that the results of the entrance test had been declared. His heart was in his mouth as he rushed towards the notice board.

Ten thousand people from across the country had applied for the three hundred B.Com seats. Of this 5,000 had been short-listed for the test on the basis of their performance in the Board exams, referral notes from their school heads and co-curricular activity track record. From this test, the top five hundred would make the grade for personal interview. At that interview, two hundred would be denied admission, and three hundred would make the cut.

There were multiple queues and the results were put up on several boards to ease the crowd. As the candidates walked up to the notice board with hope in their eyes, there were varying reactions. "Oh. Wow. Wow". "Congrats." "Great." "Bravo." And some back slapping. They were the ones who had been cleared for the next level. Then there were one-word curses. "Shit." "Sucks." "Bloody hell." Shouts of disappointment; they were from those who hadn't made the cut. A group of girls sat with their hands over their faces.

One boy was completely in tears. The lady accompanying him, probably his mother, had to console him. Tejas heard her saying, "*Beta*, this is not the end of the world. You can get into a B.Com course in some other college."

Five minutes later, Tejas had reached the notice board. For a few seconds, he closed his eyes and prayed. In those few seconds, he told himself that whatever the result, he would keep his emotions in check. The queue behind him was getting edgy. He had to quickly scan his results and move. He opened his eyes and let them run down the list. The numbers of the selected candidates were in ascending order.

His number was 1984. He suddenly realized the number matched the Orwellian year! For a moment he panicked. How absurd. Tejas, the rationalist, the one who was never superstitious, was suddenly turning superstitious. 1981 was on the list. So was 1982. Ditto for 1983. Would 1984 be the next? What would be the probability? Then something inside him said, "Why are you panicking? Look down." Well, as he looked he found nothing. It was the end of that page. So he turned right to look into the next page. The next number read 3 6 5 0. Oh God, he had lost out.

He almost slumped in disappointment. But something within him asked whether it was possible for 1700 people, one fell swoop, to not make the grade. Between 1983 and 3650, no one was on the list. Impossible. There must be some mistake. He was clinging to every possible straw. He looked down at the page number. The page number, where 1983 had appeared, was 3; the page number, where 3650 appeared, was 5. Oh, where was page 4? Ha, it had been posted to the right of page 5. It was a terrible error by some lowly clerk in the college. His hope was back.

Tejas had to look at the first number on page 4. Would it be there? Appearing first in the first column were the magical figures 1…9…8…4. He had made it to the next round. Despite his earlier decision to stay poker-faced, a ghost of a smile crossed his face. He was beside himself with joy. He wanted to jump and dance. He couldn't wait to place the long distance call to tell his parents the good news. He knew that they would be delighted.

The interviews were scheduled for 8 a.m. the following day. They would be over by 4 o'clock in the evening. Five hundred students would be interviewed in eight hours' time. How would they decide in such a short span? Would they just toss a coin?

If Tejas had known that he would actually be interviewed for less than three minutes, his heart would have sunk.

ooo

He was called in at 11 a.m. the next morning. "Good morning," he said to the panel.

"So, you are Tejas?" a panelist asked.

"Yes, Sir."

"Tejas, do you have a girlfriend?"

His eyes almost popped out of his face. What had this to do with getting into B.Com? "Sir, what do you mean by a girlfriend?"

"Don't tell me you don't know what a girlfriend is."

"Sir, I do. But what is it that you mean? A girl who is a friend? Or a friend who is a girl?"

"Now, what's the difference, son?"

"Sir, a girl-who-is-a-friend means: She is a girl. Therefore, she is my friend. A friend-who-is-a-girl means: She is a friend. She happens to be a girl."

A panelist stood up and shook hands with Tejas, indicating that the interview was over. Tejas couldn't believe it. Had he blown his chance? Okay, if they didn't admit him so be it: they were the losers.

The suspense ended the following morning. The postman brought a letter from St. Anne's. Tejas slit the brown cover with trepidation.

He had been admitted to the B.Com class at St. Anne's.

6. Inside St. Anne's – 1

Getting into St. Anne's was one thing. Shining there was another. Each of the hundred students in Tejas's class had an impressive background. They were strong in academics, great in sports and good at most co-curricular activities. To win here, you had to stretch yourself. Tejas was willing to do it.

On Day 1, popularly known as Freshman's day, the newcomers were asked to assemble at Sydenham Hall. It was a huge auditorium that could easily accommodate up to 2,000 students. This hall, his seniors told him, would be the place where he would have to take most of his tests in the months to come. There wasn't a single vacant seat. Boys and girls from all classes – Commerce, Science, and Humanities -- had turned up. The boys looked good in their outfits, ranging from t-shirt and jeans to colorful sherwanis. The girls wore either jeans or the conventional salwar kameez, some from the south wore the half sari and some of the more elegant ones wore the traditional sari. The freshness of youth was in the air! It was a sight to behold.

At 5:30 p.m. a solemn procession of poker-faced men walked onto the dais. Moments later, the traditional lamp, was lit. Why an out-and-out Catholic institution, which wore its religion on its sleeve, should do a traditional Hindu ritual was something Tejas couldn't fathom. Someday he would have to find out, he told himself.

At 5:45 p.m., the Rector began to speak. His address was a cross between a pep talk and a nanny's nag.

"Boys and girls, you have gone through one of the toughest selection processes in the country to be here at St. Anne's. You are lucky. God has answered your prayers. But remember, this is only the base camp. There is a long trek ahead. While the path will be arduous, the journey will be exciting. If you do well here, your life will be made.

"Two of India's prime ministers, one of India's presidents and three of India's finance ministers, were alumni of St. Anne's. Some of the country's top cops have gone through the portals of this great institution. Many a business icon graduated from St. Anne's. Three of the country's greatest cricketers and two of India's best hockey stars studied here. A few of America's top professors and business consultants learned their basics at St. Anne's. They have all left an indelible mark on their profession.

"Like them, each one of you should leave footprints on the sands of time."

Tejas was moved. He told himself that he would make St. Anne's proud. One day the Rector would have to name Tejas in his annual freshman's address. And he knew what the Rector would say about him. "Tejas Arya, one of India's foremost public accountants, respected and admired throughout the world of journalism, learned his fundamentals here at St. Anne's!"

Seated four rows behind him, Mike Mahi was telling himself what the Rector would say about him. "Mike Mahi rose from the coal pits to first become the poster boy and later the president of the accounting profession. Mahi, boys and girls, studied at St. Anne's."

The nanny's nag came from that point onwards.

Do this. Don't do that. Study well. This is the best time of your lives. Don't wear jeans to college. Don't wear t-shirts. Don't make noise in the classrooms. Take tests. If you bunk them, you will be reported and fined. Blah … Blah …. Blah …

Soon the Rector's address was completed; after another half an hour of homilies by the great souls who had parked themselves on the dais, the program was over.

The following day was the first day in the classroom. The Head of the Commerce Department handled the first session. It was a general session detailing how, as an autonomous college, St. Anne's would add value to its alumni. He talked about the course content, the subjects to be studied in the first semester, the grading scheme, and why the students should also focus on sports and co-curricular activities, why this and why that.

It was a warming up session. Pens raced across notebooks.

Two days later, Tejas Arya got the first hint of the kind of competition that he would be up against.

OOO

That day, Day 3, an elderly gentleman walked into the classroom. He wore a dangling full sleeve shirt, unbuttoned at the cufflinks. The shirt wasn't tucked into his loose-fitting black trousers. He had long, unkempt, oily hair that required combing. He weighed not more than fifty kilograms, was pale, puny, and wore a hungry look. If someone had thought that the elderly man had just walked out of the Intensive Care Unit of a hospital, he could be forgiven. With a duster in one hand and a bundle of chalk pieces in the other, he marched in. No one could mistake him for a student. He had to be a teacher.

"Hey folks," said the man. "I have forgotten my name."

What an opening gambit. He looked lost. "Is he Albert Einstein?" wondered Tejas.

"Look, for ages, students at St. Anne's have called me Professor Muscles, and so I shall be Professor Muscles to all of you."

Wow! To call this man Muscles required a good sense of humor. Tejas couldn't help but smile.

Prof Muscles would be handling the paper titled "Commerce". At a time when garbage cleaners called themselves sanitation engineers, this paper definitely warranted a sexier name.

The class giggled at the sight of Muscles and at his "I-have-forgotten-my- name" crack. A girl in the middle row asked, "Is this man going to teach us commerce?" She sounded concerned.

But the moment Muscles started speaking, the concern vanished. The class sat at the edge of its seat. The man was awesome. He spoke about commerce and about money. He talked about the origin of trade and of barter. He said that, but for being the medium of exchange, money wasn't worth the paper on which it was printed. The talk was mesmerizing. Tejas was beginning to understand why people craved to be in St. Anne's. In comparison, the teaching at his school was pedestrian.

Twenty minutes into the class, Professor Muscles shot his first question.

"What is a transaction?"

When the class failed to respond, Muscles chided them. "I was told that all of you have excellent scholastic records, but all that I hear is silence." Tejas wondered whether silence could actually be heard!

"What the hell were you folks taught in school?" It was a taunt, an insult that the class swallowed.

But not the lad seated two rows ahead of Tejas. He raised his hand.

"Please introduce yourself," said Muscles.

"Mike Mahi, Sir."

Mahi's face radiated innocence and that innocence lent a touch of handsomeness to him.

Muscles snarled, "Yes, please answer."

"Sir, if you slap me that is an action. If I slap you back that is a transaction." Mahi uttered deadpan.

For a second or so there was silence in the classroom. No one knew how to react. Tejas was shocked. Gosh, this was blasphemy. Would Mahi get away with it?

Then Muscles smiled. That was a signal for the class to break into a huge round of applause.

Mike became an instant hero. You don't respond in that smart, unforgettable manner and not become a star. So did Muscles. You don't take a sock like that with equanimity without becoming a superstar. The professor said, "That was a great example." He added, "Ladies and gentlemen, boys and girls, a transaction is an action between two individuals."

Tejas 1: Mahi 1

When the class was over, Tejas walked up to Mahi and introduced himself: "I am Tejas Arya."

For a moment, Mahi was short of words. "Marbles?" he asked.

"How did you know?" Not many people remembered his old writings.

"I just knew," said Mahi, not wanting to elaborate on the subject. So his nemesis had turned up at college, thought Mahi.

Something inside him told Tejas Arya that he would be crossing swords with Mike Mahi in the days ahead. He got a confirmation of that a few weeks later.

ooo

Big Ben taught Accountancy. He was everything that Muscles was not. If Muscles was 5' 3", Ben was 6' 5". If Muscles weighed 50 kilograms, Ben weighed 150 kilos at the least. If Muscles wore ill-fitting clothes, Ben sported tight fitting stuff. If Muscles looked like a chicken in need of food, Ben resembled a prizefighter. If Muscles had oily hair that needed combing, Ben was bald.

Bald, thickset, 150 kilos, 6' 5" tall, and in tight fitting attire, Ben resembled a Bollywood villain.

But the two shared one thing in common. They were terrific teachers. Big Ben knew his subject inside out. He knew every problem in the accounting Bible, *Shukla and Grewal.* He didn't need a board to solve problems; he had his own uncanny methodology for each kind of problem and explained it in such a way that even a dimwit would understand. If you paid attention in his class, you wouldn't need to do any revision at home.

The trouble with him was that he was a terrific snob. He made out as though Accountancy was the best thing to have happened to the world.

In his first class, *"Introduction to Double Entry Book-keeping"*, Big Ben gave a historical perspective on how the subject had evolved since 1494. He spoke with passion about Luca Pacioli, the priest who invented book-keeping. Ben claimed that Luca's three rules of accounting were amongst the ten greatest inventions of all time. In Ben's view, the three greatest inventions were the railways, the game of cricket, and the English language. In that order!

Big Ben then claimed, to deafening cheers from the classroom, that Newton's third law of motion, "Every action has an equal and opposite reaction," was a copy, paste of Pacioli's third rule of double entry, "Every debit has a corresponding credit." By placing Pacioli ahead of Newton, Ben was playing to the gallery.

Tejas wasn't impressed.

Before the week was out, Ben had run through his pyrotechnics, had claimed how a trial balance always tallies, and how a balance sheet was a work of art because it always balances. "Oh, what theatrics!" thought Tejas.

Mahi whispered into a classmate's ears, "Little wonder that when they croak, accountants do not die, they just lose their balance." The backbencher smiled.

Ben had seen them whispering, but hadn't heard the words. He didn't like murmurs. He asked, "Any doubts?"

Mahi stood up. "Sir, when we draw a balance sheet why is it that the liabilities are always placed on the left and the assets are always placed on the right?"

Wow. Was Mahi serious or joking? Tejas couldn't figure it out.

Even the great Ben, for all his rhetoric and flamboyance, was at a loss for words. Apparently no one had asked him that question in his twenty years of teaching. The class sensed a Mahi kill and giggled.

Ben snapped, "Shut up and sit down."

Mahi was upset. He wasn't playing games or trying to score a victory. He had a genuine question to ask. And Big Ben was shooing him off. He turned to the person seated next to him and whispered, "Why doesn't Ben answer me?"

"Maybe because he doesn't know. Maybe because *Shukla and Grewal* haven't given him an answer to this!"

"Well, do you know why liabilities are always placed on the left and assets on the right?"

"Look, Mahi. I don't. I had the same question. You had the courage to raise it. I didn't. Well, let's not worry. One day, Ben will be absent. Someone will step in for him. We will ask the other teacher."

Mahi nodded.

About a fortnight later, just as his classmate had predicted, Big Ben failed to turn up for class. He had fallen ill. No one could believe that anything could pin Big Ben to bed.

Muscles stood in for Ben and taught the class a few great tricks for cracking accounting problems. He called the session "How to muscle your way past accounting questions."

Thirty minutes into the session, Muscles asked, "Well, any questions?"

Mahi put up his hand. Everyone laughed.

"Why are you all laughing?"

"Sir, when you hear Mahi's question, you too will laugh."

"Let's see."

"Sir, why is it that in a balance sheet the liabilities are always placed on the left and the assets are always placed on the right?"

Without so much as batting an eyelid, without so much as giving it a second thought, Professor Muscles said, "Young boy, this evening, when you go home, take a look at any wedding photograph, and you will know why liabilities appear on the left and assets on the right."

Gosh, all hell broke loose. The class was rolling in laughter. Professor Muscles was enjoying his moment of supreme glory.

Mahi hadn't sat down. As the laughter subsided, he asked, deadpan, "Professor, is that why the Americans, in the vertical format of the balance sheet, place liabilities on the top and assets below?"

Goodness gracious. This was sacrilege! The class went bonkers. Muscles snapped at Mahi, "Shut up and sit down."

That day Tejas realized that Mahi would be a serious competitor for the Best Graduating Student award.

Tejas 1: Mahi 2

ooo

It was the first class test for the trimester. Two hours after the test began, Big Ben yawned. He decided to take a stroll to stay awake and to see how the candidates were faring.

The question paper carried the legend, "Question 1 is compulsory. Answer any five of the remaining eight." A relaxed Tejas was writing on the first page of his answer book, "Question 1 is compulsory". The professor spun around, stopped and said, "Hey, it's not necessary to write the questions." It was then that he noticed that Tejas was writing, "Question 1 is compulsory. You may value any five of the remaining eight." Big Ben threw his head back, roaring with laughter. The sound could be heard five classes away. He was the only one who could get away with a lion-like roar while classes were on.

Three days later the papers had been marked and Ben was distributing them.

He called out, "Tejas Arya." A voice from the last row said, "Sir, absent, Sir." Ben said, "100/100." Seven other boys and three girls had also hit the perfect score, 100/100.

He then called out, "Mike Mahi." Mahi stood up.

"You play hockey for the college, right?"

Mahi smiled, and his chest rose with pride. The adrenalin was flowing. It had just been a month, and one of the outstanding professors already knew his name and knew that he played hockey for the college. What Ben said next dashed his pride to the ground.

"If you think you joined college only to play hockey, stay on the hockey ground. Don't attend my class. Every guy with a hockey stick thinks that he's national level material. The stupid coach thinks every ward of his is a Dhyan Chand. And the Principal picks blokes with a petty academic record." Mahi had scored 12/100.

Mahi was ashamed. But Ben's tirade was not over.

"Is it to score twelve marks that your dad sent you 1600 kilometers away from home?" The next sentence was a whiplash. "Remember what a dent it must make in the pocket of a colliery worker to send his son to St. Anne's."

That was below the belt. The unwritten rule at St. Anne's was that the family background of a student would always remain a secret. Tears swelled in Mahi's eyes. Another word from Ben and they would have rolled down. "Sit down," said the professor.

Tejas 2: Mahi 2

That night, lying on the upper bunk of his hostel bed, Mahi wept. He thought of his home. He thought of his father. He thought of his mother. He thought of his brother and his sister. He could no longer hold back the tears..

He was not angry with Ben. He was angry with himself. The dressing down he had received that morning was a life-changer. He was amongst the bottom five percentile of students. Worse still, most students had scored above seventy. He had come to this college hungry, literally and figuratively. "This way I will never become a CA. And I have come here only to become a CA," he told himself as he finally fell asleep.

At home, there was his younger brother who wanted to become a pilot and his sister who wanted to be a doctor. Dad did not have the money for all that. Mahi would have to do well. He had to do as brilliantly in academics as he would in hockey. This was what he dreamt of.

7. Inside St. Anne's – 2

At the end of the second month of college, Tejas saw the large, colorful announcement on the notice board. No one could miss it. The college advertisement team had done a swell job.

"Want to be in the St. Anne's Quiz Team?" the notice screamed. "Take the written test this Friday evening at 5 p.m." Tejas was determined to make the cut. But he knew he would face severe competition as the college boasted ace quizzers.

It would be an eight-man squad. Seven from the last year's team would be competing. Technically there was space only for one new face although it was entirely possible that some of the old hands could be dropped. St. Anne's was, after all, a meritocracy.

A fat economics undergraduate named Eugene was the don of the quiz club. A remarkable quizzer, it was rumored that he rarely got an answer wrong. History dates, geographical places, the constitution, sports, inventions and discoveries, countries, capitals and currencies, media, quotes, film stars and other celebrities, music, current affairs… name the category and the guy knew all about it.

His mind was a computer. Data that was put in stayed there and could be recalled without a fuss. If at all he missed an answer even once, he would make sure to never forget it again.

When Tejas turned up on Friday for the selection, he was shocked. There were six hundred students waiting there. They trooped into Sydenham Hall. At 5:30 p.m., the instructor turned up and gave them a lowdown on how to take the quiz.

"It will be a written quiz." "Answers are to be given in one word." "Don't write your name." "Give only your St. Anne's Student Identity Number." "If any other information is found on the paper, including your gender, you will be disqualified." And, "Use only blue ink."

Tejas thought it was a bit too much.

The instructor was not done. "The quiz will run for thirty minutes. There will be thirty questions. At the end of it, fifteen of you will make the cut. These fifteen will form the Quiz Club. The top eight will form the College team. The other seven will be in the Reserve and will be sparring partners for the team to practice with."

The quiz turned out to be relatively tight. Tejas thought that he had got twenty-six questions right. There was a fifty percent chance that two more might be correct. He felt that he had a fair chance of making it. The result would be announced the following morning.

When he turned up in front of the notice board on Saturday morning, nostalgia overtook Tejas. It had hardly been a couple of months ago that he had stood in front of this very board to check whether he had made it into St. Anne's. And his name had been there. He hoped that today, history would repeat itself.

History did repeat itself. His name was on the list; but at the ninth slot. Being on the reserves was a small consolation. He had got twenty-five questions right while the eighth bloke had got twenty-six. It was a narrow miss.

Topping the list, not unexpectedly, was Eugene. He had got 30/30.

ooo

A month later, Tejas Arya got his first opportunity to showcase his quizzing skills. It was at Symphony, the prestigious Inter-College National Quiz Contest. He had been picked for the team as the first reserve. St. Anne's had made it to the finals and on the big day, one of the three quizzers had fallen sick, so Tejas stepped in. It was an exciting battle. St. Anne's was low on points but in the final ten minutes had hit the buzzer time and again, risen like the phoenix from the ashes, and at full time was deadlocked with archrivals, St. Stephen's. The tiebreaker was announced. Six questions would be asked and the team that zipped into the lead by two points would be declared the winner. At the end of six questions, both colleges were still even.

The Quiz moved into Sudden Death. There would be just one question. The team that hit the buzzer first would have to take the question. If they got it right, they would be declared the winner. If they got it wrong, the other team would be declared the winner. If no team pressed the buzzer, a toss of the coin would decide who would have to take the sudden death question. It was like Russian roulette.

The sudden death question was hurled at them: "Which Greek philosopher lived in a bath tub?"

Tejas hit the buzzer instinctively. Even Eugene did not know the answer and stared at him. Tejas waited just the fraction of a second -- enough for his teammates to hold their hearts in their mouths, enough for the college audience to keep every part of their bodies taut – before saying, "Diogenes." The quizmaster paused for what appeared to be eternity and then screamed, "RIGHT!", and all hell broke loose.

When the celebrations had subsided, Eugene asked Tejas, "How did you know?" Tejas said, "I didn't. It just came to me." Somewhere, at some time, the answer had been stored in his mind and many years later at the most crucial juncture it had been retrieved, surprising both the audience and himself. "Recall memory" had been at work.

Mike Mahi was in the crowd. He didn't like the attention that Tejas was receiving.

Tejas 3: Mahi 2

ooo

Economics was Mahi's favorite subject. The Malthusian theory of maximum population and the Ricardian theory of rent thrilled him. Half his excitement came from the fact that Muscles taught the subject.

Explaining the difference between a closed economy and a market economy, Muscles said, "Some professors take offense if you sleep in class. They walk down, tap and wake you, ask you to freshen up and tell the rest of the class, if not the whole world, that you slept. They like to control your every move, your every action in class. What book you should be reading, when you should take the test, what color ink you should use, whether you should sit at an angle of seventy degrees or ninety degrees. That's controlled economy for you. Then there are others, like me, who don't give a damn. We follow the principle of the open market economy. You sleep; that's fine with me. 'Let sleeping dogs sleep' is my philosophy."

That pushed the idea home. It also ensured no one slept in the class.

Once he wanted a report done on the topic, *"The Indian Economy – the Way Forward."* He had said, "I want simple reports. No verbiage. No theatrical nonsense. No writing funny phrases such as 'going forward' when the phrase 'in future' will suffice. No redundant phrases such as 'advance planning'; planning can only be done in advance, not in arrears. In short, no stupid nonsense. Is that understood?"

"But Professor, stupid nonsense is like advance planning. What is stupid is nonsense, and what is nonsense is stupid," said Mike Mahi. The class roared.

"Good. So long as you got that, it's fine. Now no one can say that they didn't understand what I said," remarked Muscles. The class had walked into a trap. Check and mate.

"Don't dig into the library for reports by ex-Anne's students. I know each report by heart. If you copy from them, I will be able to spot it. Now get down and do some original work. Don't quote my work in your reports. You cannot butter me up that way. I know you have lots of other things to do. I know you don't have all the time in the world to write just this one essay. But you see I have all the time in the world to evaluate it. So beware."

The man had a sense of humor.

One day, Muscles walked in unannounced to substitute a fellow teacher who had some pressing work. The classroom had a gallery type structure. Generally, the boys took up the higher and the girls the lower rows. Today the girls occupied the top rows and the boys occupied the lower ones. Muscles walked in and remarked, “I see an unusual pattern today. I am not able to place it.”

Mahi hissed from his seat, “Professor, today the skirts have gone up and the pants have come down.” It took about a few minutes before the resultant laughter subsided.

Tejas 3: Mahi 3

Prof Muscles was quiet for the next thirty seconds and made a mental note to deduct five marks from Mahi’s next answer script!

8. A Strange Election

August 1990

In their sophomore year, both Mike Mahi and Tejas Arya decided to contest for the Students' Parliament.

The Parliament consisted of a representative from each class. These representatives were the voice of the students in any student-related issue; they would run important events like the Annual Day, and coordinate with guest lecturers and summer placement recruiters. Getting into the Parliament was prestigious because it was based on a popular election, and not on teacher nomination. The representatives would then elect a President who in turn would nominate a cabinet to head key activities.

By now, both Mahi and Arya were popular: Mahi because of his genius as a hockey player who brought laurels to the college and also because of his witty responses in class. Arya won admiration thanks to his genius as an active quizzer and debater who had won several trophies for the college. He was a brilliant student. Each had his own fan following.

This election was going to be a close contest, as it would be impossible to decide between these two charismatic boys. There was a third contestant as well, Preethi Purakayastha.

The campaigning, in the best traditions of the college, was sober. Each candidate was allowed to make one speech, spelling out his vision. Arya, with his debating skills, was superb. "We need someone as articulate as him," was the refrain in the crowd. Preethi put her killer looks to great use and waved to whistles and catcalls. "We need a person like her to have our voice heard," remarked her cheerleaders. Mahi sounded pedestrian, but he was known to be a fighter. "Mahi is the right person because if he sets his mind to something, he gets it done," said many. The story of his entry into college was already part of folklore.

On Election Day, the class of a hundred finished voting quickly. The counting began immediately in the presence of the voters. As the slips were opened one by one, those belonging to Tejas were placed on one tray, those belonging to Mahi on another, and those that had Preethi's name on a third. The slips in Tejas's and Mahi's trays began to pile up into mountains, while Preethi's resembled a hillock. Soon the count was over.

Professor Muscles was the returning officer. Clearing his throat, and pausing for just that extra moment which would give him extra importance, he said, "I am going to read, in alphabetical order the votes garnered by each candidate." He sipped some water from a glass placed nearby and read out:

Mike Mahi 41

Preethi Purakaystha 18

Tejas Arya 40

There was celebration, jubilance and back patting in Mahi's camp. Muscles banged the gavel on the table twice, and demanded total silence. When that was achieved, he said, "You all know that Tejas Arya is unwell and could not come for today's polling." Someone dropped a pin and the sound of its fall could be heard. "You all will agree that had he come he would have voted for himself. In that case, the contest would have been a tie." Mahi couldn't make out what Muscles was up to.

Then he heard Muscles say, "I am therefore going to declare this election tied at 41-41."

Screams of joy reverberated from Arya's supporters. Mahi's gang jeered. Some stood on the benches to protest. Others rushed towards Muscles. The professor had to bang the gavel multiple times before order was somewhat restored. As Mahi's boys continued their protest, Muscles threw the rulebook at them. "If you guys don't allow me to perform my duties, I will declare Tejas Arya elected."

Mahi asked, "But Professor, what is the provision under which you are making this ruling?"

"There, you see," said Muscles, pointing at a fat, worn out *Office Manual, 1924* that was lying on his table. "Page 64. Clause 24."

Mahi leafed through it, read the operative paragraph, could make out neither head nor tail of the legalese, and then said, "If the Professor has understood it the way he has understood it, that's fine with me."

Muscles thundered, "It is not the question of my understanding. It is the law. Period."

"Will there be a recount?" someone asked.

"You think I, the professor of Accounting and Mathematics, would make a calculation error?" But on being pressed, he ordered a recount. There was no change in the outcome.

"Will there be a re-poll?" wondered a voter. "Or will those who voted for Preethi Purakaystha now be asked to vote again?"

Muscles stared at him and then announced. "Under Clause 24 Sub Clause 2 of the *Office Manual, 1924* there will be a spin of the coin." And then looking at Mahi, he remarked, "Since Tejas is not there, I will call on his behalf." So saying, he handed a coin to Mahi and asked him to toss it. Mahi tossed.

"Heads," said Muscles.

Mahi bent down, picked up the coin and handed it over to the Professor. The Professor looked at the coin, adjusted the mike, and slowly, in a halting voice, announced, "I declare that this year, this class will be represented in the Parliament by Tejas Arya."

Tejas 4: Mahi 3

There was a sad footnote to this story.

ooo

Three months later, Professor Muscles invited Mike Mahi to his home. Students generally didn't see teachers outside of the college. The invitation came as a surprise to Mahi. "Come to my place at 7 p.m. today," Muscles had told Mahi.

He was there at 6:55 p.m. and was guided to the first floor by Muscles' wife, a hefty elderly lady. Mahi visualized the arrow slide to 130 kilos on the weighing machine. That would make her almost thrice as heavy as what her husband weighed. She ushered Mahi into a large, spacious room, the Professor's study. Mahi had to undergo what he felt to be the longest wait of his life, agonizing over what was it that he had done that might have propelled the teacher to invite him home. Five minutes later, the freshly bathed Muscles walked into the room and sat beside Mahi.

For the next ten minutes, he entered into a monologue. Mahi made no attempt to interrupt the teacher. He was stunned by what his teacher was saying. Coming as it did from the man whom he had intuitively trusted, immensely respected and greatly admired, this information was incredible.

"I don't know what spirit entered my body that day and why I did what I did. But I can assure you that I received no illegal gratification. For a fraction of that moment, I wasn't myself…" Mahi knew that it was a weak defense.

Prof Muscles had asked Mahi to toss a coin that had a head on both sides. He had called on behalf of Arya and had called "Heads." Something had gotten into his head. No wonder the professor had seen the movie *Sholay* thirteen times and had constantly talked about what a wonderful film it was.

"Mahi, I have written my resignation letter, detailing the sequence of events that led me to take this decision. I will submit it to the Principal tomorrow and on the day after that, I'll quit college."

Once Mahi had recovered from his shock, he said, "Professor, I appreciate your honesty. I appreciate your sharing this with me. But don't leave college. Whatever happened, you are still a great teacher and this college will be the biggest loser."

Muscles stood his ground. "I have taught here with dignity and grace for the last thirty one years. I have chided people who walked the wrong path. Now, I, Professor Muscles, have strayed from that path. No, I can no longer teach with a clear conscience."

Mahi pleaded. "Sir, look at it this way. If you make this public, tomorrow every teacher will be suspected for one thing or the other. Tomorrow, when a Professor spins a coin, people will wonder whether it's loaded. When a Preethi Purakaystha gets 'A+' there will be loose talk on what prompted the Professor to give her the grade. All the respect that we have for our teachers will disappear with your resignation.

He continued: "Personally, I have nothing against you. Half the class wanted Arya anyway, and Arya has been doing a swell job. Please, please do not make this public."

Muscles refused to back down.

When Mahi left, Muscles' words echoed in his mind: "Each one of us will have to tackle the storm within us in our own way."

Tejas 4: Mahi 4

ooo

One week later, Professor Muscles tendered a three-line resignation letter, which just said, "I have, overnight, lost the spark to teach. I tender my resignation from this college. I wish the students well." At his farewell, people complimented him for living up to his words. In the past he had often flamboyantly said, "The moment I feel like I no longer want to teach, I will step down."

Mike Mahi stayed away from the farewell.

9. The Award Night

April 1991

Tejas Arya woke up with a start. Lying beside him, on his bed, was Jia Sharma. His hand was coiled around her waist, and her long leg was thrown over his body. They had been chatting last night, but he did not know when they had fallen asleep.

Startled, he jumped out and looked down at his shorts. He remembered wearing jeans the previous night. He saw that the knot of Jia's cotton pajama was disentangled and loose. It was also a shade lower than usual. Her t-shirt was crumpled and pulled up a little, showing off her flat belly. Otherwise, she was fully dressed. Of course, she had no business at all to be sleeping in his room, in the Boys' hostel.

ooo

The events leading up to her coming to his room came rushing into his head.

The Annual Fete was on. Prizes were being distributed: for academics, for sports, for cultural, and for intramurals. It had been time to announce the most prestigious award of them all, the award for the best outgoing student. The Awards committee, it seemed, was torn between two candidates, Mike Mahi and Tejas Arya.

Tejas had heard that Professor Muscles had developed a multi-dimensional model in which various inputs were placed: the academic score of every test and every exam, performance in each game on the sports field and every co-curricular activity, the candidate's response in class, his conduct, attendance, punctuality, and their ilk. If rumors were to be believed, Professor Muscles had put in 99 variables. There was also a personal interview of the candidates.

The Master of Ceremonies was saying, "But the surprise of surprises is that for the first time in twenty-five years, the 'Muscles model' has thrown out a tie. Professor Muscles is no longer with us to resolve the tie. So the committee had to take a qualitative call. Both candidates were outstanding. If Tejas was the topper in academics, Mahi wasn't far behind. If Mahi was brilliant in hockey, now having been asked to play for India, Tejas is an excellent speaker, a quality that will stand him in good stead his whole life. But an India call is an India call. Therefore, ladies and gentlemen, boys and girls, I am sure you will agree with me that the best outgoing student for the year should be Mike Mahi."

The air was rent with the war cry, "Mahi", "Mahi", "Mahi." Exactly the way whenever Mahi was on the hockey field.

As Mike Mahi, the son of a colliery worker, who had dreamt beyond his means and punched beyond his weight, got up from his seat, and adjusted his blazer, the announcer said, "But..." A few seconds later, you could hear a knife swish through the silence. "The Committee had another qualitative factor to consider. St. Anne's has always prided itself on generating leaders. While both Mahi and Tejas will surely go on to become leaders, the Committee, based on the election to the Students' Parliament, tipped the decision in favor of Tejas Arya."

"Ladies, gentlemen, boys and girls, please put your hands together to welcome the best graduating student of the college, Tejas Arya."

The ensuing claps reverberated long into the night. In one sentence, they had dashed Mahi's hopes. An overwhelming emptiness swallowed Mahi.

Tejas 5: Mahi 4

ooo

Three boys had seen the scene in Arya's room and so had Big Ben. Jia Sharma had woken, pulled up and tied her pajamas, and pushed down her t-shirt. A tall girl, she was now squatting on her haunches, her knees sticking straight up in the air and her feet almost touching her bottom. She had a shock of short dark hair, cut straight at jaw level, and a side parting. Her hands cupped her eyes as she started to cry. Ben had never seen her before on campus. Naturally. She was not a student of this College.

Tejas looked as though he were at a funeral. Ben allowed him to freshen up, change, and then took him, along with Jia, into the Principal's room. The Principal was at his wits' end. This was unprecedented.

Both Jia and Tejas swore that they had no recollection of what had transpired the previous night. Of course, circumstantial evidence was heavily against them. Rumors were already spreading like wildfire.

It was then that Mike Mahi marched into the Principal's room. The secretary stopped him, saying, "Do you have an appointment? He is in an important meeting."

"Who is he with?"

"I can't tell you. I will lose my job."

"If Big Ben and Tejas Arya are inside and if the Principal gets to know that you didn't let me in, Madam, you will anyway have no job tomorrow. I have some important information to share with him."

The bemused secretary checked with the Principal, who reluctantly agreed to see Mahi.

"Yes, Mahi. You had better have something important to say."

Mahi did not acknowledge the presence of either Big Ben or Tejas. In one glance, he took in that his former schoolmate, Jia Sharma, now had an hourglass figure, a trim waistline, and a toned structure with some meat on her bones. He told the Principal: "Sir, my room number is 207, Tejas's is 208. Last night, I saw Tejas with this girl. The door was ajar. You know that there is a connecting door to every room. I was awake the whole night, reading. They were talking about many issues. I heard them conversing until 5:30 in the morning, and then I saw them fall asleep, exhausted. As we know by now, they woke up at 6:30 a.m."

That settled it. "Thank you Mahi," said the Principal. He motioned to both Tejas and Jia to leave after giving them a lecture on how they needed to be careful in the future. "You can survive this sort of scandal only once."

ooo

Tejas and Jia rushed after Mahi. They stopped him some three hundred feet from the Principal's room. Tejas said, "Thank you, Mahi. Thank you. You saved my honor. You kept me from falling down in my own esteem. Now I know I didn't do any wrong."

"Tejas, I might have saved you the blushes, but I am not sure if I have kept you from falling down in your own esteem."

"What? What do you mean? You told the Principal that you had heard me talking to Jia and that we just fell asleep."

"Yes, I did tell him. But I didn't see that happening."

"Then why did you do it? Why did you lie?"

"Three reasons. One, what happens between you and Jia behind closed doors is your personal business. That it happened in the hallowed precincts of our college is what makes it public. But no one knows it happened. There was no need for anyone to presume that something happened." Mentally, Tejas ticked that off as a "professional" statement.

"Two, last night was the most memorable night of your life. I mean the award. I did not want innuendos to spoil the taste of that award." Tejas was touched. Tears swelled his eyes. Mentally, he ticked that off as a "personal" touch.

"And three, to me our college is a temple of learning. I feel more strongly about St. Anne's than I feel about India. A scandal of this kind is best avoided." Mentally, Tejas ticked that off as "impersonal".

It was always difficult to know the real Mahi: professional, personal or impersonal.

Jia Sharma had mixed feelings. Big Ben, who was within earshot, too realized that he could never understand Mike Mahi. He knew that Mahi had not been in the adjoining room because when he, Big Ben, had done his round of inspection, both at midnight and again at 4 a.m., he had seen that Mahi's room was locked from the outside.

Tejas 5: Mahi 5

OOO

The duo graduated in 1991. That year a superannuated politician and a retired bureaucrat teamed up to forever change the face of India, as the country dusted off the cobwebs of socialism to embrace market economy.

When the final results came out, Tejas Arya topped the graduating class. Mike Mahi was in the top five percentile. That wasn't bad for a lad who had come from a disadvantaged family and whose scholastic distinction at school had been nothing to write home about. Perhaps studying subjects that interested him had done the trick.

Now out of college, the students who wanted to do CA would have to hunt for internships. Hunt & Smith was the place where many wanted to be. The firm would be visiting their college to conduct interviews.

10. The Following Day…

YEAR: 2014
DATE: June 22
Sunday 2:00 p.m. GMT
London

The flight landed at Heathrow International Airport in London. Long queues greeted him at the world's third busiest airport.

As he waited for his baggage to arrive, Tejas Arya switched on his mobile. There were hundreds of messages and scores of missed calls. Jia Sharma had called sixteen times.

In 1998, Tejas Arya had married his long-time girlfriend, the one he had been dating since 1991. Seven years of courtship can be long and boring, but the duo finally tied the knot. By then Jia, aged twenty-six, had graduated from the National Institute of Fashion Technology (NIFT) and had gotten into modeling. With her height, her long legs and toned body, she was highly in demand, modeling first for Ritu Kumar and later for Rohit Bal.

The Aryas threw everything into the wedding of their son. It was a grand function where the crème de la crème of the city were invited. Ninety-three dishes, including sixteen varieties of desserts, adorned the tables. The rising star of the audit profession, Mike Mahi, was amongst the invitees.

This was the same Jia whose teacher had tweaked her ear in school and made her kneel, thanks to a ploy by Mike Mahi. It was the same Jia who had been found in Tejas Arya's hostel bed, and spared from the scandal by Mike Mahi. By now she had grown into a stunningly beautiful and elegant woman and to Tejas she was a valuable trophy.

Tejas looked at his mobile, and immediately knew what to do. The missus must receive priority! Tejas changed his SIM and called Jia.

"Tejas, did you watch the television? Did you see the morning paper? Did Mahi's office speak to you?" She seemed to be on edge.

"What about the television? What about the newspaper? What are they saying?" He knew everything that they were saying but did not want to take any chances. He had carefully ignored the reference to Mahi.

"Tejas, there is this **BREAKING NEWS** on Hindustan Bank. Your channel has been screaming about it since last night. They are saying all sorts of bad things about Mike Mahi. They are also saying that he could be taken in for questioning today. You must do something." By now she had slowed down.

"Jia, Hindustan Bank is a police case. Every regulator in the country, the RBI, the SEBI, the Finance Ministry, the Enforcement Directorate… name it and you have it… will descend on them. I cannot do anything even if I wanted to. In any case, Mahi knows how to take care of himself. He has the money and the connections to get the leading lawyers."

"So you knew the whole thing. You never told me. By the way, how can you be so insensitive? Have you forgotten that he once saved you from being rusticated?"

"Look here, you know as well as I do that nothing happened that night. I am not saying his statement didn't help. But if push had come to shove, we would have, even otherwise, been excused."

"You ungrateful idiot. You know that almost everything happened that night. Don't forget that you had your hand all over my body. I had mine on yours as well."

"But goddamn it, nothing more happened. We both know that for a fact. Neither of us would have done it."

"We are not sure that nothing more happened. If we could paw, we could have done it as well, drunk as we were on the whiskey and your success. We owe a lot to Mahi. He had no reason to help us out. Your equation with him in college wasn't that great."

"It's a twenty-year-old story, done and dusted, my dear scatterbrain. So what the hell do you expect me to do?"

"At least ask the morons in your paper not to publish and the idiots on your channel not to screen nonsense about Mahi."

"That's out of the question. This is the story of the decade. It's not possible to stop it. Newspapers and television channels run professionally. Each person is paid to do a job. If we didn't break this story this morning , someone would break it tomorrow. Mike Mahi is too much of a celebrity for the media to not talk about him. We could have gone on air earlier, but we wanted to confirm some details."

"At least return his call," she said and hung up.

"Damn it. First in school, then in college, later during internship, and now, this Mike Mahi is haunting me," thought Tejas Arya.

His mind raced back to the days of internship.

11. Whatever it Takes – 1

August 1991
New Delhi

Tejas Arya was on cloud nine when he got his internship. After all, he had passed out from one of India's best schools, graduated from one of India's finest colleges and was now with a top public accounting firm: Stewart School, St. Anne's, and now Hunt & Smith. Not everyone could boast of such a pedigree. The screwballs had no choice but to pick him.

In his very first week at H&S (yes the morons called it that), Tejas came crashing down from cloud nine.

Someone had once told him, "You will have to spend the first month of your internship totaling numbers in a telephone directory. You will not be allowed to use a calculator. The idea is to hone your math skills." Tejas didn't believe it. No firm could be so stupid. What he actually got to do from day two made adding telephone numbers look like high-end work. The first day was one of introductions, meeting people and getting a general feel of things. On the second day, he was assigned his first job.

"Hey, can you please go to the pantry and make us some good coffee?" asked an Audit Senior. An Audit Senior is one level above a third year Intern.

Tejas was shocked. Making coffee? Well at home, when his mom wasn't around, it was their part-time help, Nina, who did it.

"Who? Me?"

"Yeah. Who else?"

He felt like slapping the guy. But he remembered Muscles. What was it that the Professor had said? Wasn't it, "Every cloud has a silver lining." Well, he decided to put that to the test. He decided to make the best of a bad bargain.

"How do I make coffee?"

"You come from St. Anne's and you don't know how to make coffee? Go figure it out. Once you have made it, take a sip to check whether the coffee is any good."

Tejas swore silently.

He made what he thought was coffee. He took a sip, his eyes widened, his nose and mouth screwed up. He ran to the washbasin and spit it all, sticking out his tongue with his face still screwed up. "Yuck… yuck!" He coughed, rinsed his mouth and ate two spoons of sugar to get that awful taste off. What was that anyway? There was no way he could offer such coffee to his seniors. They would mock him for the rest of his life saying he had prepared kaphi.

Unwilling to concede defeat, even if it came to making coffee, Tejas walked up to the front office and asked whether he could make a call. The lady stared at him. A fresher making a call on the second day was not quite on. He gave her a number and asked her to connect the call to the pantry.

Fifteen minutes later, the call was connected. Tejas spoke to Nina.

"Nina, how do I make coffee?"

"What?"

"I asked, HOW do I make COFFEE!"

Nina knew Tejas well enough to tell that he was annoyed. "To make one cup of coffee, take three-quarters cup of milk. Add a quarter cup of water. Turn the gas on high and heat the mix until it boils. Then add two teaspoons of sugar and one teaspoon of coffee powder. Stir it and serve it."

"Nina, are you sure that it will taste good?"

"Everyone makes coffee that way. When I make it, it tastes good. When your sister makes it, it doesn't taste good. We will see what it tastes like when you make it." Tejas swallowed the jibe.

Tejas took milk and water in the exact proportion Nina told him to. He heated it and added two teaspoons of sugar and one teaspoon of instant powder. He stirred it and then served it.

The guys at the office had a cup each.

"Hmm … Not bad. But we would like it to taste better. You must improve."

"Come to the office by 8:45 a.m. and make coffee for us so that we can have it at 9 a.m. By the end of the month, you should become a professional at making coffee. Got it?"

Tejas swore silently again.

He didn't like it one bit but then if that was what his seniors wanted, well, they would get it. That night he visited a hotel, met with the coffee master, and took a quick tutorial. The tutorial lasted four nights.

By the end of the week, he had learned how to make the best coffee in town, even better than his mom's or Nina's. Better than the fare the neighboring three-star restaurant offered. Better than the downtown hotel where he had been tutored. He was mighty pleased with himself.

And the boys at the office were stunned. Tejas was now a hero.

Tejas 6: Mahi 5

When he told his mom about this, she was thrilled. His dad wasn't amused. Shakti Arya asked, "Do you intend to become an accountant or a chef?" Tejas replied, "I don't know, Dad."

The next thing that Tejas learnt was photocopying. It was the tenth day of his internship.

"Tejas, can you please get fifteen photocopies of this 25-page report," said an Audit Senior. "That's 375 pages in all: just in case your math is bad." By now Tejas knew that the word "please" was not a request but an order.

"Whom should I take it to for photocopying?"

"You have to do it yourself, dear. We don't have separate people to do these jobs."

Tejas swallowed his anger. At home, it was Nina who took it to the nearby shop and got it done. Now these guys were asking him to do it. Wasn't this ragging? Shouldn't he lodge a complaint?

"How do I do the photocopying?" he asked.

"You come from St. Anne's. You should know how to figure it out yourself."

"Shit," murmured Tejas.

He called up the front office, gave the lady a number and asked her to connect the call to the "Facilities Room". That was where the Xerox machine was placed. H&S had fancy names for its rooms.

Ten minutes later, the call was connected. He spoke to Nina.

"Nina, how do I make photocopies?"

"Take it to a photocopying shop and have it done."

"Big deal. Tell me how do I do it with a Xerox machine. And cut out all the smart references."

"Lift the lid. Place the page you want to photocopy face down. If you want three copies of a paper, press the number '3'. Then hit the 'Go' button. Got it?"

"Got it."

"Remember to switch the machine on!"

Sexy copiers in which you could punch in '100' to get hundred copies of a report done, duly sorted and stapled in five minutes hadn't hit the market yet. You could make ten copies at a time, at most. You then had to arrange them by page number. Finally, you had to staple it together. Office custom stipulated that the stapling had to be six centimeters from the left corner and three centimeters from the top. Beads of sweat dripped from Tejas's brows. He wiped them with his shirtsleeve.

For the next fifteen days, Tejas had breakfast, lunch and tea next to the Xerox machine. He knew when and how to change the toner. He knew how to get the color mix right.. His copies resembled the originals. In short, he had become an expert at photocopying.

Tejas 7: Mahi 5

His mom was thrilled. His dad, Shakti Arya, asked, "Do you intend to become an accountant or a Xerox boy?"

Tejas replied, "I don't know, Dad."

12. Whatever it Takes – 2

One thing that Tejas quickly learned was that no work was too small, or too low. Whatever you did, you did with pride and joy, be it making coffee or photocopying a sheet of paper or vouching a cash transaction. What was it that Professor Muscles had said? "If it falls to your lot to be a street sweeper, become the Picasso of street sweeping." Tejas had then dismissed it as sermonizing, but today he understood the importance of that advice.

At H&S, behind all the light banter, there was seriousness when it came to working. The best thing was that this attitude was infectious. In a crisis, the folks always went the extra mile, perhaps a couple more.. On the last day of his first month at the internship, Tejas learnt this lesson. It completely changed his perspective of things.

A multinational company (MNC) had outsourced the payroll operations of one of its branches to H&S. The contract had been bagged after a lot of effort. Two big firms and a reputed limited liability company had bid for it. But H&S, given its celebrated past, had clinched it by a whisker. The understanding with the MNC was that if the outsourcing arrangement worked well for one year, the payroll operations of all eighty branches of the MNC would be outsourced. The eyes of the big bosses at H&S rolled greedily at the thought of the money it would bring.

This was how the outsourcing arrangement worked: H&S would collate the time cards from the company every week and verify them using random sampling. Quick checks would be done with respect to sanctioned leave and holidays. Any suspicious entry would have to be reported. Next, the data would be entered into the computer; an edit list would be taken and checked for correctness. Finally, the payroll would be generated with details of gross pay, deductions, net pay, etc. There could be no margin for error as the payroll was a sensitive matter.

Once this was complete, the application would throw out the pay slip of each employee. H&S would write a single cheque favoring the bank and the "transfer letter" that would transfer money from the bank account of the company to the bank accounts of the various employees. The cheque had to be signed by two people, including a specified partner, from the firm.

The firm had a dedicated team of ten employees working on the project. The process had gone well for five months. This was the sixth month. The boys had slogged for the last forty-eight hours nonstop. Some programming bug and a shortage of personnel meant that the job that should have been completed on Thursday would only be done by Friday afternoon. That wasn't such a big issue since the transfer had to be done only on Saturday morning.

The payroll was ready at 2 p.m. on Friday. At 3 p.m., the Team Leader took the payroll cheque to the partner for his signature. And that was when the horror story began.

When he called up the Secretary to the Partner, she told him he had just left for the airport and would be away in the US for a week. There was chaos on the floor. Someone screamed, "How did we miss out on getting the cheque signed?"

"At least we could have gotten the partner's signature on a blank cheque. Later, the other authorized signatory could have signed the cheque once the amount had been filled."

"What do we do now? Eight hundred people's pay will get stalled for a week."

"Not just that. If this cheque doesn't get signed, we will lose the client for good."

"Forget the client. All of us will lose our jobs."

"But what about the partner? Should he not have briefed us on his travel plans?"

"We should talk to the bank manager, and explain to him the extraordinary situation we are in. We must request him to clear the cheque with a single signature or with the signature of a different partner. After all, we are not a small firm."

"But the bank is closed for the day and most of our partners are traveling. Will the banker listen to anyone else?"

"There is no guarantee the bank will oblige. They are government outfits and will lecture us on order, method and procedures."

A young lad put up his hand. He must have been twenty. Normally, they didn't employ anyone younger than that at H&S. But he looked nothing more than seventeen.

He asked, "When does the flight take off?"

Someone said, "Seventy minutes from now."

"How much time will it take to reach the airport?"

"An hour."

"When does the aircraft close shutters?"

"Twenty minutes before departure."

"How much time do we have before the aircraft closes?"

"Fifty minutes."

The arithmetic wasn't pleasing. Sixty minutes to reach the airport, traffic willing. And in fifty minutes the aircraft would close. It was then that the boy made an impossible statement.

"I will carry the cheque to the airport and get it signed by the partner." He hadn't even met the partner. Neither he nor the partner would know each other on sight. And before anyone could react, he snatched the cheque, rushed down the stairs (the elevator wasn't working), took the office car and told the chauffeur to break all speed limits to reach the airport ASAP.

The car raced at breakneck speed. At a few signals, it breached the red light. Fortunately, there was no cop to flag it down for speeding. Nor were there many vehicles itching to ram into their car. When he reached the airport, the check-in had closed; the passengers had passed through security and were on the flight. The aircraft had been closed. There were just another fifteen minutes to take off.

No one knew how he managed it. Maybe he had told the Airport Officer that he would otherwise lose his Internship. Maybe he pulled strings. A puny lad with a punk hairdo, he scampered through check-in, went past security, boarded the aircraft – all of course escorted by someone from the airport – identified the partner, got the cheque signed, shook hands with him and returned to office with a smile. No one bothered to ask. They were just thrilled.

There was just one word for it: astounding.

At the office, he had barely handed over the cheque when they all carried him on their shoulders, screaming and laughing. There was a victory lap. Clearly he was the hero of the month. People agreed that he was destined to go a long way in the organization. "If it has to be done, it has to be done," was the credo.

The young lad was the hockey wizard, Mike Mahi. Tejas wondered why the idea hadn't struck him. Why he, Tejas Arya, hadn't offered to do it. After all, he had made coffee and had photocopied papers. And now this guy, Mike Mahi, had hogged all the attention. Tejas was enraged. He wanted to kick himself.

Tejas 7: Mahi 6

13. Prostar

In the first year the interns learned to audit purchase, sales, cash and bank transactions. In the second year, they normally graduated to doing higher work like auditing capital expenditure.

Now in his second year, Tejas Arya was auditing Mullah & Lobo, India's top law firm. Over seventy-five years old, the firm had built a reputation for handling a variety of legal matters. Criminal law, civil law, arbitration, constitution, international law, advisory – name it and they did it. Mullah Jr., currently the National Partner and head of Mullah & Lobo, had once remarked that law was an emerging profession and that in the years to come it would be one of the most sought after professions in India. Tejas remembered Perry Mason, Della Street, and Paul Drake.

Tejas's mandate was to verify professional billing. As things stood, he could only check whether the bills that the firm raised were accounted for and if money had been received and realized against them. Verify from invoice to party account in the ledger; verify from party account in the ledger to the bank statement. Add the invoice components. A cross tick here and a straight tick there; not to forget the 'bird' tick as also the 'casting' tick. This didn't please Tejas.

By lunchtime, he was sure this was not how he wished to audit. He walked up to Tony, his audit senior, and asked, "How do I ensure that the value of the bill is correct?"

Tony had been born Samant Patnaik. He went to school as Samant Patnaik and graduated as Samant Patnaik. A year out of college, he developed a shooting back pain that did not respond to medication. When medicine failed, he turned to religion. Someone suggested he go to Church every Sunday. And so he did, week after week, with monotonous regularity. Exactly twelve Sundays later, the pain disappeared as magically as it had arrived. Thrilled beyond belief, he changed his name to Antony, Tony for short. That was his thanksgiving gesture to Jesus Christ.

Having been with H&S for six years, Tony knew its workings inside out. He smiled. Here was a second year intern who was willing to go behind the transaction. It showed a mind that was receptive to experimentation and learning. Tony decided to take him to a restaurant and explain to him over lunch.

Two bowls of soup, one Russian salad, two masala papads, four rotis and mixed vegetable curry," rattled off Tony without bothering to either look at the menu card or check with Tejas.

"Well, the firm has a client billing template. The firm plugs the details of all those who have worked on the job, along with the number of hours that they have worked, into this model. This is like the job card that you see in any repair workshop." When he had an interested audience, even if it were an audience of one, Tony tended to go on a roll.

"Wow," thought Tejas. Spotting similarities between the work cultures of a great law firm and a downtown service workshop was fun.

"The template then allows the hours worked to be multiplied by the firm's man-hour rate in respect to the category of each team member," Tony said.

"How do I know that the number of hours entered in the chart is right? Where do I get the team members' tariff rates, if I can call them that?"

"Shabash," said Tony, biting into the salad that had come along with the soup. Just then, the rotis arrived and Tejas watched Tony attack both the rotis and the audit.

"If you want to verify the number of hours the employee actually worked, you must look into each of the team member's timesheet. Each employee of the law firm writes out a time sheet each fortnight, listing the name of the client for whom he worked, the nature of work done, the number of hours worked, and whether these hours are billable or not.

"Regarding the chargeable rate per team member, it's not called the tariff card. It is just referred to as the man-hour rate.

Ask the law firm's Accounts Officer, and he should be able to provide it to you."

"That's interesting," mumbled Tejas.

"Well, that's not the end of it. When the hours worked is multiplied by the rate per hour, the firm gets the broad billing amount. To this sum, the partner concerned tops up or tops down some value to get the final number. This is what you find in the 'Partner's Sheet' as Top-Up."

"By top-up you mean that he arbitrarily adds some value and by top-down you mean that he arbitrarily deducts some value, is it?"

"Yeah."

That means that in respect to the top-ups and top-downs I must check that he has initialed them. There would be no supporting document because it's arbitrary? Is that right?

"Yeah."

"But why does he do this?"

Tony was beginning to like Tejas. He liked anyone who was inquisitive when it came to audit.

"Why does a bank charge differently for different amounts of demand draft? You see, whether the draft is for Rs 1,000 or is for Rs 100,000, it costs the bank the same. In fact, the word lakh has fewer letters than the word thousand."

"Because the bank takes more risk in case of the latter?"

"What risk? The risk, if any, is for the customer. He has parted with the money."

"Ha, it's based on the principle of what the traffic can bear."

Tony was surprised. Those were the exact words that his professor had used while explaining this idea in his marketing class. He who can afford to pay more must be made to pay more. He who can afford to pay less must be made to pay less—that was the underlying logic of service pricing.

Tony was glad that with his small talk he had given Tejas some insight into service pricing. One lesson well taught indeed.

By then the dessert arrived. Tejas had chosen ice cream. Tony settled for fresh lime with soda.

Over dessert, Tony went into lecture mode. "An application called 'Prostar' is used to do the audit. The data in respect of all invoices is transferred from the client's database into 'Prostar'. The software classifies the invoices into A, B and C. A category would be invoices with the highest values and C category would be invoices with the lowest values. The intern would then have to specify three things: one, the total sale value he wishes to audit; two, the number of transactions that he wishes to review; and three the confidence levels he desires. Based on these inputs, 'Prostar' would identify the transactions to be audited. These transactions may flow from any category and from any of the twelve months. You have to audit only those transactions chosen by 'Prostar' and you cannot skip one and pick another."

"So we have significant technology intervention that helps us audit?" Tejas asked, taking another scoop of the ice cream.

"You don't have to check all invoices. We go by trust, but we also check. When you buy chocolates you don't check all of them; you check some of them and if those 'some' are fine, you buy the whole pack. Ditto for Revenue. Remember, 'trust but verify' is our tagline."

Tejas wanted to yawn. After all, he had been with the firm for one year and he knew all this jazz about sampling. He was annoyed at Tony not getting his point.

"In short, 'Prostar' guides us through the audit. If you know English and have an open mind, you don't have to be an expert to conduct the review," said Tony, sipping his fresh lime soda. "The audit process, rather than the auditor, would be the hero of the audit."

"Well said. Well said."

The waiter brought the check and Tony settled it. Of course it would be given to the client for reimbursement later!

Tejas decided that he would test his newfound knowledge by verifying whether, Mullah & Lobo were charging a differential price for the same service to different customers. He also wanted to check whether the same service to the same client showed differential rates at different points of time, whether there were any budgets for completing client assignments, and whether payments were obtained by the due dates.

His dream was to take audit to the realms of management consulting.

ooo

In the third year, Mahi was turning out to be brilliant at work. If he audited debit notes, the client would have to make corrections worth several crores. If he checked credit notes, he could spot omissions and commissions running to several lakh rupees. If he set his eyes on capital expenditure, he would find instances of revenue expenses being capitalized and capital expenses being charged to income. Once, when a senior asked him to audit treasury operations, he came out with a stunner of a report. Even the client was floored.

Work was always fun. But fooling around was better!

The boys had a ball when they toured the coffee estates. Work stopped at 6 p.m. No planter worked after that. At 7:30 p.m., they were invariably at the club, playing squash or cards. The planters drank in gallons while the audit team sipped in a few drinks. They could go to the spa, the pool, the gym or the pub. The only thing that they didn't indulge in was horse racing.

Some of the audit guys played cards for money. The stakes were pretty high. Auditors were supposed to have money! Mahi and Tejas weren't really interested in booze or cards. They wanted to learn a new game, squash. After four days, they were good enough to take on the local juniors.

One day, the trial balance wasn't tallying by an annoyingly large number: 3,10,31,993. The company hadn't as yet fully automated its accounting. After eight agonizing hours of struggle with the trial balance (on which four people worked in sets of two), someone threw the paper at Mahi.

"You are great at math. Now crack this. We have spent long hours on it."

Mahi took one look at it and said, "The number resembles the date of the last day of the year: 31-03-1993. Check if it has, by mistake, gotten added to one side of the trial balance." It turned out to be the case and Mahi became a darling.

Tejas 7: Mahi 7

The CA final exam came soon enough. The interns went on study holidays and then took the National Level exam. They needed to pass it to become CAs.

14. Five Days Before Results Day

"Gosh, how time flies," said Mahi, realizing that it had already been forty five days since he wrote his last paper for the CA final examination. And this morning, July 25, five days before the announcement of the results, he had received a letter, which was unmistakably from NICPA. You could recognize the cover from a mile.

Your result is being withheld because Form 102/62/52A has not been filed with us. Have it deposited in the next two days so that your result can be announced as per schedule on 30th July.

NICPA announced the results of its exams on 30th Jan and 30th July. Mahi had always asked himself why NICPA announced its results on Martyr's day.

Mahi knew that he had given them every document, including Form 102/62/52A. In fact, he had an acknowledgment from the Institute with respect to the paper in question. His dad suggested he take the train to the regional headquarters, meet the officer-in-charge and get the thing sorted out.

It was thus that Mahi found himself on a train to Calcutta, which was where his studentship was registered because the partner he had signed under practiced in that city.

His mind wandered back to his exams. He knew he had done well and should by all rights sail through. But you never knew; this course could take anyone by surprise. The night outside was dark and chilly. That and the persistent lullaby of the train helped Mahi crash out fast.

He was in the midst of his cost accounting exam and the problem on variance analysis looked like French. Although Mahi had mastered the inimitable format that his professor had so assiduously taught, the silly examiner had managed to throw in a googly. Beads of sweat ran down his face, his hands were trembling; he leapt up, and his head hit the upper berth … Mahi was now wide-awake, his body shaking!

"Thank God, that was not real," thought a relieved Mahi. This was the sort of nightmare that his friends had often talked about, and Mahi was experiencing it for the first time.

The train chugged into Howrah in the wee hours of the morning. Most of his co-passengers were just beginning to wake up. Mahi got off the train. The porters ran after him, offering to carry his suitcase. His dad had taught him the virtue of carrying his own luggage.

"Dalhousie… Dalhousie… BBD Bagh… BBD Bagh…" The encore of half-asleep bus conductors sounded like a cacophony in the silent surroundings. They were calling out names of destinations. Mahi boarded a bus that took him to his hotel. It was a small but functional hotel, with clean rooms and a nice restaurant that served good breakfast.

By 9:30 a.m. he had shaved and showered in steaming hot water and had a quick breakfast that included cornflakes, toast and piping hot tea. He slipped into a new shirt and clean trousers and set off for the Institute, carrying a file that had all the relevant papers. He reached at 9:50 a.m. There were reams of paper stuck on the Notice Board, which looked like results. "Is NICPA so wonderfully inefficient that they are carrying results that are six months old?" he wondered. He had a strange habit of checking whether his number had appeared in an examination that he had not taken! For instance, he would look at the results of the medical school exam to see if his Class XII or his B.Com roll number appeared.

He went up to the board.

Gosh, it was the result of his examination! He couldn't believe his eyes. Hadn't the letter from the Institute suggested that the results were at least five days away? A young man walking past him hissed that the results had been announced late last night. Anyway, he was sure his results would have been withheld. After all, Form 102/62/52A was not with NICPA.

But if the Institute was wrong regarding the date of the result, it could also be wrong about withholding his result, thought Mahi.

Butterflies in his stomach, his eyes automatically wandered to the list to see if his roll number was there. His heart raced like that of an Olympic athlete who had just completed a hundred-meter dash. An atheist at heart, he was now praying like a seasoned sage. It was his first attempt at praying.

His fate was written on that sheet of paper.

He eyed the results. Goodness gracious, they were in a really tiny font. He struggled to read it, wishing he had brought a magnifying glass.

"116216. There it is, 116216." A look at the hall ticket and then at the result sheet, then again at the hall ticket, and again at the result sheet and yet again at the hall ticket... In his anxiety, he didn't notice that this time around the name of the candidate was also printed. Ah, there it was. "Mike Mahi." Wow.

Graffiti covered the sheets. "Well done, aunty," someone had written against a lady's name. "G8 show dear," someone scribbled against a guy's name. Another wrote, "Stupid Institute. Me to write again?" The graffiti was innovative and at times invective. They spoke of the joys of the winners and the disappointments of the losers. A few years later ICAI started putting the result on the Internet. With that the fun and joy of seeing your exam result was partially gone.

Mahi still wasn't 100 percent sure. After all, he had been trained in auditing in one of India's finest firms. The internal evidence (the letter from the Institute) was inconsistent with the external evidence. He wasn't willing to take chances. He decided to meet the officer who had sent the letter. The man was at his post, reading the day's *Telegraph.*

Mahi went up to him. "Sir, here is your letter which says that some of my documents are not with the Institute. But here is my acknowledgment copy."

Keeping to the traditions of *babudom*, the man didn't look up. "Well, if you have an acknowledgment, it means the Institute has your paper."

"The notice board says I have passed. But your letter says my results are going to be withheld."

Again, without looking up, the man said, "Does your name appear on the list outside?"

"Yes Sir."

"Then you have qualified."

"But your letter tells me my results are being withheld."

"Forget the letter. If your name appears on the list outside you have qualified."

"Sure?"

"If it appears there, then sure."

The guy hadn't lifted his gaze from the newspaper. He didn't utter a word of congratulation to NICPA's newest member.

As he walked out of the Institute, the full weight of what had happened hit Mike Mahi. The son of a colliery worker from distant Rampur Collieries was now a CA. He screamed with his hands thrown up in celebration. A war cry reverberated through the atmosphere. Inside the Institute, that shout would be passé; CAs are known to celebrate in odd ways. One guy was reported to have removed his t-shirt and swung it around, the rock star way. Outside, on the road, people stared at Mahi.

Mahi desperately tried to call his dad's colliery. But there were serpentine queues at the post office where he went to place the call. You see these were the pre-mobile days. He took the earliest train and reached home late in the night, anxious to break the news to his parents.

He stepped into the house. The door was open, but the house was silent. He put his bag down. "Papa? Mamma?" He nearly jumped out of his skin when his Mamma caught him from behind and stuffed his mouth with sweets. She whispered:

"This morning, around 8:30, your cousin sent you a congratulatory telegram saying that you had cracked the CA examination. And your dad has gone around the colliery distributing sweets."

Mahi let the tears of joy flow.

ooo

He would soon learn that Mr. Marbles, the guy whom he had saved from certain expulsion, the one who had been elected to College Parliament thanks to a maverick teacher, the one who had walked away with the best outgoing student award by a whisker, had outsmarted him again.

Tejas Arya had topped the rank list, yet again, finishing all-India first. First in Intermediate and now first in Final. "Did the jackass ever finish second," wondered Mahi.

Tejas 8: Mahi 7

A few years later the NICPA began posting the results on the Internet. The joy of watching other people's performance and scribbling graffiti would be gone!

15. Uncle Krishna Ignites the Spark

Tejas had many choices. Newspapers were carrying plenty of advertisements for CAs in different sectors.

He could join a bank. Or he could join the company where his dad, Shakti Arya, worked. They would be very eager to take him. Or he could try his luck with a few multinational corporations that had sent him interview letters on the strength of his finishing first. If he was lucky, he could become Executive Assistant to a CEO. Of course, the Middle East with its tax-free megabucks was an attractive choice. Mom suggested that he see Uncle Krishna before he decides what to do next.

Now in the evening of his life, Uncle Krishna lived with Aunt Seetha in the hills on the outskirts of Ooty. The 72-years old had been consulted by Tejas's family, right from the days of his late grandfather on matters of business, inheritance, marriage, and everything the family considered important.

"There is no harm in giving it a shot," thought Tejas. "At least it would make Mom happy and I could do with fresh air in the hills." So, off to Ooty he went.

Driving through the curved roads and scenic tea gardens, Tejas arrived at Uncle Krishna's house. It was his first visit to the hill station. The chill breeze cut through him like a scalpel. After the crowds of Bombay, the traffic of Delhi, the heat of Calcutta and the humidity of Madras, this was heaven. Uncle Krishna lived on a small plot with a landscaped garden with beautiful flowers in every second pot. At one end of the plot stood a house made of red bricks.

"Wow! What a beautiful house," exclaimed Tejas, as he unloaded his suitcase from Uncle's old Volkswagen Beetle. The two-door, four-passenger, rear-engine car had been sent to pick him up from the station, at the foot of the hills. Uncle Krishna had used the car right from the day he first stepped into the Madras High Court four decades ago.

"She has been with me longer than your aunt has," said Krishna, tapping the hood of the Beetle.

A couple of hours later, the duo was out in the garden, teacups in hand, where the wind blew gently, caressing their faces softly. It was the ideal place to contemplate life.

"So what next, little one?" asked Uncle Krishna. He had never outgrown the habit of calling Tejas "little one."

"Well, I am not sure, Uncle."

"Ah, so that's what brings you here," said Krishna, smiling. Tejas had only a vague idea of what he wanted to do. The internship at a Big Six firm had given him an idea of what he did not want to do instead of what he wanted to do.

"Fame or fortune? What is it that you want?" asked the legal eagle.

"I prefer a slice of both," answered the new CA, as if Uncle Krishna was asking him about his choice of ice cream.

"Well son, you will have to make a choice. Life is about tradeoffs."

"What would you suggest?"

"Well, when you earn lots of money you can spend them during this life time. But if you want to earn fame, which would last beyond your life, you may have to sacrifice on earning money. Fortune is of this life. Fame is of the next," said the knowledgeable lawyer.

"Fortune is knocking at your door; you have got some great offers from the industry. If that's your cup of tea, get into either banking companies or manufacturing companies. You could look at working in MNCs. There you will get a good grounding in the operating procedure, the micro picture. But remember, seven times out of ten, your identity will be crushed in these places.

You will have to work within a system until age turns you gray," he added.

"How?"

"You have to be a grandfather before your opinions are considered in the corporate hierarchy. And given your boyish looks, after some years you may even have to dye your hair a shade gray to make an impression."

Tejas smiled. Being a reformer by nature, he would certainly suffocate in the systems the corporate world was sustained by. In one of the companies that he had audited, a CA was in charge of maintaining the fixed assets register. In another, a CA handled bills. He couldn't see himself doing such jobs.

Tejas hadn't spoken much for the last twenty minutes, only uttering the occasional sentence or two. The aspiration in his voice, however, did not go unnoticed.

"So what is it that you would love to do if you were sure that you would not fail in it?" the lawyer asked.

Tejas looked up at the sky, rubbing his palms together. "Never fail, right? Sure of success, is it?"

"Yes."

"Well, I would like to be a renowned journalist. Investment banking and the silky world of the stock markets excite me. I would like to be looked upon as a serious financial journalist. I would like to travel from city to city, far and wide on business," said the dreamer, visualizing walking down the airport aisle surrounded by admirers.

"A public figure is what this boy wants to be," thought Uncle Krishna. "If that's what you want, go ahead with it," he said aloud.

That was how Tejas Arya joined *New Delhi Times*, a media group that first ran a newspaper and later a television channel. The pay that they offered was a fraction of what a top multinational company had promised him as a CA. But what was it that Professor Muscles had said? "Every man makes his choices public and keeps the reasons private."

ooo

Three days after Tejas Arya left Ooty, Mike Mahi quietly checked into the Queen of hill stations. His mandate: meet Lawyer Krishna.

Many years ago, his dad had been amongst a handful of people for whom Krishna had fought a case against the Colliery and won. Both monetarily and otherwise, the case had been crucial to the colliery workers. And surprise of surprises, the lawyer who usually charged by the quarter-hour refused to take a fee. Mahi Senior had been very, very impressed. So when Mike decided to embark upon a career, Senior told Junior that he must seek the lawyer's advice and blessing.

Junior didn't seek an appointment with the elderly man. He didn't have his number. His dad told him that if you asked for Lawyer Krishna in Ooty, anyone could guide you to his house. He wasn't wrong.

Profusely apologizing to Krishna for turning up unannounced, Mahi told the septuagenarian that he was looking for advice. The lawyer let Mahi speak uninterrupted for half an hour, listening as Mahi outlined his economic background, his stint at St. Anne's and later at Hunt & Smith and how he was now torn between industry and practice. His heart, he said, lay in "practice", but his head told him, "industry." And that was why he was here, he confessed to Krishna.

"Start working towards your dream. Set up your own practice, do things the hard way, you will succeed. But remember, practice is for long distance runners, not sprinters. Struggle on, sacrifice your fees, but never sacrifice your integrity. "

Mahi's eyes brightened. At least here was someone who believed in him.

"It will be very difficult in the beginning. There will be mistakes and there will be failures. Your classmates will be working in cushy jobs, drawing fat salaries and commanding respect and awe in their respective organizations. But stay focused. You will make it. This is the way towards your dream. You have it in you to do it. The country needs people like you."

Now, how could the words of a man who had been in legal practice for over four decades be doubted? Mahi decided that getting into professional practice was the way to go. He was getting into entrepreneurship.

Tejas 8: Mahi 8

That year, Formula One racer the Brazilian Portugese Anyrton Senna, Mike Mahi's personal favorite, died in a car crash.

PART 3: GROWING BIG
1995–2012

16. The Day after … Cont'd

YEAR: 2014
DATE: June 22
Sunday 06:30 a.m.
Mumbai

A copy of the morning's *New Delhi Times* lay beside him. The news was on Page 1. Appearing in bold black headlines, in the only way journalists know to report, were the words: **Financial scandal hits Hindustan Bank. Mike Mahi under the scanner**. Followed by reams and reams of what Mahi saw to be "analytical" hogwash and "expert" opinion.

The first paragraph read: "Hindustan Bank, the country's top bank, fiddled with derivative transactions and under-provided expenses by using questionable practices. Experts point out that it overstated its profits by not marking investments to market. A few offshore investments were not recorded in the books. Loans were granted to doubtful parties against inadequate security."

There was a boxed item on how Mike, Mahi & Associates had looked the other way while authenticating the accounts.

Hands trembling, Mahi flung the paper seven feet away.

Mahi was surprised by some of the details reported. "How did they get access to them?" he wondered. He seethed at parts of the writing that showed a clear lack of research. They had not noticed that his firm audited Hindustan Bank jointly with another firm. Surely his firm could not be held accountable for the negligence, if any, displayed by another firm. Of the areas named, only loans came under his firm and Mahi was sure that his star Director, Doc, would have documented them well.

Mahi did not think all journalists were a pain in the neck. There were extremely competent guys in the field: professional, unbiased and accurate. Like Tejas Arya, whom he held in high regard.

Mahi tried to reach Arya on his mobile. It was still switched off.

Irritated, he paced the room. Right now, he wasn't sure which way the wind would blow. The more he thought about it, the more he felt his initial assessment was wrong. This story, if not handled properly, could spin into a huge scandal. The accounting empire he had so painstakingly built, which spanned countries and continents, could come crashing down.

17. Mahi's First Assignment

Mike Mahi had not risen to stardom overnight. He had built his practice up, brick by brick. It had taken him 20 years to reach his current position.

YEAR 1995

Mumbai

The firm was called Mike, Mahi & Associates. Yes, there was a queer little comma sitting between Mike and Mahi. "Numerology," was his explanation; not that he cared to explain!

It was a one-man, one-table, one-typewriter office. Mahi couldn't afford the luxury of a secretary. He engaged a commerce graduate, but that was more for looking after the office whenever Mahi went to visit the tax office. Mahi was the boss, the secretary, the assistant, the office boy, all rolled in one! He bicycled to work in a city that was fast becoming traffic-snarled. It had nothing to do with being health conscious; it had everything to do with economics.

Mahi's first client was a doctor.

The doctor had had a run-in with his earlier auditor as the latter had failed to file the doctor's Income Tax returns on time. This was despite the fact that all the necessary paperwork had been completed well before the due date for filing. The firm had confirmed to the doctor that the return had been filed.

So when the notice came from the Tax Department, seeking interest and penalty for belated filing, the doctor blew his top. Why engage a professional if things weren't done on time? What got his goat was that the firm had been economical with the truth. He had called up the CA's office and while the secretary put him on hold, he overheard the CA say, "Tell Dr. D'Souza that I am not in office."

That was when the doctor made up his mind to let him go and hire another auditor. He decided to engage a fresher who could get things done for him rather than a senior who had little time for him. That evening, at the Golf Club, he enquired about young auditors and a fellow golfer suggested Mike Mahi's name.

Two days later, he was on the phone with Mike Mahi. The voice at the other end said, "Mike, Mahi & Associates."

"Can I speak to Mike Mahi?"

"Speaking."

"My name is D'Souza. I work for King's Hospital. I am a doctor. I am looking for a CA. Stephen Raj referred your name. When can I meet you?"

"Any time, at your convenience, Doctor," said Mahi. The doctor was impressed. He had expected something like, "Well, let me check my schedule." He knew Mahi was looking for work and was happy he hadn't put up a show. Mahi had passed D'Souza's first test.

"Will 3 p.m. tomorrow be convenient? I will take only twenty minutes of your time."

"Yes, Doctor. I look forward to meeting you."

Mahi cleaned up his 12ft x 10ft office. He hung an imposing picture of Abraham Lincoln on the wall. He had spoken to a contact at King's Hospital to get an idea of the doctor's likes and dislikes. The contact told Mahi that the doctor often quoted Lincoln's Gettysburg Address. The research was important. It was a practice Mahi would use to great effect in future. He bought some chinaware so that the doctor could be served tea. "You don't get a second opportunity to make a good first impression," was Mahi's favorite quip.

Promptly at 3 p.m. D'Souza knocked on Mahi's door. Mahi was pleasantly surprised. He had been expecting a well-built man in his fifties with professorial looks. But Mahi found it difficult to place the balding man anywhere above his mid-forties.

"You have a beautiful office," said the doctor as Mahi escorted him to his seat. There was genuine warmth in his voice. Mahi's eyes moistened. He knew his office had a long way to go before it could even be called presentable. However, it was his only pride, of-course besides his CA qualification, and he knew it would, someday, transform into a beautiful office. From that point on, he decided he would always say good things about others.

"Thank you, Doctor."

The doctor was impressed. He had been expecting something like, "Oh, Doc! You are charitable." He was happy Mahi was proud of his office, no matter how small it might be. Mahi had passed the second test.

"Will you handle my account?" He had gone straight to the point.

"Sure, Doctor. Do let me know what it might involve."

"Well, my secretary keeps tabs on all the receipts from my private medical practice. I receive cheques for consulting work from hospitals. Then there are my investments. You should make sure that dividends and interest have been received and recorded. I would expect you to give me a monthly statement of net income. You will also have to advise me on tax and tax-related investments. It will mean your office will write my books of accounts, prepare my income tax returns and file it on time. For now, I will take the final call on my investments."

"Sure, Doctor."

"What will be your fee, young man?" Again, he was to the point.

"That would depend on the volume of work," Mahi said matter-of-factly.

"I will need you at the most for two days a month, including the advisory and filing." The doctor had obviously done his homework.

"Rs 15,000 per quarter, Sir."

"Well, the work is twenty four days a year, give or take. That's about a month's work. I understand that a fresh CA gets about Rs 5,000 a month. You would naturally like to add some overheads, but I trust that you would not want to load a lot of it on me! I don't like bargaining, but let's say Rs 10,000 per quarter."

"Okay, Doctor."

"Do a good job, and I will ensure you get a lot of referrals."

"Thank you, Doctor."

The doctor stood up to shake hands.

That was how Mike Mahi, the man who aspired to be the President of the National Institute of Certified Public Accountants (NICPA), the country's apex accounting body, secured his first client.

18. Mahi Loses His Virginity

He walked in unannounced.

"Can I meet Mike Mahi? I have a reference from Dr. D'Souza."

"Sure, Sir. Please take your seat. He is on the phone, and will meet you in a couple of minutes. Meanwhile, can I serve you some coffee?" asked Rupa. Rupa was fresh from college and was the young lady that Mahi had recruited to provide secretarial support.

"Sure. That would be great." His parched lips could definitely use a cup or two. He looked around the small office and wondered why Dr. D'Souza might have chosen Mike Mahi. But he trusted the doctor's judgment.

Rupa breezed in with piping hot coffee. Her short t-shirt that ended just below her hip and the tight jeans fit her perfectly. The man loved it: the coffee. Once he was through, Rupa escorted him to Mahi's cubicle. At someone's suggestion, Mahi had recently carved a small space for himself within his tiny office. It gave him a semblance of privacy.

"I want some papers to be filed in the office of the National Registry of Companies. Dr. D'Souza asked me to speak to you."

"No problem, Sir. It will be done tomorrow."

"Actually there is a problem. This document is now time-barred. I want it to be filed and backdated."

"I am not sure if that can be done, Sir."

"Let's give it a shot. Dr. D'Souza has a very high opinion of you."

Those words energized Mahi. "Sure, Sir. We will visit the Registry tomorrow, meet the officer in charge and see what can be done. If you could join me for the meeting, it would be a big help."

"Done."

"Thank you, Mr. Simon."

The man literally jumped from his seat. "How did you know my name was Simon? I never introduced myself!"

Mike said, "I have my ways. That's some proof that Dr. D'Souza is right to trust me, Mr. Simon."

Andrew Simon pressed his lips hard. He nodded, his face flushing. He couldn't do anything else.

The following morning, Mike Mahi and Andrew Simon walked into the office of the National Registry of Companies.

ooo

The National Registry is a wing of the Government of India. Anyone who wishes to form a company has to get clearance from this office. This is also the office where all legal documents relating to companies are filed. There are deadlines for the filing of these documents. In some cases, failure to meet those deadlines can be condoned; in other instances, there are severe penalties, and in some other situations, any delay renders the original transaction void. These documents are also available for viewing by the general public.

Mahi hadn't slept the previous night. He had been thinking of how best to backdate the document. He had gone through the Companies Act and court judgments but had found nothing of help. "Is it possible at all? Or does Simon actually want me to do an underhand deal?"

Still battling with a hundred questions, Mahi found himself in front of the Registry Officer. The man sat behind a cluttered table and had a surprisingly pleasant personality. He gestured to Andrew and Mahi to sit. Over time, Mahi would learn that most officers of the government were seemingly pleasant. Corruption was never written on their faces.

"Yes, how may I help you, Mr....?"

"Mike Mahi." He gave him his visiting card.

"Yes, please go ahead."

Mahi presented his case to the officer.

"What my client is asking for may not be within the letter of the law but it is within its spirit," he said, sounding quite uncomfortable. After a pregnant pause, he continued, trying to sound more confident, "The delay in filing is a technicality. A technicality should not come in the way of natural justice." It was a smart argument that kept all options open. "I would request you to allow the document to be filed, backdated."

"Do you have a precedent to back this?"

"Well, I looked for it all of last night but couldn't find one on record. Perhaps, Sir, you with your vast experience could help us find one, but if there is no precedent and you are convinced of our logic, then you must set the precedent yourself." Mahi remembered what the hockey captain had told Coach Mukherjee many years ago.

The officer smiled.

Any appointment of a person as director of a company had to be filed within thirty days at the office of the National Registry. The delay would not necessarily invalidate the appointment, but if it could be shown that the document had been filed by the deadline date, it would help Andrew Simon in his battle for directorship of the company.

Mahi was right. There were no recorded precedents. The officer liked Mahi's persuasive argument. Anyone else in Mahi's place would have invariably begun by discussing the price. This young man was talking about the law, which the officer found refreshing.

"Okay," he said. "We will do it as a special favor to you."

"Thank you so much, Sir."

As Simon and Mahi stood up to leave, the officer raised his hands, showing his palm. Mahi blinked.

"Not Rs 5000. Not Rs 500,000. Only Rs 50,000," said the officer.

"Right here, or elsewhere?" asked Simon.

"Oh, this place is perfect," said the officer, smiling.

Mike Mahi stared wide-eyed at Simon, who smiled back at the officer. "Is this really happening?" He was watching corruption unfurl before him for the first time. He had just lost his virginity.

The officer turned to Mahi and said, "Now that you know me, should you want anything done at this office… absolutely anything… you come straight to me. No need to meet anyone else. Let's consider ourselves to be in business." The badge on the officer's shirt read: R. Harishchandra.

Mahi was shaken. It was not that he did not know money changed hands in a not so legal way. But he was witnessing it first hand. In one way, he was a party to it. It hurt his integrity.

The moment they stepped out of the Registry, he asked Simon, "Why did you agree to pay him?"

"Because he got the job done."

"Is he not paid a salary by the government? Why should we bribe him, especially when the law was on our side?"

"Are you sure we bribed him? Are you sure the law was on our side? Now, even if it were so, what could we have done if he had sat on our papers? Naturally we are thankful to him. Don't forget he's told you that you can have direct access to him. Relationships open doors. This helped you as much as it helped me."

Andrew Simon added, "Mike that was a gift. That wasn't corruption."

Though he wasn't convinced, Mahi didn't argue. He had grown up in the lap of honesty. His dad wore honesty on his sleeve and was dead set against corruption. If he were to come to know of this, he wouldn't approve at all. But then again, Simon was one of Mahi's clients, a new one at that, and Mahi didn't want to antagonize him.

That night, a distraught Mahi decided to call Uncle Krishna. He was sure the lawyer would help him fight the inner demons on a day when he had actually won his first case.

"In life, there is no black and white, there are only shades of gray. Remember, you had a choice, and you chose to pay," said Krishna.

"No, I did not have a choice. The officer spoke directly to the client, and the client decided to pay." His voice was a little high and he was breathing heavily over the phone.

"Well, you could have stopped him. Remember, acquiescence is also a crime. Watching something taking place and letting it happen is called 'accessory after the fact.' But don't worry too much. If your client's giving him Rs 50,000 was the reason why the officer gave the verdict in your client's favor that surely qualifies as corruption. But if your client paid because he was happy with the outcome, and the amount was not large, it would qualify as a gift."

"I don't buy into your explanation, Sir. How would you define small or large?"

"Well," said Krishna. Mahi could sense his smile. "That's a choice you make. You see, life is about making choices." Mahi still disagreed, but then coming from Uncle Krishna, there must be something deeper to it, he told himself. He tried his best to calm down. When he woke up the next morning, he would be okay.

OOO

Six months later, Andrew Simon was back at Mike Mahi's office. He had been served a tax assessment notice by the Tax Department.

The Tax Department is the place where tax returns are filed, assessments handled, appeals made, and judgments delivered. Every citizen of the country and every business entity operating in India has a unique Tax number on the basis of which the government tracks down who paid how much tax, who was defaulting, and the entire financial history of a person.

Andrew Simon had received a notice for assessment of his tax. He wanted Mike Mahi to handle it.

Mahi was no tax buff. This was his second case of tax assessment. He had completed his debut assignment with the help of a medium-sized firm that specialized in taxation. One day, the firm's partner called him up saying the client had approached them for further tax work, and they were going ahead with it.

It was Mahi's first brush with poaching, a practice that others of his profession had already perfected. So this time around he decided he would handle Simon's case himself.

Over the course of the next week, Rupa and Mahi worked at Simon's office, collating all the information the Tax Department wanted. Every little detail was taken into consideration. The work extended long into the night. But Rupa didn't mind and Mahi made it a point to drop her home himself.

Once the papers were ready, Mahi suggested, like on the earlier occasion, that Simon accompany him to the Tax Department. "At the hearing, you should come with me. I will do the talking. If there is any need for you to respond, I will give you a cue."

"Done."

At 10.30 the next morning, Mahi and Simon were ushered into the officer's cabin. The man appeared stiff and standoffish. He gestured to the duo to sit down.

"Good morning, Sir," said Mahi.

There was no response from the officer. He was busy scribbling something on a piece of paper. The table was littered with files with titles like "Urgent," "Top Secret," "Immediate." Mahi didn't know how "Urgent" could be different from "Immediate", or why there was a "Secret" and a "Top Secret". He made a mental note to ask Mr. Stiff later.

Suddenly, Mr. Stiff sprang to life. Running through the papers, he asked a range of questions. Between Mahi and Simon, they answered them all. They also agreed to present those replies in writing. Whenever Stiff wanted data "for my file", Mahi agreed to give it. When he excused himself to visit the restroom, Mahi whispered to Simon, "Once we give the data, they won't even go through it. But if we don't give it, he might scent something amiss!"

Three hours later, the assessment was coming to a close. The officer promised to look into all the details and issue a "No-addition" order by the end of the fortnight. A No-addition order would mean that the return filed was perfect and that no further tax was payable.

After that, the conversation got down to small talk. Mahi was pleasantly surprised that Mr. Stiff was communicative.

"I recently read the book *How to Win Friends and Influence People* by Dale Carnegie," said the officer.

"That's a lovely book," said Mahi.

"The principles laid out there are applicable at all times, at all ages. Every young boy and every young girl, every young man and every young woman, should read it."

"I understand Carnegie committed suicide," Mahi said.

"I am not too sure if that's true. Even if it is, it does not take away the inherent merit of whatever he has said in his book."

"Very true, Sir. I have two copies of another Carnegie book. I shall send one of them to you."

"That would be nice."

"I have heard a lot about you. People say you are one of the few officers who never takes money." As usual, Mahi had done some background check.

"How can you say that when you haven't even made an offer?"

All of them, Stiff, Simon and Mahi, had a hearty laugh.

"For sure, honesty is the best policy, but those who follow that policy are not necessarily honest. In fact, I might even say honesty is the lack of opportunity," said the officer.

As they came out of the Department, a confused Mahi asked Simon, "Is he fishing for money?"

Simon responded, "He said it, right? Offer and check."

Mahi laughed.

19. Arya Rubs it in

Around the time Mike Mahi picked up his third assignment, Tejas Arya was receiving many job offers. It pleased Shakti Arya that his son Tejas was now hot property in the corporate market.

A leading FMCG company wanted him to take responsibility for the pricing of cosmetics and detergents. "It isn't my idea of fun," Tejas told his dad. Another offer arrived from the National Oil Corporation, a Fortune-500 company. "Who wants to prepare invoices day in and day out?" asked Tejas. When a large financial institution gave him the position of a credit officer, a role that he loved, they placed him in Grade A while the IIM grads got into the higher Grade B. "They can't treat a top CA with disrespect," he told everyone who was within earshot. Dad asked him to meet the company and explain, but Tejas felt that if they could not spot talent right away, there was no point meeting them.

Six months on, India's top ranking student of accounting still did not have a job. "Hey, Tejas, what's the plan?" asked his dad.

"Dad, I intend to apply to *New Delhi Times*."

"But it isn't a popular choice and it doesn't pay much."

"Doesn't matter. You have earned enough to last three lifetimes!"

Tejas was a big fan of an investigative journalist, who happened to be a CA, who had unleashed a train of events that had brought down two national governments. The man wrote with the kind of clarity and precision not usually given to accountants. His dad reluctantly agreed to his son's choice.

His mother wept that night like she had wept when he had chosen to do commerce.

"My mother, wife of my father, don't keep crying," said Tejas, smiling as he set out to Mumbai to try his hand at being a journalist. The paper was only too happy to take him. They had ambitious plans. In a few years they would be starting a television channel and promised Tejas that he could straddle the two ventures.

OOO

The first Press Conference he attended was a revelation.

It was in a five-star hotel. At the entrance, an usher in a large red turban, freshly starched trousers and loose kurta opened the glass-paneled door and greeted him with an elaborate bow. He turned to check if someone was behind him and found none. Tejas was distracted by the spacious front office where smartly dressed, pretty young ladies wore beatific smiles. "Ah, hmm…" he nodded in acknowledgment.

He walked up to one of them, "Where's the presser?"

"This way Sir," said the lady, guiding him to the room. She walked too close to him for his comfort. He could smell the jasmine perfume on her dress. Soon a large ballroom beckoned him. It was huge and well lit by twelve sparkling chandeliers.

"Why is the company spending so much money?" wondered Tejas. A man in a gray safari suit led him to the table where drinks were being served. Tejas looked left, and looked right to see if he could locate any known faces. His editor had told him that deals were struck at such parties. Soon, he spotted a senior and began making small talk.

An hour later, the meeting began. There was a large turnout of media personnel. The company outlined its financial performance and its plans for the future. Then the chairman asked rather perfunctorily, "Any questions?"

An investment analyst asked what was obviously a planted question. After a few other friendly questions were fielded, the executive who had earlier guided Tejas to the drinks table announced, "Well, folks, let's break for dinner."

That was when Tejas put his hand up, with an "Excuse me," annoying both the company and the media. He wanted to ask a question.

He had noticed a small change in accounting policy tucked away in a little corner of the published accounts. Line 12 on

Page 37 had given him the clue. The company had changed the method of accounting for depreciation. He asked, "If you had not made a change in the method of accounting for depreciation would the profits, the reserves and the net fixed assets not have been lower?"

"Well," said the CFO, "the law allows a change in the method of accounting for depreciation."

Tejas looked down as his senior stuffed a chit in his hand. He read and tore it into four pieces.

"But can you tell us the reasons behind making the change? Is there any logic to it, or was it done to report higher profit?" The atmosphere was getting tense.

The CFO said, "Well, the law allows a change in the method of accounting for depreciation."

"Sir, I repeat my question. What were the specific reasons for making the change?"

The CFO said, "No specific reasons. The law allows it. Period."

An elderly journalist stood up. "Mr. CFO, I think the young man has a point. We would be happy to have your direct response to that. Do you or don't you have a reason for the change in the method of accounting?"

The CFO responded with, "Well, the law allows a change in the method of accounting for depreciation."

After one more question, dinner was announced. The reporters from the vernacular press and from non-financial papers surrounded Tejas to ask him about the implications of his question. He had become nothing short of a hero to them. The investment analyst gave Tejas a piece of gratuitous advice. "Your point was good. I noticed it too! But we should not ask embarrassing questions."

Arya later learned that it was Mike, Mahi & Associates who had advised the company to alter the method of accounting for depreciation to report better profits. Later, a Big-Six firm had seconded it. It was perfectly legal. But he was surprised that Mahi would suggest something like that.

Tejas made it a habit to go to every presser, well prepared. He would do his homework and if hard questions had to be asked, he would ask them. The senior who had passed him the chit politely told him that it wasn't fair to ask contentious questions. Tejas smiled. He soon developed a reputation for being a journalist who couldn't be trifled with. He had enthusiasm, he had courage and he had chutzpah.

ooo

A week later, Tejas Arya ran into Mike Mahi. It was their first meeting after leaving Hunt & Smith.

"Hi, Tejas? How's life? What are you up to these days?"

"I am fine, Mahi. I am working with *New Delhi Times*. No, not as an accountant, as a journalist."

"Oops, India's top accountant shifting streams to journalism? Great! By the way, I am now in CA practice."

One thing led to another and soon Mahi was talking about speed money at the National Registry of Companies (NRC) and about the "did-you-offer-me" officer at the Tax Department.

Tejas wanted to know whether everything had a price tag at the NRC and at the Tax Department. Mahi wasn't too sure and said, "It takes two to tango. After all, if the client's hands were clean or if the client were willing to fight it out, there would be no need to grease someone's palm."

That Sunday, the *New Delhi Times* carried a story titled **"Shopping Cart: CAs play middlemen".** The byline: Tejas Arya. It carried an item-wise service list at the two government offices along with a price tag. Veterans of the profession were taken aback by the accuracy of the figures. Arya indicated that all information had been sourced from CAs and from government officials and that they were all on tape.

Mahi was fuming. Was his conversation on tape too? "That jackass thinks like a journalist and talks like a journalist. Then why didn't he study journalism?"

Tejas 9: Mahi 8

20. Mahi Meets the Young Lady

The year was 1999. India had tragically crashed out of the World Cup Cricket in England. Mike Mahi was now 27 and his parents wanted him to get married, but he had other plans. He first wanted to put his professional practice on a more even keel before thinking of setting up a family.

It was another typical evening when he entered the squash court, whistling to himself. He often practiced here, mostly to keep himself physically fit and mentally sharp. He noticed a young lady jumping up and down, as though springs were attached to her shoes, as she waited for her opponent to take a shot. Her ponytail too popped up and down. She wore black shorts ending two inches above her knees and a loose blue t-shirt.

She was a splendid player. To Mahi, her game was breathtaking. When she finished her session and was walking past him, sweating profusely, the CA used his racquet to tap her back. She whirled around, her cheeks turned red as she screamed, "What the hell?"

He extended his hand, "Hi, My name is Mike Mahi. Don't get annoyed. You play wonderful squash."

The color on her face changed to pink. "Wow. Mike Mahi, the man Dad speaks about so often. The rising star of the accounting profession who had let slip the opportunity to play for India in the hockey World Cup, because it would clash with his preparation for the CA final examination!" Thoughts raced in her mind.

"You play very well."

"Thank you, Sir. Are you really Mahi, the auditor?" Her smile was captivating.

"No, I am Mahi, the chartered accountant."

CAs preferred to be called that way. That was because in rural India tax practitioners who hadn't qualified as CA were called auditors.

"In some countries we are called certified accountants."

She smiled.

"Let me buy you a cup of coffee to celebrate your excellent game," said Mahi.

"Yup. Sure, sure. But coffee alone won't do. You number cruncher, you will have to buy me cheeseburgers as well."

They walked down to the cafeteria. Mahi chose a table that gave a good view of the garden outside. She refused to sit and stood up to her full height, alternating between standing on her toes and standing on her heels. In awe of Mahi, she made small conversation. Okay, he was not a rock-star. Okay, the city at large would not recognize him. But she had heard a lot about him from her father, and she liked what she had heard.

He ordered a chocolate pastry for her. "Ooh! My favorite!" She sank her teeth into it. The silky icing melted in her mouth. The cake was so soft, she didn't have to chew, just swallow. She finished every bit of it leaving nothing on the plate, licking her fingers and smacking her lips as she craved for more! Mahi couldn't help but smile, and offered to buy her another one.

Soon she became bold enough to ask, "I heard that you sacrificed an India cap to prepare for your CA?"

Mahi was surprised at how these bits of information traveled. After all, his skipping the World Cup had been more than five years ago. And he was only a rising star then. "Well, that's right."

"But how could you have done that? How could you have let India down? Doesn't the country come before the self? "

Mahi grinned. It reminded him of the torment that had raged in his mind when he had to make the difficult choice.

Playing for India had been a dream. But how long would he be able to play top-flight hockey; five years, six years? That glory, even if he were to be draped in the tricolor following a World Cup or an Olympic gold, would soon be forgotten. Also, he couldn't make a living from playing hockey. CA was a different game. He knew that if he performed well he would get a swell job or he could practice. If he did it with dignity and grace, he might one day bring laurels to the country through his profession. That would be the long-term plan, the greater patriotism. Playing hockey and doing CA simultaneously was impossible. Both were full-time efforts. CA was no walk-in-and-write-it exam. Thus, in the end, the head won over the heart. CA won over hockey.

He didn't tell her all this. She was too young and wouldn't understand. He smiled at her. "Some choices are difficult to explain. Another day, another time, when I have gotten to know you better, I will."

"Wow. So we will meet again? Great."

"Hmmm… I will drop you home on my way back."

"No, it's okay; I will take a bus."

He either didn't hear her or simply didn't want to take no for an answer in this case. He slid into the driver's seat, opening the passenger side door and said, "Get in." She did. He started the car and when they had pulled out of the parking lot, he asked her, "Where do you live?"

"Victoria Castles."

Mahi wanted to kick himself. Castles, as it was called, was in the opposite direction. If he were to now take a right, he would be on the road to his home. If he were to take a left, it would lead to Castles. It would be a thirty-minute drive. So if he were to drop her at her house, it would be a full extra hour of travel.

He turned right.

"I will get down here," she remarked. "Nope, you should get down a kilometer further down this road," he said.

"But Victoria Castles is in the opposite direction," she cooed.

"So what?" he asked. "You can catch a bus and come back this way!" His eyes danced in triumph. She raised an eyebrow at him but didn't say anything.

They were now driving at a steady speed of 30–40 kilometers per hour. You couldn't drive faster than that in this traffic. Vehicles often overtook them from the wrong side, the left. Some overtook them from the right. Mike had even placed a sticker on the rear of his car that read, "Do not overtake on the left, it is not right." No one cared.

Though the traffic lights changed, he continued to drive. She said, "Hey, red, red." With deadpan seriousness, he remarked, "That's amber; not red." It really got her goat.

"I know. I know. I was saying it would soon turn red." He sighed, "Oh!" She frowned. "What the hell does he think of himself? Does he believe that he alone has a feel for the language? How egoistic he is."

The one-kilometer drive was over. He slowed down. "Your bus stop is about a hundred feet from here. 16 J goes to your place."

She was angry. She had grown up in this city, and he was now telling her which bus to take. As she got down, she wondered whether she would ever really become friends with him. The thought didn't even cross Mahi's mind. For all that he knew, this might have been the last time that he saw her.

He could not have been more wrong. Yes, he would meet her many more times over the next three years. He had never dated during college, and in his CA the gender ratio was too skewed. This was the woman with whom he would spend the rest of his life. In the third year of their friendship, the two got married.

She was Tanya Roy.

ooo

Tanya chased Mahi like a lively kid would chase her dad for candy. She would scandalize him with all the happenings in her life, including what happened in college, her plans after her post graduation, who was seeing whom in the film industry and all the trivia one could imagine. Her infectious enthusiasm appealed to him, but he never imagined that he was interacting with his future wife. He would drive her to the beach or to a restaurant whenever he felt he could no longer avoid her or when he thought he needed a break!

Then one day, in May 2002, she called him when he was at work. "I got through! Yes, man, I got through!"

"Tanya Roy. Don't get on my nerves. You got through what?"

"My dear Mike Mahi, I got my admission to the University of Pennsylvania to do my doctorate in Psychology" Mahi could imagine her jumping with joy. He heard her say: "Now listen, I'll meet you tonight at your place. Let's go out for dinner. My treat."

Mahi sighed. It was peak season for him at work. Leaving office just like that wasn't on. But when Tanya was on a high, she was difficult to handle. He was excited too, but deep inside, he felt a little empty at the thought that he might not see her for the next few years.

He went home and readied himself for the date, if he could call it that. The doorbell rang as he was engrossed in his thoughts. Tanya stood there, dressed in starched cotton sari and a pair of sassy heels. Mahi whistled, even as he scanned her from head to toe. "You look ravishing!"

For no apparent reason, she took off the shoes. Then Tanya stood on her toes, rising to her full height, reaching a shade under Mahi's neck. Mahi bent, his hands now on her shoulders and an electric wave passed through her. He pushed her chin up and she looked him in the eyes. He surprised himself by gently kissing her forehead. A feeling of Godliness swept through Tanya. They then left for the restaurant in his car.

The ambience at the Chinese restaurant was great. Both of them loved Chinese food. He ordered some noodles and mixed vegetable curry. They started by sharing a sweet corn vegetable soup, dumplings and spring roll. He looked at the soup and wondered how this little lady would be as a psychologist.

That was when she said: "Mahi, should we get married?"

Mahi choked on his soup, rushed for the napkin and spilt the water he wanted to drink to stop his coughing.

"Huh?"

"Will you marry me?"

"Seriously?"

"No I was just practicing on you!" The sarcasm oozed out, and Mahi caught it and smiled.

"Tell me one good reason why I should marry you."

"Because no one else will, and in that case you will stay a bachelor all your life."

He held her hand, even as he looked into her eyes. She blushed.

"Yes, my dear. I will marry you."

He wasn't sure if she was serious or joking. He was still flabbergasted that she had asked. When she leapt up in joy and put her hands around his neck in a tight embrace, in full public view, he knew that she meant it. Six months later the two entered into wedlock in a simple function, where their parents, a few close friends and relatives were present.

She was 25 and he was about 31 years old.

21. Mahi's First Networking Assignment

Mahi's business had moved into its fifth year. There were a few individual accounts, some tax advisories, a happy quantum of bookkeeping work, some small partnership and corporate audits, a few certifications, a couple of secretarial maintenance jobs. It was good; it could be better.

His office space was larger than before, about 1500 square feet.

There was Doc, the audit manager who did a splendid job as Mahi's Man Friday. The guy swore by documentation; hence the name Doc.

"Are there backup workings?" "Have you taken a photocopy of the rental agreement?" "Have you date-stamped the papers?" "Have you made notes on the Directors' meetings?" "Have you recorded the sample size and the methodology for selecting the sample?" "Have you indexed the file?" Have you done this, and have you done that?

If something wasn't on paper, that something didn't exist for Doc. Sometimes, his requirements bordered on being extremely eccentric. While publicly they all called him Doc, in private conversations, people referred to him as Cranco Doc. He lived by the paper. No one dared to say, "He would die by the paper."

Doc wasn't a CA. A postgraduate in quantitative techniques, he had done his M-Stat at the National Institute of Science. Mahi had hired him because Doc was awesome at sample selection and breathtaking in data analytics, long before that term had captured the audit profession's imagination. Dark of complexion and curly haired, he wore thick glasses that were the outcome of years of poring over endless documents. Mahi once suggested he switch to wearing contact lenses. Doc refused. Looks didn't matter to him. Books did. A first-rate bookworm, he spent most of his waking hours in the firm. People believed that when he talked to his engineer wife, he talked about Company Law, MRTP Act and Nash equilibrium.

There were a couple of interns. One of them, Dina Iyengar, now in her final year, showed great promise. Smart, she came from a convent school background, was well-mannered and did her work with joy. She had done her Intermediate examination well and Doc was sure she would get an All-India rank in her Final.

Then there was Rupa, Mahi's Executive Assistant, who helped him with office maintenance. She was 5' 5" in socks; her high-heeled footwear added two inches to her height. She had thick, beautiful hair and a slim body. She had studied in an expensive international finishing school and this was her first job. Her big smile made her the darling of all those who interacted with her. She wore a mix of ethnic, modern, and formal clothes, and was someone people looked forward to seeing each day.

The sixth person on the team was an office assistant.

Mahi, Doc, Dina, Rupa, a second intern and an office assistant; well, that was the full size of the office.

Mike called a meeting. The agenda was simple. He wanted Doc to prepare the firm's profile for circulation.

"What?" exclaimed Dina, scandalized.

An audit firm drawing up its profile reminded her of wannabe actresses, clutching their folder of photographs, walking up and down from the offices of film producers. Could there be anything more demeaning, she wondered.

Mike looked mildly surprised. "What 'what'?" he asked.

"How can we circulate our own profile?" asked Dina.

"There is an advertisement in the *Economic Times* from a top company asking audit firms to present their credentials."

"But we can't respond to that. The code doesn't allow us." Clause 6 of the *Code of Conduct* of the NICPA which read, "A CA will be guilty of professional misconduct if he solicits client or professional work either directly or indirectly, by circular, advertisement, personal communication or interview or by any other means.," came blinking on Dina's radar." Without realizing it, she had actually spoken those words!

"That's okay," said Mahi, a little annoyed. "Our firm has received a mail from the company asking us whether we are interested." That was a lie. Which top company would write to this one-horse firm? But Mahi was now okay with half-truths. He didn't believe in the adage that a lie is a lie is a lie.

"Mahi, should we respond to an ad? Imagine: would the world's top neurosurgeons rush to put in their CVs if the head of a state wanted urgent medical attention? Would they be saying, 'Hey, I have done 500 surgeries'? Or would you expect someone like management guru Peter Drucker to advertise his credentials for running a seminar?"

Mike cut her short. "That's good for them, Dina. With us, there is no other way to tell potential clients that we exist. Anyway we are not soliciting, we are responding. Period." His irritation was palpable.

Dina couldn't resist. "From here, the step towards direct soliciting will be small."

"Madam, I have a living to make."

Dina wouldn't give up. After all, it was Mike who had taught her the virtue of never giving up on a point of principle.

"So the line between profession and business has waned. How would it look if doctors, lawyers and teachers took out front-page advertisements?"

"That will do, Dina. We can discuss the pros and cons some other day. Today, we will get down to the business of how to respond to this ad."

He listed what would go into the profile. "First, we must give them a list of the firm's top clients and the annual billing."

"Would Dr. Denton Cooley, the world's top heart surgeon, give a prospective client a list of his patients, and how much he charged them?" Dina asked herself.

Next, Mike wanted the head of the audit and the composition of the audit team to be named.

"So Denton Cooley would have to name his operating team. He would have to say who picks up the scalpel, who stitches the heart, and who swabs the blood?"

Mike was saying, "One partner, one Principal Associate, two Senior Audit Managers, one Audit Manager. That makes for five qualified staff. Three interns, three support staff, five administrative staff. A total of sixteen."

The office had only six people, well, seven if you counted the boy who served them tea!

"Annual billing: Rs 60 lakhs." That was a 200 percent lie. The office billing was Rs 20 lakhs, if you included the expense reimbursement.

"Number of clients: 30." That was about double the number that Mike, Mahi & Associates serviced.

Mike knew that the numbers surprised both Doc and Dina.

He explained. "I have spoken to a fellow practitioner. For the purpose of bagging this assignment, our two entities will be sort of merged. Our firm's name stands. My fellow practitioner will be designated Principal Associate Partner. We will execute the task. He will take 30 percent of the fee. The staff of his firm will be considered staff of our firm. That should explain the increased number."

"You are talking as though this assignment were already in our pocket," said Doc.

"My gut feeling is that, given the regulations, no major firm will apply for this position. The smaller ones will think hard and long before they decide. By being first, we will have an advantage. Once we get the call, it is anybody's game."

With the reference to "regulations", Dina smelt a victory of sorts. "Does the ethical issue of responding to an ad not apply to us?"

Mike was curt. "We will cross that bridge when we come to it."

Dina's dad worked in the corporate sector. He had told Dina that you can quarrel with your boss, give him your input, and argue with him endlessly but when the boss finally takes a decision you will have to abide by it and execute it.

"This is no longer a profession. This is becoming a business. Like selling soap and detergent. Like selling contact lenses and condoms." Dina kept these thoughts to herself.

Doc and Dina finally prepared the profile and sent it to the advertiser. Three days later, the phone call came.

ooo

"I am Paul. Sabrina Paul from National Tea Corporation. Can I speak to Mike Mahi?

Rupa connected the call to Mahi.

"Would it be convenient for you to meet our Accounts Manager in connection with some audit certifications? Will tomorrow four in the evening be okay? He will take only fifteen minutes of your time."

"Yes, madam. I look forward to meeting you and him." The "you" before the "him" was a carefully chosen order.

That evening, Mike Mahi went to Sajjad Ali, the city's top outlet for readymade attire. He bought himself a new khaki-colored trouser and a sky blue full- sleeved branded shirt and matching tie. It cost him a small fortune if you added the blazer that he impulsively picked up at the shop. From the nearby bookstore, he also helped himself to an expensive file, in which he placed his firm's profile.

The following day, sharp at 3:55 p.m. he, along with Doc, walked into the reception area of National Tea Corporation. Someone had once told him about the virtue of being neither too early nor too late. If you turned up for an appointment twenty minutes before time, people might think you had nothing better to do. You may have nothing better to do, but why let the world know?

Sharp at 4 p.m., Sabrina Paul walked in and escorted Mahi and Doc to the office of the Accounts Manager. Wow! This office was a lot richer than some of the top offices he had been to during his internship. Mahi was taken in by the opulence. He promised himself that soon he would sit in an office of such splendor.

"Hi, I am Venkat. Welcome to my office." Mahi was tongue-tied. He had expected an elderly man. What he instead saw was someone a lot younger, maybe in his thirties. Mahi gathered his wits just in time to say, "Hi. Thanks."

Venkat got down to business immediately. "I was surprised when a small firm like yours made an application for this assignment. I liked the ambition and the speed with which you responded.

"That's why I wanted to meet you, and tell you in person why we cannot offer the assignment to you."

Doc's rare, slight smile was wiped off completely.

Mahi did not show his disappointment. "But can you let us in on what this assignment is. Then I could explain our credentials."

Venkat felt he wouldn't lose anything in talking to Mahi.

"We want stock verifications done each quarter at sixteen locations across India. This would include test check of material movements and 100 percent verification of inventories. Two persons will be needed to work four days on the job. Some previous direct experience will help. It calls for proper documentation and organized working."

Mahi turned to Doc. "Doc, can you explain to Venkat how we handled a similar assignment for Greenwich Soaps?"

Doc went on to explain the process, the methodology, the stratified sampling adopted, the documentation, the working paper maintenance, and the report writing. It was professionalism at its very best. Venkat was impressed. He was beginning to feel that he was dealing with a bunch of real professionals.

Of course Mike, Mahi & Associates had done no such work for Greenwich Soaps. For all that one knew, there was no such entity. It was a name Mahi had picked out of thin air. What the firm had done the previous night was complete research on stock verification and stores audit.

The "you" before "him" had helped Mahi learn from Sabrina Paul that the assignment here was related to stores and stocks.

"So you have the experience and the skill set. But we want to hand it over to one firm, and your firm does not operate at so many locations. This is something that only the biggies can handle."

"Venkat, none of the big guns have offices in sixteen places. A research report done by us," (he had looked into NICPA's register of firms the previous night) "tells me that the biggest of them has six branches. They will have to travel to ten places and your company will have to pick up the tab. I have a network of associates in all sixteen places. You can easily save on peripheral costs without sacrificing the quality of performance."

Doc spilled the water he was drinking. Mahi had no network of friends in sixteen centers. He was shooting from the hip. He hoped he wouldn't end up shooting himself in the foot.

"But we don't want to deal with so many firms."

"You don't have to deal with them. Mike, Mahi & Associates will do it. We will be your one-point contact. We will draw up the audit program with your help. We will rope in the fifteen firms. We will interact with them; mentor them. We will file all the reports to you. Within the first three months, we will visit all locations at least once to verify whether things are on the right track."

Venkat was beginning to get interested. "What will it cost?"

Mahi made some rapid back-of-the-envelope calculations. "Sixteen locations. Two men for each location. Four days per location. That's 128 man-days each quarter. If you take Sunday as a holiday, that's approximately five man-months. A graduate gets a salary of Rs 5,000 per month. So our manpower cost on that score would be Rs 25,000. Sixteen qualified hands will have to look at the report for a day or two. That's one man-month. That should cost about Rs 20,000. Total Rs 45,000 per quarter.

"If I use a ratio of 4:1, which is what we typically use for pricing, I would like to quote Rs 180,000 per quarter for the sixteen locations. I am not counting the audit program design which I would put on my account. For one year, we can, therefore, look at Rs 720,000 for sixteen locations put together. You could add our travel cost to the sixteen locations separately. We will travel functionally and lodge functionally."

The man had spoken non-stop.

To Venkat, the costing looked sexy. The nearest figure that he had received from a couple of firms was twelve lakhs. He had been willing to settle for ten lakhs. And here was Mike, Mahi & Associates, prepared to do the job for 7.2 lakhs plus modest expenses. It made sense financially. His company had given him a budget of ten lakhs. But would Mike Mahi be able to deliver?

Looking at Mahi and Doc, it was clear they were aggressive young men with a dream. He thought he could take his chances. After all, under the incentive plans, 20 percent of cost savings would accrue to him.

"I don't like to bargain, but make it Rs 500,000." Mike had heard a similar remark when he had picked up his first assignment from Dr. D'Souza.

"Venkat, my costing is tight. Can we close at Rs 600,000 since we are building a relationship?"

"You will hear from me within a week."

Mahi was all smiles as they shook hands and walked out. Doc kept his own counsel. "Are we going to start scouting for sixteen people now?" he asked.

"Yup. And beginning today you are Chief Head of Audits." As though there were various heads! Mahi was learning to live by bluster. "Your first job is to line up associates in sixteen different centers. And get it done pronto."

OOO

A week later, Mike, Mahi & Associates received a letter from National Tea.

Dear Mike Mahi:

I thank you and your colleague for spending your valuable time with me last week and sharing your experience on stock audits. I respect your knowledge and wisdom and look forward to working with you some time in the future. For the moment, the stock check is being assigned to Hunt & Smith.

Regards,

Venkat

Doc was crestfallen. Mahi said, "No issues Doc. Let's go ahead and build our network. This model will take the firm to greater heights."

OOO

A few days later, Mahi called National Tea Corporation and asked for Venkat. Sabrina connected him to the busy executive. "Sir, Mike Mahi is on the line. He wants to speak to you."

"Now, pray, who is he?"

"He is the one who met you last week on the stock audit engagement along with his colleague."

"What does he want? He is pushy. I did a background check on him. There is no company called Greenwich Soaps. He had spun a yarn. You think I should meet him?"

"I think you should. After all, you liked his yarn until you came to know it was a yarn, which means that he had done his homework. Not everyone has work experience. Everyone needs an opening. Hear him out."

"Hmmm… the man seems to have made an impression on you. Connect him."

Mahi came on the line. "Hi Venkat, I called to invite you to dinner some time this week. It would be great if you could join me."

A surprised Venkat asked, "But what's the occasion?"

"Nothing unusual. I thought Doc and I would celebrate a little success that we have had this week."

"But I am tied up with work. You know my office doesn't allow me the luxury of private dinners."

"Doesn't matter. Let's make it an official dinner."

"I didn't mean it that way. I said that I only attend dinner parties, held publicly, especially when it's an invitation from service providers or prospective service providers."

Mahi let that jibe slide.

"Venkat, it's just an informal evening together. If you are busy, we can go another day."

That was how Mahi's friendship with Venkat began and over the years, it blossomed.

22. Trouble at Titanic

On the 14th and 29th of each month, someone from Mahi's office would turn up at Dr. D'Souza's clinic to meet the doctor's secretary and collect the invoices, the expense bills, the cheque stubs, the updated passbook, and other documents related to the fortnight. The doctor put them all in a large manila envelope. Mahi wondered at the meticulousness of the physician's efforts. He rarely had to call the doctor or his bank for any clarifications.

On the 4th of each month, at 11:30 a.m. sharp, Mahi would meet D'Souza with the month's accounts drawn up: the cashbook updated, the bank statements reconciled, an invoice-wise payables statement prepared, and the doctor's income and expense statement along with the balance sheet. Each quarter, a profit projection for the rest of the year would be made in order to compute and pay the advance tax.

If the doctor was meticulous, Mahi was no less. When D'Souza's credit card statement had an expense for the purchase of two saris, Mahi marked it to his personal account. He received a hand-written note from the doctor thanking him for doing the right thing.

D'Souza introduced a fellow doctor to Mahi, and asked him to carry out similar services for him. Over the course of the year, he introduced ten more. Over the next year, these ten introduced about ten each and by the end of the fifth year, Mahi was providing accounting services for 610 doctors. He kept the price static, engaged graduates, introduced technology and provided top-class, error-free service. He half-jokingly told the doctors, "You take care of patients, and I will take care of your money."

This Accounting Service was the first vertical that he opened in Mike, Mahi & Associates.

Cranco Doc oversaw the operations. He introduced processes and defined defects. For instance, if the date were wrongly entered, it was a defect. If someone had debited the wrong expense head, it was a defect. If the wrong amount had been entered, it was a defect. Quality checkers were appointed. Errors were flagged. Every graduate went through a training program and was rewarded for defect-free working. The permissible errors were fifty for handling a million transactions. The vertical operated at five-sigma and the firm planned to touch six-sigma soon.

It was a roller-coaster ride. A few clients suggested booking fictitious expenses. Some would have one car but would want to book expenses for payment to three drivers! Mahi would have none of it. Some would want Mike, Mahi & Associates to get spending-bills from third parties and offer to pay five percent on it. Mahi would have none of it. Some wanted to write off personal expenses as professional expenses. One said that he worked sixteen hours a day and hence two-third of what he paid his barber would have to be tax-expensed. Mahi would have none of it.

If you wanted it, accounting could be so dishonest.

A client once asked Doc, "You are doing accounting, not auditing. Book whatever bills I submit." Doc thought there was a point there, but Mahi explained to him the firm's credibility would be on the line. It was Mahi's hope that if an assessee filed a return and attached an accounting statement that had the stamp "Prepared by Mike, Mahi & Associates" affixed to it, the Tax Department would approve it immediately, knowing that the firm would not be resorting to skullduggery.

The firm lost clients. These were the ones who were upset at Mahi taking the moral high ground or at his sitting in judgment over what was an appropriate expense and what was not, as if he was from the Tax Department. Nevertheless, Mahi managed to sail through year eight with 1010 happy clients!

His network of professionals helped. He shared his fee liberally. He was keener on having a high top-line and to have a large client base than on retaining huge net profits. Over time, the Tax Department came to trust Mike Mahi. He developed a spotless reputation. Mahi could not but help remember what a senior in the profession had once told him, "Whatever you do, make sure you never do accounting work. It's beneath the dignity of a professional accountant. You will be competing with non-professionals."

Meanwhile, the contact with R. Harishchandra at the National Registry of Companies was bearing fruit. In double quick time, Mahi got to know almost all the senior officers of the Registry personally, including the Registrar and the Regional Director. In all professional interactions, he made it a point to discuss only the law. Doc ensured there were extensive notes in the office files documenting these discussions. Among senior officials, Mahi came to be known as a man of substance. His networked associates made the necessary contacts with the Registry's regional offices in other metros.

Money did change hands in crooked ways, but the clients handled these transactions. In the early days, Mahi refused to entertain those clients who had once gotten their cases cleared by monetary inducements, despite having received Mahi's solid professional advice. With time, Mahi decided that this was no concern of his. Of course, he would change his tune years later.

ooo

Venkat had now started giving him leads. Mahi made it clear to his clients that he could handle any work anywhere in India at a reasonable cost. He fed this work, as it came in, to his network of associates. Sometime in 2005 he had his next big break that took him and his firm on to a whole new orbit.

A new CFO had just taken over at Titanic Ltd. He invited Mike, Mahi & Associates to do a process study of traveling expenses. Doc was leading the assignment. The two-member team of Doc and Dina stumbled on a fraud of gigantic proportions.

ooo

As the signal turned green, she walked briskly along the zebra line, confidence personified.

It was 7:30 in the morning. She flashed her ID card and checked past the security gate of Titanic. "Morning, madam. You look good," said the man at the gate. The beige-salwar and the off-white kameez that she was wearing had apparently made an impact. "Good morning, Paul," she replied, taking a quick look at the nameplate that the security officer had pinned to his shirt. Mahi had told her that people loved the sound of their name.

With her spectacles perched on her nose, she marched off to the audit cabin. There was very little time for small talk.

Titanic was in the FMCG business. In the manner typical of Indian factories, it worked around the clock, workers moving in three shifts. Its accounts department would be in, full house, at 8 a.m. While the working hours officially ended at 4 p.m., the bean-counters would stay back until 8 every night. God knew what kept them back that long.

The working hours for Mike, Mahi & Associates would begin only 90 minutes later at 9:30 a.m. But today, Dina was early as she wanted to be alone while preparing the draft report on an extremely sensitive matter.

She had got a whiff of a racket a week ago. She was auditing "travel" at the Rs 1,750 crore company that was struggling hard to retain its market share. The competition was tough, and employees traveled extensively to fight competition in the marketplace.

Employees' travel bills included taxi fare from their residences to the station and from the railway station to the hotel. They all claimed this as a matter of course. No documentary evidence was attached. "What if they traveled by bus and pocketed the differential?" she asked herself.

She looked at the company's travel policy document. It said, "Actual cost when backed by evidence or Rs 250 flat if no evidence is adduced." So, technically the employees were right in their claim. But Dina argued that this technicality would fall flat if they had not actually incurred the cost. "There can be no reimbursement in respect of an item if expenditure is not incurred," she had read somewhere.

For that, she had to prove the expenditure had not been incurred. She decided to dig. And what she saw, she didn't like one bit.

Her boss, Mahi, had set the tone. If he were to travel with his wife on business trips and if they were to check into the same hotel room, he would always pay out of his pocket for the difference between double occupancy and single occupancy. This despite the fact that he was the co-founder and the principal owner of the firm. Similarly, if he traveled economy class with his wife, he would pay his wife's fare and not the difference between total fare and the business class fare that he was entitled to. That way, he wouldn't be subsidizing her travel. His friends suggested that his brand of honesty had crossed its sell-by date. But Mahi stuck to it.

Like Mahi, Dina had her own notions of right and wrong.

When she looked into the tour plans, tour reports, and tour bills, she noticed that the executives traveled in groups of five. They all stayed in the same hotel. She reasoned that from the station to the hotel and back they would be hiring only one cab. If true, they should be spending only Rs 500 but between them they seemed to be claiming Rs 2,500, and thus pocketing Rs 2,000.

Her audit firm, Mike Mahi & Associates, had drilled into her the virtue of sampling and of extrapolation.

She conducted fifty verifications and found in thirty of them that this was the case. She did some quick math, making estimates of the number of travels, attached a probability to the figure and estimated the excess payment could be about Rs 144 lakhs. Of course, there was an outside chance that all those employees might have actually spent the money.

Dina had checked into work early so that she could have the undivided attention of Ghosh, the Finance Officer at Titanic, who handled travel payments.

ooo

"Morning, Mr. Ghosh. Can I have ten minutes of your time?" she asked.

"Is it urgent or will around twelve be okay?"

"Now would be good," said Dina, speaking in a prim and proper tone, unlike many of the interns who tended to either giggle or say, "Okay Sir, no problems."

Ghosh escorted her to his cabin. The table was strewn with travel papers he had to clear. He had the ten-page travel policy document with him.

"Mr. Ghosh, do we have proof that the taxi fares from residence to station and from hotel to station to residence were actually incurred?"

Mr. Ghosh had a reputation for being a stickler for the rules. "According to the rules of the company, proof of expenditure is not required." He spoke each word slowly and clearly.

"True, but in that case they are required to attest that the expenses have been incurred."

"That's true. They do give such a statement. You must have seen it attached to the payment voucher."

"That's correct, Mr. Ghosh. What if the declaration is false?"

"You will have to prove it, Dina. It's difficult for us to make a charge without evidence. Anyway, it is okay since they must be drawing only what they are entitled to draw."

"By that measure, is it okay if one of your bosses travels by overnight train and claims airfare merely because he is eligible for it?" That wasn't a polite question but when Dina spoke her mind she never minced words.

Ghosh half smiled. "Find out," he said.

Now sure that shenanigans were being practiced, Dina decided to check on the air travel. She was back in her audit cabin. She sifted through a maze of travel documents and was shocked to find senior executives at Titanic had checked into their hotels at 6:00 a.m., attended meetings at 9:00 a.m. but claimed airfare for flights that would have arrived only at 10:00 a.m.!

Clearly, they had traveled by train. Boarding passes and flight tickets weren't required to be enclosed. A declaration would suffice.

Some six hours and fifty transactions later, Dina, and a colleague working with her, decided that on a conservative estimate, the company had lost around Rs 2 crore. They had all the proof properly stacked up. A couple of hours later, a draft report was ready.

At 7:30 that evening, she called Doc, her Audit Head, and fixed a meeting at their office for the following day. The meeting was short, just twenty minutes. Doc shot off a few questions.

"Are there backup workings?" "Have you taken a photocopy of the travel documents?" "Have you made notes?" "Have you recorded the sample size and the methodology of selecting the sample?" "Do we have samples of the transactions audited?" Finally he said, "Okay, leave the papers with me; I will go through them and then speak with the management."

Dina came out of the meeting, dumbfounded by Doc's lack of enthusiasm. She wondered whether the story that used to do the rounds among interns about how the auditor of a large firm picked a client's three-year-old car at the written down value was true. Or how the external auditors mysteriously dropped an audit qualification and it later transpired that they had picked the audit of a group company.

Glum-faced, she shared her experience with a friend who worked as a reporter.

"So your boss chose to look the other way?"

She couldn't forget the gossip at the newspapers. She told Dina of how editors traveled extensively around the world thanks to companies sponsoring expensive all-paid trips for them.

Surprised, Dina asked, "Do you think there is something fishy?"

"No, the editor writes only what he wishes."

"But why should he accept these travels? Surely the companies would be expecting a quid pro quo."

Her friend explained. "Titanic had the money to spend and was willing to spend. What if the employees spent the money and got reimbursed or didn't spend the money and collected it? Either way the company didn't lose. Similarly, companies have a budget to spend on editors."

Dina remembered her dad's comment: "You scratch my back, I will scratch yours." That was the philosophy that drove businesses. He had advised, "Little one, when you step into the world tomorrow, you must stand up for what is right even when the rest of the world is against you."

A fortnight later, Mike, Mahi & Associates, after a confidential discussion with the company's Board of Directors, filed a Special Report on Travel. Another week later, some twenty high-performing marketing stars were shown the door at Titanic.

At Mike, Mahi & Associates, Dina became a hero.

It was an object lesson for her. Don't draw hasty conclusions about anybody. Someday in the future she would apologize to Doc, she told herself. The following day, *New Delhi Times* carried a sensational first page report titled, **"Trouble at Titanic. Giant travel fraud unearthed"** under the by-line of Tejas Arya.

Mike Mahi wondered from where he picked the information. He had every number right, till the last rupee.

23. Spreading Wings

Mahi picked up several offbeat assignments in the next few years of practice.

One of them was a consulting work from David Das, who produced a sixteen-page stock market newsletter, *Stock Talk*. The paper was running at a loss and there was pressure to close it down. *Stock Talk* had been in business for fifteen years. David was quite attached to his magazine. He now wanted Mahi to advise him on whether to continue with the newsletter.

Mahi hadn't handled such consulting work before. He could crack audit, tax and corporate legal cases, but the fuzzy world of management accounting was a different ball game. Yet Mahi wasn't someone who would give up an assignment that was falling into his lap. He called Doc for a meeting and explained the situation.

Doc said, "Boss, we have Ham, who has already completed his cost accounting qualification. We will use him. I will brush up my knowledge of cost accounting. It is not rocket-science."

"Perfect. Make Ham the head of the assignment, give him full responsibility and authority, and let him deliver. If he does a good job, we could give him a small bonus. You mentor him."

"Done."

Three days later, Ham discussed his findings with Doc. The essence of the findings was that the magazine was only a short way from breaking even. Ham told Doc, "David Das should procure advertisements from a few companies for the full year and place them in *Stock Talk*. There should be no investment recommendations regarding these companies for the full year. That way, the magazine need not compromise on its editorial independence. Then the magazine will stop losing money.

"I know a thing or two about the stock market. I believe in the next few months the market will see an upswing, and then the subscriptions could soar."

"So?"

"So, it would be a shame for the company to close now. Ask him to try our suggestion and a year later, if things don't hold up, it can down shutters."

Doc crosschecked his recommendations. In his signature style, he documented every little number: the cost of paper, the cost of honorarium, printing, stapling, postage etc., to ensure the arithmetic was right. Finally, he accepted Ham's figures. He ran the numbers past Mahi. Mahi liked it. He also liked the idea about advertising. "This lad, Ham, has brains. He will go places."

Mahi made the presentation to the client. Both Doc and Ham sat through the meeting.

The client applied the report in letter and spirit. They opted for advertisement income as well as advertised the magazine to promote the sale. They decided to stay around for six months, anticipating the market turning around in their favor.

Six months later, the client was laughing all the way to the bank. The market went into a bull run. Investor interest in the stock market shot up. The magazine subscription tripled. David Das was profusely thankful to Mike, Mahi & Associates.

Mike sent in his invoice. Three months later, after watching the brilliant run of events, he sent a second invoice for the same amount. Dina wondered if the client would agree.

She was surprised when the client happily paid.

With that, Mike, Mahi & Associates opened their management accounting division. David Das sent in cartloads of referrals, and the division that Ham had innovatively christened MAD soon turned out to be a cash cow.

As business grew exponentially, Mahi opened offices in two other cities.

ooo

It was Venkat of National Tea who gave him the reference.

Mohammed Haider was running a successful enterprise called Max Inc., but the company was being foxed by foreign currency transactions and Haider wanted professional advice. Venkat suggested he get in touch with Mike Mahi.

Mike, Mahi & Associates had no experience in such jobs and the office was skeptical about their ability to deliver. But Mahi pooh-poohed them saying, "We need to grab every opportunity that comes our way."

A large part of Max Inc's turnover came from exports and half its purchases were through imports. Its dollar denominated sales were five million and its dollar denominated purchases totaled three million, in short, eight million exposure. "Not chicken feed," Mahi said in his first meeting with Mohammed Haider.

Thirty minutes into the meeting, Haider made the offer on the strength of National Tea's reference and his own first impressions of Mahi.

"I will give you access to everything you want. Within a fortnight, you must come out with an action report. If I like the advice, I will give you a blank cheque; otherwise I will pay you nothing." Mahi gladly accepted, conveniently ignoring NICPA rules that prohibited one from getting paid on the basis of results.

Doc and Dina got on the job the very next day.

Doc's first round of discussions threw up major insights. After careful analysis, Doc recommended that in respect of purchases, the company should buy forward cover at prevailing rates for the period of credit. He worked out a sensitivity analysis for all major products, indicating how much every rupee of dollar appreciation would shave off profits. This would act as a good ready reckoner.

Next, the team analyzed exports. Doc recommended that the company should sell dollars forward at the rates that they had assumed as the exchange rate for pricing. Doc worked out a sensitivity analysis indicating how much every rupee of dollar depreciation would shave off profits. This would act as a ready reckoner. He also asked them to net foreign receivables against foreign payables before taking forward cover as they provided a natural hedge.

The recommendations were made in a slim, sleek report peppered with easy- to-navigate tables and understandable graphs, and very little verbiage.

A year later, Mohammed Haider congratulated Mahi, telling him that his report had helped him save a few millions.

With that, Mahi opened a forex-consulting wing in Chennai and in Mumbai. The firm was beginning to grow as Haider brought in an army of clients to Mike Mahi for forex and related advice.

At Mahi's suggestion, a three-man in-house team was set up, which had expertise in assessing when to take forward cover and when to stay exposed. A man who had worked in the treasury operations of a foreign bank headed it. More currency games were played as the forex business grew stronger. All these transactions were handled by Hindustan Bank.

Mahi picked up consulting engagements in management accounting, foreign exchange, transfer pricing and the like. He never let go of an opportunity even if he had no previous experience. His approach was to line up the right people at short notice, to ask Doc to supervise the engagement and share revenue with all of them liberally. Slowly, business picked up and by the time he had completed ten years in his practice he had set up quite a few verticals. He had also begun auditing many medium-sized companies and a few large ones as well. He had already established three offices in India.

In 2006, *Business Today*, one of India's largest business magazines, named Mike, Mahi & Associates as one of the twenty firms to watch. Mike Mahi was on the cover page.

24. Birth Pangs

Tanya tried reaching Mahi on his private line. It kept ringing. "Why don't these husbands understand the urgency when there's one? Try a million times, but the blessed fool never picks up his private number."

She then tried the switchboard.

"Hello," came a voice from the other end. It was Rupa.

"Is the big man around?"

"No Ma'am. He's gone for a meeting. He didn't tell me where."

Tanya rolled her eyes in disbelief. Rupa knew every little thing Mahi said and did in his office. After all, she wouldn't be called "shadow" for nothing. Yet the man had given even her the slip.

This was it! "Work, work and work; he knows nothing else. I'm never allowed to go to his office parties. Don't know when we last went out, either for a movie or to a restaurant or on a holiday. And now he doesn't care if his wife is alive or not!" she grumbled to herself.

Pain shot through every inch of her body. It was 9.30 p.m. She asked the hospital to send an ambulance and dialed Mahi's switchboard again.

"Rupa, do me a favor please. Ask Mahi to call the hospital as soon as he gets out of the meeting." Hope the busy bee remembers the hospital name and number.

"Are you okay?"

"Yes Rupa, I am fine, thank you."

The pain only grew worse. The twelve-minute wait and the ten-minute ride to the hospital felt like eons. They rushed her into the delivery room. She did not have a very good feeling about it, something was not right. Examining her, the gynecologist placed a hand on her shoulder and told her not to worry. The C-section would not take time. Tanya was sweating. The nurse inserted an IV line and the anesthetist, the pediatrician, her gynecologist and a couple of nurses wheeled her into the operation theater. The little one inside busily kept kicking her, itching to come out into the big, bad world outside, but the silly doctors showed no signs of hurry!

Soon the anesthetist administered an injection and Tanya's body lost all sensation. And there, standing with the pediatrician with his charming smile that had first attracted and later haunted her, was Mike Mahi. He was coolly signing the mandatory consent papers. He hadn't told her he had come and hadn't even asked her if it was okay for him to sign! How had he managed to get inside the theater? Well, the idiot had his ways.

She lay half-conscious while the surgery was underway. She tried to keep her eyes away from the television screen that showed what the doctors were doing to her and the baby, as she started getting a sickly sensation in her stomach. Disgusting! The doctors chatted amongst themselves, cracking jokes.

"Is there any magazine here that I might read?" asked Tanya, shocking them all. One of the doctors screamed, "What the hell?" Another whistled. She loved it.

The long wait would soon be over. Would it be a boy or a girl? They had told her it wouldn't be twins. Mahi smiled. She wondered if he already knew. Boy? Or girl? The anesthetist gave her another shot.

"It's a boy!" said the gynecologist. The time was 11:11. Tanya wanted to jump out of the bed and see the innocent face, hold the delicate body and feel his soft skin. She felt proud. Her prince was so tiny! His skin was pink and he had a frown on his face! "Like father, like son!" she thought.

She felt a needle pierce her. She heard the nurse saying, "You need some rest." Somewhere, in the distance she heard Mahi saying, "Ugly fellow, not at all like his mother." And "The little one will play hockey for India some day."

25. Mahi Builds

Mahi was getting noticed. Some loved him, some hated him, but no one could ignore him. Tales of how Mike Mahi picked audits, how he networked, how he sourced work from fellow auditors, how he undercut without undercutting—all these started doing the rounds.

The story of the manner in which Mike Mahi bagged the external audit of one of India's most premier automobile companies became part of audit folklore. It was meticulously planned and executed with élan.

It began when Mike opened an Intelligence wing. He called it the Research and Analysis Wing (RAW). The entire office was in peals of laughter when the name of the new department was announced!

An ongoing project at RAW was capturing data on who audited which company, who was on the board of directors, what was the company's annual audit fee and its annual turnover. This data would then be fed into a computer. The software would convert the raw data into information. Mahi would get a report on "Audit fees as a percentage of Sales". He would get a director-wise list of companies. If a person happened to be a director of a client of Mike Mahi & Associates, that information would be separately filed.

Once that was done, a letter went to each of the directors of Mahi's clients, documenting the nature of work done for them by Mike Mahi, the audit fee ratio and the audit fee ratio of other firms that were auditing the other companies in which the person was a director. The letter would be worded ingeniously.

Dear Sir,

We thank you for the opportunity given to our firm to be professionally associated with your company. You might like to have a brief note of the kind of contribution that we have made to your organization. The enclosed note provides an executive summary.

[The note gave out the major suggestions on cost savings and the process improvement initiatives besides the key audit findings. Each suggestion was backed by an impact on the bottom line. The clincher would be the information on the audit fee ratio of the company along with that of the other companies of which the addressee was a director]

You might also be aware that our firm operates from six locations, has twenty-four associates and seven practice areas, each of which operates as an individual profit center manned by high-end professionals. A note on each of the practice areas is enclosed.

Should you require any clarifications, we would be most happy to meet with you in person.

Yours truly,

For Mike, Mahi & Associates

If anyone from the level of Senior Audit Manager and up was introduced to a person in any meeting, seminar or conference, and if that person held a position of influence, a letter would go out from Mike, Mahi & Associates detailing the meeting and briefly indicating the nature of work the firm was doing. Couched in informal language it would simply state, "We are documenting the conversation between us." Audit managers were trained to speak to clients and say, "If there are certain certifications, do let us know so that we can strengthen the relationship between our organizations."

Mike Mahi appointed corporate liaison officers, a phrase that could mean anything. They were lobbyists. The idea struck him after learning that in the US, companies had people working in that capacity lobbying with the Congress. While others generally worked on the basis of no brochures, no advertisements, Mahi engaged a marketing team and appointed Field Representatives. Their job: call on prospective clients and socialize with existing clients. The objective: update them on what the firm was doing. Talk to them about the firm's new initiatives and present capabilities. The result expected: bring in new clients and new assignments from existing clients. The idea was outrageous, but Mahi said, "If pharmaceutical companies can have medical representatives, why can't accounting firms?"

Mahi roped in clients under the guise of sharing ideas. In a seminar attended by industry honchos, he sprung a surprise on everyone by suggesting that there should be a system of rotation of auditors. "Familiarity breeds contempt," he argued.

One morning, three weeks later, the CEO of a large drug company invited Mike Mahi to a discussion on replacing Hunt & Smith.

When irate auditors charged him with being dishonest to the profession, he said with undiluted candor: "I retained an audit by not qualifying a financial statement which I ought to have qualified. Why? Because I was scared the company would not retain me. Of course, I backed it with a flurry of legalese to save my skin. Tell me how many of you wouldn't have done the same thing?" Not a single hand had gone up.

He continued, "If we had a fixed tenure, companies wouldn't be able to sack auditors at the drop of a hat. Fixed tenure ensures that you wouldn't bother much about being on the right side of the client. I am saying this not in my interest alone. I am saying this in the interest of the profession.

"A firm gets to know a client after perhaps three years of work. Rotation would be professional suicide," someone remarked. Another added, "It takes us time to build a client relationship: how can someone unilaterally demand rotation?" Mahi smilingly said, "I am suggesting this to clients beyond a certain size."

The following day, in a private conversation, Doc told Mahi, "You cannot force a customer to choose his supplier."

Mahi grinned. "Is the relationship between the statutory audit firm and its client one between the supplier and the customer? Or is it one between the 'judge' and, for want of a better word, the 'accused'? While the accused can select his lawyer, can he select his jury?" He added, "Look, audit firms have to make their living. Things like marketing for clients, retention of clients etc., are existential dilemmas, which cannot be swept under the carpet." Mahi could be persuasive when he chose. Doc felt that Mahi was crossing the thin line between profession and business.

Mahi was crazy about human relations. If clients came first, employees came a close second. He recruited with care; never allowing limpets on the rolls -- employees whose intention was to forever stick to the organization! "Take only the best guys; don't worry if they later leave us for greener pastures," he constantly told HR. He had once famously remarked, "You can rent a brain, but you can't rent a heart."

The employees and interns were paid well by industry standards. But more than the money, it was the bonding he encouraged among them. He regularly communicated with his employees, giving them a feeling of belonging and making them feel as though they were part of the family. In the annual office outing, the best rooms in hotels were allotted to the junior most members and the partners stayed in the lowest-tariffed rooms.

Mahi chased clients. It was not the money that propelled him. There were other engines. His favorite example was cycling. "Do you remember the elation you felt when you first learned cycling? Nobody gave you a penny. You did it because it gave you joy. Similarly, in business, the applause, the public adulation, the recognition, the joy of creating, the feeling of having arrived – these are the ultimate turn-ons."

He had by now established ten branches and had a strong networking arrangement with thirty-two firms. All of them used the Mike Mahi brand. He was now a significant presence in the country having either an office or a networked office in each state.

He decided to put in place an impressive Board of Advisors. One day he told Doc, "Let's get a Board in place. Let's bring in people from different walks of life: architects, doctors, engineers, lawyers, artists and so on. This will bring in new ideas and trigger growth."

This was something that was not in NICPA's scheme of things in terms of how accounting firms should be run. But Mahi wouldn't be Mahi if he went with everything NICPA said. "What is not explicitly disallowed is allowed," was Mahi's view. His choice of the Board depended on what they could bring to the table.

Once, he wanted someone on the Board and told Doc to get him in.

"But he isn't an authority on anything. What will we gain?"

"He will open doors for us. You need introductions to big corporates. He will do that for us."

"You think he will agree to work with us?"

"We haven't asked him. So how do we know? Anyway, ours is not a kirana shop. There is no need for us to be apologetic."

"But the guy has a streak of madness in him."

"No wonder he is a genius."

"He doesn't come for a small price. He charges a fortune. He is a guy who puts himself up for sale in the marketplace."

"So be it. Knowledge has a price."

Mahi had ambition. He had guts. And now he showed that he had vision as well.

26. Back to the Breach Candy Hospital…

YEAR: 2014
DATE: June 21
Saturday 10:30 p.m.
Mumbai

Tanya Roy could not forget him. Ronnie, her brother, was many years younger than her and the apple of her eye.

As he grew up, she savored every little success of his. When he first chanted "Twinkle, Twinkle, little star," she was speechless. When he learned how to tell the time, she was amazed. When he finished second in class, she rejoiced. When he won prizes in athletics, she went bananas. When he scored a quick fire fifty in school cricket, she was thrilled. The only thing that would break her heart was when he toiled long into the night to finish his homework.

Ronnie was in first grade when he came home and told her that he could now ride her bicycle. She refused to believe him.

"Hey, you mean you can now push my cycle without help?"

"No. I can ride it. The way you can."

Her questions came in a flurry. "Are you sure? How did you learn? Who taught you?" She had seen him push her bike with some help over the last few weeks as if he were escorting someone on a walk. Now he was saying that he could ride it? Impossible!

"Hmm… I learned myself."

"Come on, don't bluff. You won't even be able to sit on the cycle seat. You are too short!" His mouth curved into that radiant smile that no one could resist.

"Come see for yourself," he said.

Tanya's eyes and mouth opened wide in sync. Perched on the seat, his two legs couldn't touch the pedals simultaneously. Her guess about his height had been right. But she hadn't guessed his ingenuity. He pushed the right pedal when it was high. Once the pedal was down and the left pedal came up, he would push the left pedal, bringing the right pedal up. Tap. Tap. Tap. The cycle slowly moved forward, and he had got his balance perfectly!

There was uninhibited joy in Ronnie's eyes. Tanya danced in excitement. When he got down, she hugged him, showering him with kisses. He wiped his cheeks and grinned.

Ronnie was generally reticent, but he was a playful child. He loved all games. Cricket, football, hockey, table tennis, athletics – name it and he was into it. He also made sure that his studies were never affected.

And then it happened.

One evening, during a football game, he collapsed. His friends and the coach rushed to him and tried to revive him, but he didn't budge an inch. His body felt heavy. The coach called the ambulance and Tanya.

"Hello."

"Tanya, something's wrong with Ronnie. He collapsed on the field and isn't responding. Please come to the hospital."

Tanya went pale. She slumped down into a chair. Her hands were shivering, but no tears would flow out. Her mom noticed.

"What happened, Tanya?"

Gathering up courage, she looked at her mom and said, "Mom, let's go to the hospital. Ronnie's not okay."

The doctors said they would have to keep him under observation.

After seeing no improvement even after two days, he was moved to a specialty hospital. His parents and Tanya were beside him.

As Ronnie lay there in the Intensive Care Unit (ICU), hovering precariously between life and death, the family tried to come to grips with what was happening. The doctors had identified the ailment and concluded Ronnie would be a vegetable for life. Tanya now began praying that the gods take him away, though he was too young to die. She wanted to remember him as the bubbly young boy who played games, won hearts and studied hard. She did not want to see him lying here like this, lifeless.

Ronnie answered her prayers.

On the 30th of December at ten minutes to ten, he gave up the battle for life. Tanya didn't cry. Nor did her father. Grief choked their tears. Her mother was inconsolable. At the funeral, his friends made lovely speeches about him and his accomplishments. She was suddenly very, very proud of her brother, prouder than she had ever been.

When Tejas Arya walked into the hospital that night and her Chief stood in attendance, she was shaken. He had brought those memories back, and she remembered Ronnie and those events of so many years ago.

ooo

Tanya wasn't sure what to do. She had placed Arya.

Tejas Arya was her senior at school and the sight of him gave her goose bumps. They had a five-year age gap. One day, when someone had bullied her, he had protected her like an elder brother. Every time she met him, her heart used to race.

He was the school's star debater, the ace quizzer, and the lad over whom the lasses swooned. When she won the sports champion title in Class V, he mischievously winked at her. It was a wink she cherished and remembered till date with goose bumps. They had kept in touch with each other thereafter too, but in a subdued way. She knew he had topped the NICPA exam, had become a journalist and now enjoyed a big reputation. He knew that she had become a psychologist. They rarely met, and whenever it did happen it was for a brief while and during parties.

Today as she saw him walk down, she wondered whether she should go up and greet him. She was in two minds about it. Finally, her curiosity overcame her.

It was then that Tejas Arya saw her. He stopped in his tracks. She thought for a fraction of a second that he hadn't recognized her. "My God, will I have to introduce myself?" she wondered.

She didn't have to.

"Hey, Tanya," he said, the sheer joy on his face dissolving every misgiving that she had harbored. "How are you? Where have you been all these years?"

Tanya smiled. She liked his new look. The hair on the top of his head was cut pretty short. The hair on the side and back of the head was cut short too. It made him look athletic. There were some specks of gray hair, but they made him more appealing.

He was India's master storyteller: his facts well-researched, presented without bias and without political affiliation. He had written about things that mattered to the citizen: unsafe roads, defensive treatment by doctors and corruption in the corridors of governance. He had journeyed to Kashmir and written about terrorism. He questioned the quintessential nexus between shady politicians and corrupt cops and tracked corporate shenanigans.

He had written about the bright side of life too. When a woman had broken the glass ceiling to become the chairperson of a multinational bank, he was the first to interview her. When ordinary men and women jumped the odds to lead extraordinary lives, he would somehow find them and interview them. Each of his stories was a classy tale. His best, in Tanya's opinion, had been his moving and gripping story of how a young boy, twenty-something, facing death in a hospital bed, had sought euthanasia.

Tejas wasn't the wishy-washy writer averse to taking positions. He wasn't the kind who would say, "On the one hand this is good, on the other, that is good." With most things, he took a stand, including in the story of euthanasia.

In that story on euthanasia, he had championed the cause of mercy killing without downplaying the medical profession. He had suggested that while he didn't want individuals to play God, they should be given the freedom to die just as they had the freedom to live. He had laid down in a crisp, no-nonsense style, the conditions and circumstances under which mercy killing should be allowed.

He met the patient and the parents. He documented the plight of the mother. She was a career lady hopelessly and helplessly dedicated to her son, who wished that he would be allowed a decent death. Tejas had researched the number of cases of people living in a comatose state in the country and actively canvassing for mercy killing.

The story, carried both in the newspaper and on television, won him the National Award. When Tanya read that story, her eyes had gone misty.

"Hey Tanya. It's me, Tejas. How are you?" Tanya snapped back to reality.

"I'm fine," she said, her hands outstretched. "Tejas, what brings you here at this ungodly hour?"

"Meet Dr. Michael D'Souza," said Tejas.

The D'Souza!! Tanya couldn't express her enormous surprise. India's most respected general surgeon was escorting Tejas Arya. Any other time she would have given her right hand to meet Dr. D'Souza. But today Tanya's heart raced. "Why is Tejas in D'Souza's company? What is the problem?"

Tejas was saying, "Dr. D'Souza, this is Tanya Roy, a budding psychologist, soon to be one of India's best."

Tanya wasn't ready for the small talk. "Tejas, why are you here?" she asked, her concern very visible in her voice.

Tejas smiled. "You must ask Dr. D'Souza."

Dr. D'Souza stared at Tanya. "Later, madam," he said as he and Tanya's boss hurried along with Tejas to the Chief's chamber.

27. The Twilight Zone

Tejas Arya sat before the doctor, clad in blue jeans and a yellow t-shirt.

Ironically, Tejas was wearing a dress that he didn't like seeing a doctor wear. He believed that bankers, CAs, doctors, and teachers should not sport casuals while they were at work. Customers, clients, patients, and students lost trust when faced with professionals who wore casual clothes.

Tejas was here to collect his medical reports before his visit abroad. The doctor was a pleasant man, always smiling, always calm and courteous. He never displayed any other emotion. But today, as the physician was going through the papers that presented the final test results, Tejas saw a frown cross his face.

"Is everything okay?" he asked.

"You are fine, but you have to be careful in the future." Tejas tried to let it sink in. "With proper medical care and lifestyle alterations, we can manage this."

Tejas belonged to a profession that exaggerated things in the battle for readership, eyeballs, and TRPs. But he also knew accountants and doctors invariably underplayed events. He knew the physician was softening the blow for something.

He didn't want any beating about the bush. There had been signs of an impending ailment even earlier. He might as well face it. He said, "Doc, I can take it. Tell me, how many years do I have?"

The doctor had always admired Tejas, the thoroughbred professional bleached in innate honesty. He had a very high estimate of Tejas's intelligence quotient, but he was stunned that the iconic journalist could read so quickly between the lines.

"We never know. Medical science can come out with innovations that can dramatically alter both diagnosis and dispensation. Things over which we have no control today will be conquered with ease in the future. Pneumonia was once incurable; today it is not. Tuberculosis was once incurable; today it is not."

"That's fine, Doc. But given the present availability of medical wisdom, what's the status?"

Before the doc could reply, Tejas asked, "Five years?"

"Tejas, we could still be very wrong about the time frame."

That was the closest the doctor would come to telling him. As Tejas realized the significance of that, his face changed color.

He smiled. "Thank you, Doctor. That sets the deadline for a few things that I have always wanted to do. I had postponed them, pressed by professional commitments. Now I will do them."

The doctor returned the smile. "You will live to achieve them, Tejas. Remember, every moment, every situation and every issue has a positive side."

"Thank you, Doctor."

"Thank you, Tejas. Take care."

Tejas Arya looked fresh as he exited the doctor's cabin. But a storm was raging within him. This was no age to fade away.

But then, it wasn't in his hands. Tejas had to get a few things done at top speed now. He knew he would feel hurt on and off; but he would learn to take things in stride, positively. People die. Once that is understood, everything else appears insignificant. He decided to continue to dream. He would make some friends, if it were possible. Most importantly, he would understand human failings. Greed for money; hunger for power.

But first, he would have to write a will.

28. Brush with Advertisement

YEAR 1999
Mumbai

In his fourth year at *New Delhi Times,* Tejas had his first brush with bad advertisements and with how his profession worked.

The first thing that Tejas did every morning, even before he got out of bed, was to take a peek at the newspaper. Not his paper, the rival's. One such day, a catchy advertisement stared at him from the paper. There was a ladder. At the bottom was the investment instrument, National Savings Certificate, followed on successive higher rungs by other investment instruments, namely National Savings Scheme, Monthly Income Account Scheme and Public Provident Fund. Perched at the top was "Our Corporate fixed deposits". The coupon rates were displayed prominently: 9%, 10%, 11%, 12% and 14%.

The advertisement added, "Come, Invest with us. We offer the best rates."

Tejas jumped out of bed and sat himself down straight in front of his computer. No brushing teeth, no face washing, no morning tea. He was furious with the claim, explicit or implied, that the company's corporate fixed deposits were the best of the investment pack.

The advertisement had conveniently forgotten several things, such as the fact that NSC entitled the investor to tax rebates. Its interest was eligible for both tax rebate and tax concession. The investment in NSS was like expenditure and reduced the taxable income. The interest on the MIAS was eligible for a tax concession. The investment in PPF was eligible for a tax rebate, and its interest was wholly exempt from tax. As opposed to all this, corporate fixed deposits were fully taxed. With some quick arithmetic, Tejas figured out that instead of being at the top, the fixed deposit investment should be at the bottom of the ladder.

He lost no time in shooting out an article that drew attention to the advertisement and the thoroughly misleading nature of it. He immediately sent it to Sam Allen, the Editor of *New Delhi Times*.

Two days later, the editor called him. "The guys from the company have come and they have some points to discuss." A suave, genial, soft-spoken gentleman with an aristocratic mindset, he never spoke above a whisper.

"Sorry, Mr. Allen, I didn't get you."

"It's about the piece you wrote."

Tejas abhorred the phrase "piece". His article wasn't a scrap of paper.

"What about it, Mr. Allen?"

"They are here with me. They agree to what you say. Their claim is it was designed by an overzealous ad agency and cleared by a very senior operating manager who did not understand its implications. Incidentally, the person from the advertisement company is also here. So is a representative of the paper that carried the advertisement."

"Are you suggesting that we kill this article?" Tejas asked with a mix of concern and anger.

"No, definitely not. I have told them that as their advertisement is now in the public domain and as they agree our analysis is right, we will carry the article. We can also carry their explanation."

"Thank you, Mr. Allen. What is the explanation they are offering?"

"Nothing. They are disappointed that we want to carry it. They are nice blokes and have agreed not to carry the ad again. The newspaper has indicated that they will drop it from now on."

"That's good, Mr. Allen. I am sure they have also agreed not to carry this advertisement anywhere else in the country."

"Yes, Tejas."

ooo

The day *New Delhi Times* hit the stands with Tejas Arya's article, the number of letters the editor received was far less than what he normally received. But one thing did happen; the advertisement stopped appearing in the paper. Apparently both the company and the newspaper had kept their part of the bargain.

Four weeks later, Tejas Arya was shocked to find the advertisement reappear, but this time in *India Happenstance*, a national magazine based in Mumbai. It was a breach of trust. Tejas Arya wrote to the Editor of *India Happenstance*, outlining the circumstances under which the ad had been pulled out in his city. He documented in detail the outcome of the meeting that had taken place between his Editor, the newspaper's ad agency and the company. He sent in an article for publication, outlining how the advertisement had been in bad taste.

Tejas did not receive a reply. He tried to call the magazine's editor, but couldn't get beyond the secretary. "He is in a meeting." "He is with the Big Boss." "He will call you back in an hour." Short of saying he was in the restroom, the lady used all the other excuses. Many attempts later, Tejas reached a man who identified himself as assistant editor. The guy said the Editor couldn't take calls, but that he would look into the matter and respond.

A week later, Tejas received a letter signed by the Assistant Editor (AE), stating the magazine had checked and that they stood by their action. Of course, the Assistant Editor had made no reference to the inappropriateness of the advertisement or to the article. Tejas called and was politely told they wouldn't carry his article. When asked why, the AE remarked, "The decision to carry or not carry an article is the sole prerogative of the magazine."

"Does the Editor know about this?"

"Nothing happens in this magazine without our editor's diktat."

It was clear that advertisement revenue was more important than journalistic integrity.

That evening, Tejas Arya lost his respect for the Editor of that magazine. He finally understood why Allen's paper never made tons of money. An uncompromising owner-editor was an anachronism in a business driven by ad revenue.

He checked with Sam Allen about the next course of action. He wasn't willing to let the magazine go scot-free with a dangerous ad. Allen suggested that he move the Advertisement Standards Council of India. The ASCI responded after three weeks, saying that they had extensive talks with the advertiser and with *India Happenstance* and that both had assured them that the advertisement would not be carried in the future in any medium. Hence the Council wouldn't be proceeding with the issue. Bravo!

Some years later Tejas Arya had another experience by which he learnt how the media works.

29. Whom Shall We Hang?

In 2004, the television channels carried the news non-stop. A man had been rotting on Death Row for the last ten years and the jail authorities had forgotten to hang him. The official explanation for the delay: the national hangman wasn't available to carry out the execution. The real reason: the jail authorities had forgotten the convict existed! After all, he was a lowly gardener who worked in an apartment complex.

A super cop told Tejas Arya that jail conditions had improved dramatically over the years. He even suggested Tejas do a story on it. When Tejas set out to visit the prisons to study the conditions first-hand, a major surprise greeted him. The convicts attended yoga sessions in the morning. They did hard field work during the day. They studied in the afternoon. The evening closed with a game of football. They were given moral lessons after dinner and once a month they were allowed to watch a late night movie. It resembled a remedial school. Tejas was bowled over!

He decided to visit Death Row. It was a visit that would reschedule his life for the next six months. It was here at Death Row that Tejas met Satyam Raut.

Satyam had been convicted of a rape and murder that had happened twelve years ago. The courts had sentenced him to death. In an animated one-on-one conversation, Tejas learned the execution had been postponed thrice; twice, a day before the execution and the third time, the date just came and went, with no intimation of postponement or otherwise. Tejas tried to imagine how devastated Satyam would have been that day. Now everyone else had forgotten about it.

Tejas abhorred capital punishment. This was a chance to bring this anachronism to center stage. Here was a story tailor-made to capture national attention. Satyam Raut was thirty-six, which meant he had just been twenty-four when imprisoned.

He had been married for less than a year. His aging parents lived on the verge of poverty. His wife who stayed with them had met him on only six occasions over the last twelve years.

An eighteen-year-old convent schoolgirl who resided in the apartment complex where Satyam worked as a gardener had been raped in her home and then been brutally murdered. The police had cracked the case with remarkable speed. Satyam was arrested within twenty-four hours of the crime. The circumstantial evidence was overwhelmingly against him. A witness claimed Satyam regularly stalked the girl. Someone saw him come out of the apartment a few hours before the girl's body was found. He should not have been inside her house. He had no explanation as to why blood matching the girl's was on his dress. No lawyer was willing to defend him. Who would defend a man who couldn't afford it?

The court took less than a year to pronounce Satyam guilty. The judge held that this was an instance of the "rarest of rare cases." Satyam appealed to the higher court, claiming that he was innocent, but the judgment stood. The date of the execution was fixed.

A day before the execution, the jail authorities found that the national hangman was unwell and no one else was available to carry out the execution. A second date was fixed for six months later. Meanwhile, Satyam applied for presidential pardon. The country's first citizen had other pressing engagements and pardon wasn't atop his list. A day before the second date, there was the inevitable postponement because the President had not come to a decision yet.

A year later, after seeking legal advice, the President ordained that Satyam should die. A third date was fixed for the next quarter. That date came and went, but Satyam wasn't hanged.

Tejas Arya wrote a moving story about Satyam's ordeal. "There can be no greater punishment for a man than living in a solitary cell on death row for twelve long years, waiting to die," he wrote. "There can be no greater stress than knowing that you will be hanged tomorrow without the hanging actually taking place.

"Look, it hasn't happened once. It hasn't happened twice. It has happened three times. No society can ignore this, even if the man is a convicted rapist and killer. He has been punished enough."

Tejas met Satyam's aging parents and was moved by the abject conditions in which they lived. Hell would have looked like heaven compared to their home. Tejas closed his piece by saying, "If we believe that mercy is twice blessed, Satyam should be released."

A new President was in office. He was known for his humaneness and for his pragmatism in dealing with issues. Tejas asked Satyam's parents to petition the new President for clemency. They were unwilling to do so. Finally, an NGO came forward to help.

Tejas's story had unintended consequences. All the leading newspapers carried editorials on it. There was a singular sense of unity in approach. Every editorial and every article exhorted the President not to show any mercy.

Public interest groups followed the newspapers' lead. They were on the streets, baying for Satyam's blood. The wife of the head of a state told television reporters that Satyam Raut must be hanged. The hangman, who made a living from an occasional hanging, ruled that the convict had no right to live in a civilized society. The school where the girl had studied voted for execution. It did not matter that most of those children hadn't even been born when the crime had taken place.

It was then that Tejas decided to play his trump card. He wrote a letter to the parents of the girl. It appeared on the front page.

Dear Mrs. and Mr. Jain,

I am Tejas Arya. I have been a journalist for ten years.

Today I want to talk to you about what will inevitably bring forth memories of one of the most horrific times of your life. I know your daughter was raped and killed. I am very, very sorry for that. But I believe twelve years is a lot of time. I know that nothing can diminish the memory of a loved one, more so a daughter and still more so one who has been snatched away in the flower of youth. But I believe that time is a great healer.

Satyam Raut has been on death row for twelve years. Had he been given life imprisonment, which is quite a usual punishment for rape and murder, he would be a free man in another two years. While that is not the law, it has been the general practice. I met his aging parents. They live in abject penury. They love their son as much as you loved your daughter. Their daughter-in-law has stayed with them through thick and thin and hopes to one day be united with her husband.

Mr. and Mrs. Jain, it's time to move on. Satyam's hanging would only amount to an eye for an eye. It would in no way bring back your little girl. His parents have suffered a lot.

No, I do not justify Satyam's act. Yes, he did not commit a traffic offense. But that does not mean he should be hanged. The state should not play God. Capital punishment is state-sponsored murder. By staying silent, we would all be abetting the crime. We should give him a chance to live. And the one who can set the ball rolling is you.

You already know that there is a growing national opinion against Satyam. I am not even asking you whether the response would have been much the same had he been well-educated, well-heeled and had connections in high places. I am just asking you to give a thirty-something man the opportunity to live. It would place you in the pantheons of the great.

I request you to write to the President of India for clemency for Satyam Raut.

Yours sincerely,

Tejas Arya

Arya let a week go by, but received no reply. He allowed another week to pass by. Nothing happened. It was a closed chapter for the girl's parents.

The country's most famous journalist was pilloried. Angry letters came from all over India. The near unanimous view: Satyam should hang. "How can one nation hold so much venom?" wondered Tejas.

Magazines and newspapers weren't far behind. Their view was simple. A pardon would send the wrong signal. An example should be made of this man. Satyam must hang so that a message went out to all rapists and murderers that they would not get away with their actions. It was a firm and fair argument.

Arya wrote, "Research claims that executing one criminal translates into ten fewer murders that the criminal might commit. In ten years, there have been 150 additional executions. Hence, there should be 1500 fewer homicides. But there have been only 500 fewer murders.! The death penalty hasn't acted as a serious deterrent."

Tejas Arya was fighting a losing battle.

Two months later, the President of India, a genial man, consulted his lawyers, went by the rulebook and denied Satyam Presidential pardon.

Forty-eight hours before execution, television cameras were stationed inside and outside the central prison, capturing every second of the man's final hours. Cameras were placed outside Satyam's house, capturing the trauma of his aging parents and his heart-broken wife. No one cared about privacy. A graphic detail of how the hanging would take place and how the head would fall once hung was shown on the idiot box.

An NGO held a nightlong vigil for Satyam. In the wee hours of the morning, Satyam Raut was hung. Tejas Arya had lost.

ooo

By 2005, Tejas had been in the newspaper for ten years. He had rapidly risen up the ranks and was now Editor. He had also won a number of awards. Newspapers were once exciting but television was changing it all. It was exploding in a big way and Tejas realized that the future of journalism lay in television. There the public would see you, unlike in a paper where they only read what you wrote.

Even as he was contemplating quitting the paper and joining one of those channels, an opportunity arose when his paper decided to expand into television. The call came from the owner. "Tejas, will you like to lead our initiative into television." Arya needed no prompting, "Yes, Sir." He however continued to write a column for the paper; it would appear twice a week. The romance of reporting was being replaced with the joy of analyzing.

30. The Thin Dividing Line

Of course, not everything thus far had been smooth sailing. While building the firm, Mike Mahi realized there were enormous seeds of conflict.

The first big conflict of his career happened during the first decade of practice. Mukul Sharma, an extremely well to do businessman, turned up at Mahi's office. He wanted Mahi to make an application to the Tax Department for a No-Due certificate, which was a pre-requisite for selling a property. Someone from Mahi's office had to liaise with the Department and then obtain the license. A small payment would have to be made, but that was par for the course.

The form was simple. One of the questions to answer was, "In which Circle are you assessed to tax?" Sharma hesitated when Mahi sought a reply. "We will say, 'New Case', isn't it?" Mahi was taken aback. "But it can't be that you haven't been having taxable income and haven't been filing tax returns," he retorted.

Sharma, clad in a dhoti and a matching white shirt, looking every inch a politician said, "No, no. I do have income and have filed returns, but there are some dues that I will settle in the next few months. If I give those details now, I will have to pay it immediately and I don't have the cash flow to do that."

Mahi hesitated, but only for a moment. "We can't say, 'New Case.' It will not be correct. Also, the consequences that follow can be dangerous."

"How much do you usually charge for such work?" Sharma asked.

"Rs 10,000," said Mahi not quite sure what was going to come next.

"I will pay you Rs 50,000. Have this done."

Mahi froze for a moment, trying to gather his thoughts.

"Okay, I will pay you Rs 100,000. Have this done."

Mahi was now sure that he didn't want to get into this. "It may not be possible to do this, Sir."

"What's your problem? Surely, you are not signing anywhere. After all, I am giving the declaration. Actually, you are acting only as a liaison between the Department and me. So what's your concern?"

"Well, I have a long career ahead of me."

"You know I could get half a dozen guys to walk into my office in the next hour who would be willing to do this for Rs 1000?"

"I know, Sir. You should get in touch with them."

Sharma smiled. "I wish you the best of luck in your profession." Under his breath he swore, "This guy will never go far."

Mahi said, "Thank you, Sir."

ooo

A few years later, the scene was replayed, but with a very different customer, S Raghavan.

Raghavan was moving the Tax Department for a one-time settlement. According to the law, the Department offered every assessee a once-in-a- lifetime opportunity to come clean.

Raghavan fixed an appointment with Mahi. Mahi was in his office, poring over an audit case. It was two hours past the appointment time, and Mahi had almost given up on Raghavan. He heard a knock. "Come in!" A pot-bellied man with long oily hair, unbuttoned shirt and a devil-may-care attitude walked in. The office wasn't sure whether he had come to the wrong place. But he was clear. He wanted to meet Mike Mahi.

"Hello."

"Hello, I'm S. Raghavan."

"Oh, I was expecting you! Please sit down," Mahi said, shaking hands.

Mahi first tried to understand the problem and then he painstakingly got down to explaining what he needed if he were to take up the assignment. It went on for thirty minutes. After the preliminaries were over, Mahi gave Raghavan a list of forty documents that he needed. Raghavan agreed to see him a week later.

A week went by. So did a fortnight, and then a month. Mahi had completely forgotten about him when the man called and turned up, hours behind schedule. Out of the list of 40 he had information for five and left the other thirty-five blank. Mahi wanted all forty.

"See I don't have the time to get them all. You make out the papers. I will sign wherever you want."

"Sorry, Mr. Raghavan, that's not the way I operate."

"How much do you usually charge for such work?" Raghavan asked.

Mahi had a sense of deja vu. "Rs 5 lakhs," he fibbed, a little circumspect of what was going to come in next.

"I will pay you Rs 25 lakhs. Have this done."

Mahi was thrown off gear, his experience notwithstanding. He gave Raghavan a fleeting look, put the papers down and kept both his hands on his chin, staring.

"Okay, I will double that amount. I will pay Rs 50 lakhs. I understand you are the best in the business. Work for me."

Mahi leaned forward, both elbows on the table and almost hissed in amusement, "Sorry Mr. Raghavan, I don't work that way. I can refer you to my colleagues. You can connect with any one of them." He stood up and held his right hand out.

"If that's how you feel, so be it."

"Yes, that's how I feel about it."

31. Crisis in Marketing

It was bound to happen, sooner than later.

Mike Mahi's network of firms helped him bag several assignments. To start with, most of these firms were independent, but as Mahi brought in more and more work, many of them merged with *Mike, Mahi.* Those who merged operated with full autonomy as Strategic Professional Centers (SPC) and would receive more assignments.

Someone asked, "What's in it for you, Mahi?"

"Increasing the top line substantially and fattening the bottom line significantly," said Mike without batting an eyelid.

Some of the independent firms called themselves Networked Associate of Mike Mahi. It was a phrase Mahi had conjured up as an idea of brand building.

He charged 30 percent for any assignment that he passed on to his associates. The client was billed and 70 percent of the fee was paid to the networked associate. Any firm that did not carry the tagline Networked Associate of Mike, Mahi was paid 50 percent. It was his way of pushing people to come into the network.

The networked associates never got in touch with others except when it was officially warranted. There was no sharing of information of clients serviced or potential clients targeted. Each one jealously guarded his territory.

One of the networked associates, Stephen Gupta and Co., was pitching for an assignment and was in touch with the CFO of the prospective company. The task was to value a firm. The associate had no expertise in valuation but was confident that once the assignment was in the bag, they could get Mahi to help them out.

"What would it cost us?" the CFO asked Stephen Gupta, the young head of Stephen Gupta & Co..

"Rs 500,000 all told."

"But that's a bit stiff for us. Why don't you rework your numbers and give us a revised quote?"

Stephen Gupta didn't like bargaining over professional fees. Can a patient negotiate with a doctor, he wondered.

"Well, I remember my costing well. The best price would be Rs 475,000."

"Think it through, Stephen. We may be sitting on many other quotes far below the sum you indicated."

The CFO wasn't sitting on 'many other quotes'. He was aware that CAs, especially those relatively new to the profession, almost always looked to gain a client rather than earn the rightful sum of money.

"I shall call you back," said Stephen.

Another networked associate, Khemka & Kabra, was also working towards picking up the very same valuation assignment. They also didn't have experience in valuation. Learning on the job was fine, but clients don't pay you to learn at their expense. Khemka & Kabra reasoned that they would approach Mike Mahi for help once the assignment was in the bag.

"What would it cost us?" the CFO asked S. S. Khemka, the head of Khemka & Kabra.

"Rs 495,000 all told." Khemka believed in psychological pricing and felt that hitting the Rs 500,000 mark might look offensive.

"But that's a bit stiff. Why don't you rework your numbers and give us a revised quote?"

S S Khemka didn't like bargaining over professional fees either.

"I remember my costing well. The best price Rs 425,000." He was shaving off a cool 15 percent and felt that anything lower than that would send a wrong signal.

Just like he had done in the case of Stephen Gupta, the CFO indicated that they had many other 'offers on hand'.

Over the next week, unknown to each other, Stephen Gupta and S. S. Khemka kept cutting their prices and at one point Khemka offered Rs 300,000.

"I have someone who wants to do it at Rs 300,000," the CFO told Stephen Gupta.

It was a ridiculously low fee. There was no margin. There was just about no way that Stephen could go below that.

"Just out of curiosity, may I know who is offering to do it at that price?"

"Khemka & Kabra."

Stephen Gupta almost sank to his knees. Oh God, two networked associates had bid against each other and literally shot themselves in the foot. "Give it to them," he told the CFO.

A week later, Khemka turned up at Mike Mahi's office seeking staff support and technical help on the valuation assignment. Doc asked Dina to handle it.

"This profession is going to the dogs. A valuation assignment for which I had quoted Rs 500,000 has gone to someone else at Rs 300,000," Gupta told himself.

Gupta met Mahi.

"Look Mahi, I don't mind losing the assignment. That's routine. But two associates fighting in the marketplace for the same client is horrible. It is like two dogs fighting over dinner. Or like two friends fighting over the same woman."

"True. I am confident the CFO must be smiling behind our back. You see, our letterheads indicate that we are networked firms!"

"We must put in some checks and balances to ensure this kind of accident does not happen again."

Mahi spoke to all the networked associates. He suggested they keep Mike Mahi informed if they were bidding for a particular assignment. Some were uncomfortable about disclosing whom they were negotiating with.

"What is the guarantee that with that information, another networked firm might not approach the same client for the same work?"

Mahi appreciated the point. True, professionals shouldn't be waging war for a client, but if push came to shove he knew they were capable of it. Sadly many people understood the language of rupees better than the language of professional relationships.

"We will maintain a Red Book where we will list the assignments being bid for. Anyone can call up and ask whether a particular assignment is in the red book. There will only be a 'Yes' or 'No' answer. If the answer is 'Yes', they will not bid for that assignment. If the answer is 'No,' they can go for it."

"What's the guarantee someone at Mike Mahi will not breach our trust and bid?"

"Let the red book be maintained by an attorney's firm," said Mahi to thunderous applause.

Three months later, the firm plunged into another crisis.

ooo

One of Mahi's networked entities, the Hyderabad-based Moon Das & Co., was the internal auditor for the Bangalore-based Super Good Food Products. A fraud of gigantic proportions had taken place in the company, arising out of a perfect error of judgment.

The company drew large sums of money from the bank and kept it in the office at the end of every month. There was no insurance cover for cash–in-transit. The company would not be able to recover any amount if the cash-in-transit was stolen while being moved from bank to office. Similarly, there was no fidelity insurance. If Mr. Cashier decamped with the money, Super Good would not be able to recover it from the insurance company. They had insurance for fixed assets and for stocks, but not for cash.

One bright morning, the cashier didn't turn up for work. He didn't come the next day, or the following day. The keys to the cash box were with him. He wasn't reachable. The Security Officer reached his residence but was told the Cashier had left for good two days ago.

The management had no option but to break open the safe. They called in the police as witness. A sum of Rs 150,000 was missing. A quick verification took the tally higher because a few withdrawals from the bank hadn't been recorded and some expenses had been recorded twice. The accountants spent some time working the numbers. The Cashier had walked away with half a million Rupees. A police case was filed, and a hunt began for the missing cashier.

The management promptly sacked the internal auditor, Moon Das & Co.

"You should have warned us about the perils of not having taken insurance. You should have spotted that cash drawn had not been recorded. How could you have reconciled the bank balance without spotting these shenanigans?"

Moon Das had no answers and tendered his resignation. That's when the crisis opened up at *Mike, Mahi.*

Super Good Food Products approached a Bangalore-based public accounting firm, Richmond Associates, to undertake the internal audit.

Joseph Richmond was the partner-in-charge. With his playboy looks, he should have been an actor, not an auditor. His work ethics were pathetic. Legend had it that he once signed the accounts of a bank branch merely on the strength of the branch manager's words. Of course, he did turn up at the branch with an assistant. While the assistant spent the day counting gold, as he loved the yellow metal, Richmond chatted with the manager.

After assessing the volume of work and terms and conditions of the assignment, Richmond quoted his firm's fees, which after the usual haggling was accepted at ten percent less. The fee was significantly lower than what Moon Das had been drawing. Richmond hadn't checked whether the firm had already been subjected to internal audit and, if so, who the auditors were and why they had left. Richmond didn't consider it necessary because NICPA required this information only if he were replacing an external auditor.

To Joseph Richmond, if doing something wasn't mandatory, it was best not to do it.

He accepted the offer of internal audit with Super Good Food Products. Richmond Associates was a part of Mike Mahi's networked firms. Moon Das did not like what Joseph Richmond had done. Mike Mahi came to know of it.

Das wanted Richmond Associates to resign from their new position. Joseph Richmond would have none of it. He had never interacted with Das before and, therefore, there wasn't a snowball's chance in hell he would do something to soothe Moon Das's bruised ego.

Mike Mahi invited them for a meeting.

"What's the bloody point in having a networked arrangement if we are going to poach each other's clients?" asked Moon Das.

"Hey, hold on. First, I didn't poach the client. Your assignment with the company had already been terminated."

"Even so, how could you take it up? What about my credibility?" asked Moon Das.

"I didn't know you were the internal auditor. We haven't met each other in the past, nor have we worked together."

Mike Mahi intervened and proposed an arrangement. All of them would share their client base in a Blue Book. The client base would be pooled and placed with the Attorney, the one who handled the Red Book.

Anyone meeting with a prospective client would have to check whether the client name appeared in the Blue Book.

If 'Yes', then he would be barred from approaching the potential client.

Stephen Gupta butted in. "I think that would be unfair. For one thing, I might place a few companies on the list without them actually being my clients."

"Would you do that?" asked Moon Das.

"Okay, I might not do it. But someone might be tempted to do it. Also, what's the point if you are doing audit work and I was offered tax work and I don't accept it and it goes to a third party"?

Mahi understood the logic. He suggested that they change the rule regarding the Blue Book. "The Blue Book will have the list of clients and the name of the networked firm. If Richmond wants to do business with a Moon Das client, irrespective of how the client approaches Richmond, it would be incumbent on Richmond to check with Moon Das whether he has any objection. Moon Das should not have an objection unless he is doing identical work for the client".

Everyone agreed it was fair.

Someone asked, "What if Moon Das objects?"

Mahi said, "It would be Richmond's call."

Das added, "Once I lose a client and it goes to a firm not on the network, I will have to remove the client's name from the bluebook."

"Perfect" said the group, in chorus.

This was how Mike Mahi constantly played the role of a leader, stitching together an alliance and keeping it on a balanced keel.

32. Into the Council

YEAR: 2006

Mumbai

"Why? I am quite comfortable doing things the way they've always been done."

David Kocher was talking to a group of students after he had completed a teaching session at NICPA. The group had met him, suggesting he should also handle classes outside the NICPA banner.

Kocher hadn't got into teaching because he was out of work. He had got into teaching because teaching was his passion.

"You see, Sir, you are handling only a few topics on accounting for us, which means we don't get to be your students for the other topics."

At NICPA, democracy dictated that a team of teachers would teach a subject. Six teachers taught a 120-hour subject like Accounting, which meant 20 hours per teacher. By the time a student got the feel of a teacher and the subject, the teacher would have moved on. You had to be a scene-stealer like Kocher to make an impact in that short span.

"So what? They are knowledgeable teachers, extremely competent professionals." David Kocher was known to be diplomatic.

"Sure they are, Sir. We aren't questioning that. But we want you. You inject practical inputs, not just the theoretical knowledge. You make it enjoyable. The only way we can learn the whole subject from you is if you start teaching outside the NICPA's radius."

Kocher agreed that their demand massaged his ego. But he wasn't sure whether he would be able to handle sessions outside of the support system an institution offered. Private enterprise involved administration and marketing, both of which he abhorred. And then there was the issue of fees. Charging a fee for students was something he wasn't comfortable with.

He politely changed the topic, smiled at the group of students and walked away. He thought that was the end of it.

Kocher had underestimated the seriousness of the group. They were a persistent lot. They called him up three times after that. Once, they walked into his office unannounced. It was time for Kocher to decide one way or the other. He told them he would get back to them within a week.

The moment they left, he called up his friend, Mike Mahi.

"Mahi, Kocher here. There is a lot of pressure on me to handle private classes."

"So? Go ahead and do it. What is stopping you?"

"I can't charge them a fee."

It almost took Mahi's breath away. "Why? Have you become a hermit? Or is it that you have a fat cow at the office that you are milking dry?"

"You know me well. It is none of that. It is not that I don't like money. And I don't have fat cows. It is just that I believe knowledge must be disseminated freely. I can't bring myself to accept fees from students directly."

Mahi believed his friend. But he had to find a way to ensure his friend earned. He knew if Kocher taught on a payable-if-and-when-able basis, it would send a wrong signal.

"I don't want to debate whether teaching should be priced or not. You are entitled to your views. If you don't teach because you don't want a fee, it is not going to stop others from teaching for a fee. So, in the end, knowledge will continue to be disseminated for a price. It will not advance your cause. And importantly, you will be seen as being boorish." Mike was at his convincing best. "If you wish my office can handle the administration."

"Fair point," said Kocher. "No, I won't trouble you. I will do it myself and will seek support, if necessary."

ooo

Slowly, Kocher's Classes (as they came to be known) gained tempo. His lectures were peppered with examples and humor, making the subject lively. Some of the humor was staid, some raunchy and some intellectual; altogether, it was great. People loved his classes as he used stories to drive home points.

Slowly, he began receiving invitations to lecture in different parts of India. He received calls for professional seminars as well. These brought in new relationships, and Kocher nurtured them with great care.

When he returned from each trip he would send out a personally signed thank you note to all those who had interacted with him. He would add tidbits of the conversation to drive home the fact that he remembered the person.

His popularity soon turned him into an icon.

ooo

Somewhere down the line, around 2006, Mike Mahi's desire to get elected to the National Council and one day become president of the NICPA gathered momentum.

His inner circle of friends was shocked.

"Goodness gracious. You have spent so much time and energy building a firm of substance. Why do you want to get into a thankless job?"

"Given the way power is structured at NICPA, you will never be able to leave footprints at the Institute!" counseled a second.

"Even if you became president, you would only have a two-year term, and that's too short a time to bring about reforms in the world's second largest accounting body. It's a long enough period, though, for someone to throw enough muck at you," proffered an unsolicited advisor.

Mike Mahi turned to Kocher for his views.

"Look Mahi, there are always two sides to an argument. I have some very strong views on the subject. I won't push you to go by my views."

"I know that. But I want to have your input so I can take a call."

"You tell me why you want to get into the Council. I will play the Devil's Advocate and tell you why you shouldn't."

"Well, why do good men get into politics? It's because they want to serve a nation of more than a hundred crore people. Why do men get into high positions in social organizations? It's because they think they can give something back to society. Why do people want to get into professional bodies like the NICPA? So that they can lead an army of experts and wannabes."

"So, the Chair is what you are after?"

"No, you got it wrong. I don't have to become President although that would be the logical culmination. Getting into the Council will do; it will help me implement many ideas. There are lots of changes that we must bring about at the national level."

"How do you know that?"

"In the last one year, I have traveled extensively. Everywhere, everyone has grievances, right from the students, the management committee, and the members. I think that these complaints can be quickly sorted out. But to do that, one must have power."

"Mahi, are you telling me everyone who gets into the Council is there for altruistic reasons? Do you mean to say no one is there because he is hungry for power and because it would help further his professional work?" David Kocher was in full flow.

"I am not saying that. Of course there is an opportunity for professional growth. Yes, one's contacts can increase. Visibility does go up. If in the process some audits drop in, most people won't refuse them."

Kocher decided to rub it in. "So, wouldn't holding office at the NICPA and being in professional practice at the same time not be a conflict of interest?"

"Not necessarily. The extra professional work that comes by would have come anyway."

"Come on, Mike. There are enough stories of how National Members conduct themselves. Don't you know Sid Khosla? It is an open secret that whenever he turns up in a city on NICPA work, he does the rounds to all the banks. He presents his credentials, both his professional card and his NICPA official card, to seek a place on their panels. Bankers usually point out that such work can be given only to a local CA because of logistical issues. He goes ahead and develops a contact with a local CA."

"One drop does not make a monsoon."

"You know it is not 'one drop'. There are many such drops. The NICPA office provides the perfect setting to help you foster relationships with tax officials and government *babus*. You can surely build a Chinese wall around you but despite all that, someone can always point the accusing finger at you."

"Like how?"

"Like, even if you bagged an audit in the ordinary course and it turned out to be a fat one, people would say 'Hey, it was because he is a National Member'. If you get a favorable judgment in the Tribunal and someone you enjoy a good relationship with is sitting on the bench, people could turn around and say, 'Hey, it was because he is a National Member'. You will be damned if you do and damned if you didn't."

"Well, when I go on NICPA's work, I will not give my professional card," Mahi said.

David Kocher remarked, "Let us be practical. If the bloke shaking hands with you asks for your professional card, will you say no? And once you give it, you would open yourself to abuse."

Even as Mahi mulled over it, David served an ace.

"You need to campaign extensively for the election. Look at the costs. You will need an eye-catching brochure, then there is postage; you need to do two to three dispatches. You have to personally visit the branches. You will need a running mate. Travel, boarding, lodging and local conveyance for the two of you will cost money. You will have to visit at least twenty-five branches and throw in some parties. It will set you behind by at least ten lakhs."

Mahi felt that the figure was reasonable. He wasn't sure whether Kocher felt the same way. "It's high for sure. But since the expense is tax deductible the pinch will be a lot less. I can also look at it as an investment." He was playing it safe.

"Investment for what? If you are using it as a platform to market your firm, you are wrong. You can propel your firm forward even without that 'investment'. If you are looking at it as an opportunity to save the accounting profession, God bless you."

Mahi agreed that there were merits to what David said.

Kocher continued. "Normally, you get to become President only in your third term. It means you will spend six years in the Council to reach a position from which you could effect change. To my mind, that's too much time."

Mahi saw Kocher's logic. Mike, Mahi & Associates was on the growth trajectory. Audits were coming its way; people were turning to the firm for tax representations. In many cases, his firm was the first choice of the new generation. Consulting assignments were on the rise. The networking idea that he had initiated years ago had begun to reap enormous rewards. He now had offices in several locations across India. Logic suggested that he build on these and take the firm to the next level instead of testing uncharted territory.

He was undecided. Then something happened that took the decision out of his hands.

33. Candidate Mike

It happened at the Oberoi Sheraton.

Three hundred of the profession's most influential men and women had assembled in a conclave titled *Frontiers of Accounting* at Ball Room 1. Speaking at the plenary session was Kris Manchandani, NICPA's outgoing President and one of the country's most revered names in accounting.

"The world has changed in the last two years. The rules of business have transformed. The profession is rapidly globalizing, and it is time for us to leave behind the baggage of the past." If someone thought that it was a pep talk, he was wrong. There was a whip in Manchandani's voice.

"We have to think beyond audit and tax to stay afloat. New opportunities will come our way; opportunities not thought of by many, even of our generation. We need leaders, not caretakers, in the National Council, who will orchestrate these changes. We need opinion builders, not dealmakers. We need men of intellect, integrity and imagination, not that there aren't any. We want people who can invest time."

Kris was known to be a no-nonsense president, yet even by his standards, these were very harsh words.

He wasn't actually saying anything people didn't know. It was just that someone was voicing these thoughts for the first time in public and the "someone" happened to be the president of the top accounting body. A clap sounded from some corner of the room. It turned to two, three, ten and then there was thunderous applause.

"Don't clap, act," said Kris sharply. "The tall pillars of our profession need to come out of their comfort zones, to contest for the council and take the profession to the next level. I know many of the three hundred assembled here have it in them to do this."

Mahi did not hear the rest of the talk, as he was lost in introspection.

Over tea break, Mahi sipped his coffee and bit into his biscuit, his eyes following Kris. The president was busy chatting with someone Mahi didn't know. And things took an unexpected turn when Kris walked up to Mahi and said, "You must contest. The profession needs men like you."

Mahi's face flushed. "Thank you, Sir. I will give it a thought."

When a man of Kris's stature sees leadership material in you, especially at the national level, it's a big compliment.

Mike Mahi decided to weigh the pros and cons. He analyzed the scenario to assess his chances. Like in a consulting assignment, he split the candidates into three categories.

In the first category were the popular and well-known faces. Some like David Kocher were popular because they taught thousands of students. Others like Rex Alwaris were well known because they spoke extensively at conferences and were highly knowledgeable.

Reuben Patnaik, a former candidate, had once remarked, "People tend to remember their teachers and vote heavily for them." Doc was sitting with Reuben. Doc's body language indicated that he didn't buy the argument.

Mahi later demonstrated it. "Doc, close your eyes for a moment." Doc closed his eyes. "Now think of the teacher who taught you English in Class V." Doc did that. "Does his face flash before your eyes?"

"Yup."

"That's the power of a teacher! Teachers leave footprints in your mind particularly when they display other qualities of the head and heart, like being punctual, committed, and staying dignified."

Reuben had told Mahi, "Men like Kocher and Alwaris do not have to hit the campaign trail. Given their extraordinary goodwill, they have only to let the word spread, sit back and win."

Doc asked, "Why then do such men campaign?"

"To demonstrate their strength. Finishing at the top massages one's ego. It also comes in handy when you interact with the officials at NICPA."

The second category belonged to candidates who were associated with well-established firms. People like Alka Varma of Hunt & Smith, or someone like J Sabharwal, also from one of the Big Six. They commanded respect in the accounting fraternity based on the sheer size and scale of their firm's operations. These firms produced thousands of CAs, and the alumni bond was strong. If you were the only contestant from one of the Big Six, you could expect the alumni of the other big firms to vote for you!

Mahi chipped in. "I understand the firm's clients issue whips to the CAs working with them to go and cast their franchise. This is important as the polling percentage has always been lower than even during the elections for the Parliament!"

These men had an advantage when it came to canvassing. National politics was such that you voted on party lines; you didn't care to learn about the individual candidates. In NICPA elections, there were no parties. A candidate was voted in on the basis of his personal strength, his academic and professional accomplishments. The bottom line: the electorate has to be wooed. Voters expect candidates to visit them to seek votes.

Mahi believed you could be excused from personal campaigning if you were from a high-profile firm. People understood that you wouldn't have the time. You could even get them to come to you. One way was to throw a large party in a fancy hotel. The idea was to address your electorate on what you could do and learn what their expectations are. It could cost a bomb, but it would help to save time.

The third was the category to which Mike Mahi believed he belonged. These men weren't electrifying teachers or outstanding speakers. They didn't belong to large firms with deep pockets.

They were contesting because occupying positions to serve organizations was their passion. These men had to soil their hands while campaigning. The campaigning had to be intense, both within and outside their network. Mailers and door-to-door canvassing were a must. You needed an army to help.

OOO

The NICPA election process was based on a complex system of single transferable vote and secret ballot. It involved first preference votes, quotas, selections, eliminations, sequencing, transfer of votes on selection, transfer on eliminations, etc. The funny thing was that you could draw more votes than a fellow candidate and yet turn out on the losing side!

Mahi pored over reams of material to understand the election mechanism. He assessed the past voting pattern, the possible first and second preference votes that he could garner, potential election strategies that he could use and finally threw his hat into the ring. There were six slots for the National Council from his region. He was reasonably sure that if he planned and executed things well, he could get in.

Once Mahi made up his mind to compete, he got into the act. He realized each of the three categories of candidates had their advantages. He wanted to align his candidature into all three categories. He would get Kocher, who belonged to the first category, to campaign for him. He would take the help of Alka Varma for the second category. And of course, he fell into the third category.

His first step was to rope in David Kocher as his campaign manager. Till date, no one had done that. The job of the campaign manager was to act as Mahi's public face, plan his strategy and help him execute it. It would be a high profile, near full-time role. His friends were skeptical of whether Kocher would accept the job.

Their concern was genuine. If Kocher became Mahi's campaign manager, he would get branded as Mahi's man. Kocher had other friends who might be contesting. They wouldn't like to see him spearheading Mahi's campaign. It also might not have made sense for a man of his standing to be seen taking sides in a free-for-all battle. Kocher wouldn't stand to gain.

Mahi wouldn't know until he asked Kocher!

Mahi wanted to have Kocher for many reasons. He was a great mascot and attracted crowds. His word carried weight. But merely telling people to vote for Mike Mahi might not be seen as showing much support. Acting as a campaign manager would bring him more securely into the election process and would send the right signal, he thought. It would be difficult to pull off a campaign without a manager of Kocher's stature. He wanted to make it worth Kocher's while to accept this role.

Mike Mahi made a five-point charter as the first step towards a poll manifesto and took it to David Kocher. The charter included exam reforms, poll reforms, professional growth, self-regulation and brand building. There was a brief explanation as to why these were needed and how they would be achieved.

By articulating these views, voicing concerns and promising to put them on the right track, Mahi hoped to strike an emotional chord and also convince David Kocher that he meant business.

Mahi fixed a meeting at Kocher's office. He explained to Kocher the five poll planks. Kocher listened to Mahi's plan intently. Finally, Mahi asked, "I want you to act as my campaign manager. Will you?"

"Yes. Good people should go to the Council. You are a good man," came the quick reply. Mahi couldn't believe his ears. He wondered why he had huffed and puffed before asking him the question. In later years, Mahi would know that Kocher had been impressed by his five-point agenda, held the belief that Mahi meant business and would do the profession a world of good by getting into the National Council.

The two shook hands, and Mahi left Kocher's office with a feeling of accomplishment.

Mahi's next stop was Alka Varma. But the partner at the Big Six, while agreeing to vote for Mahi, refused to be drawn into any form of campaigning. "You will agree that I am not cut out for this," she said with great tact.

34. On the Campaign Trail

The NICPA was broken up into seven regions. Each region comprised of a few geographical states. Each state was broken up into branches for ease of administration.

Kocher lost no time in strategizing.

He appointed a core team of four deputies. Mike Mahi was contesting from 'Earth', which had five states and twenty-five branches. These branches were broken into big, medium and small on the basis of the size of the electorate. A professional was roped in to write a software program and do analysis to plan the campaigning strategy. A database was created of the entire electorate, based on a hard copy of NICPA's list of members!

The campaign team had Deputy Heads. Each deputy was given a set of branches on the basis of the size of the branch, the state to which it belonged, past voting turnout and past voting pattern. The branches where Mahi or Kocher had spoken in seminars and areas where Mahi had major clients were identified and marked.

Each deputy was asked to recruit branch campaigners to work under him. Four campaigners for large branches, two for medium branches and one for the small branches; adding up to forty. Each branch campaign head was given a free hand to enlist any number of volunteers. The idea was to create an army of two hundred volunteers. They would personally meet each one of the 30,000-strong electorate at least twice over the next three months.

A dossier was prepared for each voter, carrying name, occupation, marital status, spouse's name and occupation, their personal predilections relating to the Institute and its activities, grouses, etc. The volunteer was expected to know the voter assigned to him inside out with the help of this dossier.

It was also planned that Mahi and Kocher would visit all twenty-five branches in the course of the next three months. It was the job of the deputy to organize private programs. Here Mahi and Kocher could deliver addresses on a range of topics like "How to run a firm like the Big 6" or "How to Network" or "Vision 2020" or "Improving professional opportunities". The idea was to showcase Mike as a thinker and a doer.

The plan was to keep the campaign professional without appearing aggressive.

Incidentally, Kocher had maintained an impressive database of his alumni. He wrote individual letters to each of them, saying that he was acting as campaign manager for Mike Mahi. The gist of the message was that Mike Mahi had built a firm from scratch, that he was a great visionary, that whenever Kocher had any professional issues he had always turned to Mike Mahi for help and that Mahi would be a major asset to the Council. These letters were placed on David Kocher's letterhead and were personally signed by him.

Mahi wrote a one-pager talking about his background, his rise in the profession, and his five-point plan. It was an extremely readable manifesto that answered some of the most frequently-asked questions about how the NICPA could be taken to the next level.

Meanwhile, the volunteers met all the voters personally, at least twice. During the second visit, the campaign deputy also accompanied them. And when Mahi visited the branches he met as many people as possible. Kocher almost always accompanied Mahi.

Tanya managed the household. Whenever Mahi left for a campaign she made sure that his luggage was ready and packed. When he campaigned in the city, she ensured that his shirt looked spotless and his shoes were dirt-less. She had her own professional life to live but she was madly in love with him and desperately wanted him to succeed. She wouldn't let maids work on his dresses and at times he was too disoriented to ensure that he took care of all these. Tanya was turning out to be a great asset.

Tanya was also adept at speech writing. It was she who wrote Mahi's famous catch line, where referring to his Spartan upbringing he talked about "the audacity of hope, the magic of dreams and the sheer breadth of possibilities…"

As a psychologist Tanya was popular. Young boys somehow liked to share intimate details with an attractive looking lady who would hold their hand, pat them on their back or run her fingers through their hair; and they had a sense of comfort dealing with her. She was good at talking to the struggling students that helped them heal from the memory of failing an exam or being blanked out of a relationship. Her combination of matronly and petite looks made it easier for the kids to confide in her what they wouldn't dream of confiding to their parents, their teachers or even to their friends. Among her clients were several CA students, who living as they were in hostels and seeking to cope with a very demanding and punishing course had their fair share of problems.

The turnout at the seminars was impressive. The presentations were professional, and the message that Mike Mahi was the right candidate to go to the National Council was driven home effectively.

Mahi felt the campaign was going fine. It was then that David Kocher came up with a masterstroke.

"Let's arrange for a public meeting of CAs in the metros. You tell them about your vision for the profession and what you will do and won't do if elected."

"But that's exactly what we have been doing at the branches. What's new about your suggestion?"

"This time we will invite the other candidates too and give them an opportunity to present their case and let the electorate grill them."

Mahi agreed. Kocher was confident that Mahi would be a runaway winner in public debates. And if the show were recorded and shown throughout the region, it could be a killer idea.

"What will happen if the others do not accept the challenge? Don't expect the current vice-president to take this gauntlet. Don't expect the seniors who have been on the Council for two full terms to accept this public debate."

"I think the sheer novelty of the idea would make them accept it, especially if we can mobilize public support. If they refuse the offer, word will spread, and it would hurt them."

A local accounting association organized the debate with stupendous success. Most candidates did very well. Mike Mahi was outstanding.

He had said, "Over time, audits in India will no longer be conducted only by the members of the NICPA. It is not just the CPAs of USA who will carry out audits of US firms. Nor will the audits in England be restricted to members of the ICAEW. You will see an umbrella body of which all the public accounting institutes will be members and any member of an institution holding a membership in the global umbrella will be eligible to audit any firm anywhere in the world. This will open up global professional opportunities, enhance quality and knock the bottom out of our profession if we don't stay updated." The audience roared in appreciation.

Days before the election, the whole electorate thus learned that Mike Mahi was a man of substance.

It was then that Kocher told something, which really irritated Mahi. "I suggest you should give up your certificate of practice. You should retire from your firm and work for the Council full time. You would then become the first man to do so. There will then never be a conflict of interest charge."

"But isn't that unfair. I know about my conscience. I will not do anything wrong."

"I know that but why take a chance. By focusing only on the council you will also be sending out the right signals.

Mahi was taken aback. His nostrils flared and his face turned red. Surprising himself he said, "But that's impossible. I won't be in the council forever. When I come back wouldn't my firm have suffered?"

Kocher sat unperturbed. Leaning back on his chair and picking the tall glass of chilled orange juice that was on the table, he said, "My sense is that this will be a big surprise. No one has done it before and as the first one to walk out of a firm in its high growth phase you would have taken the winds out of your opponents' sails. You will win hands down."

Mahi didn't reply. He was weighing the pluses and minuses. And then he said, "I appreciate the point. But I will stay with my firm.

35. Member, Mike

The CAs went to polls on 13th and 14th December, 2006. Twelve candidates were in the fray in the Region from which Mike Mahi contested. Six of them would be elected.

Shekhar Baruarkar, the incumbent vice-president, if elected, would automatically become president. No region had ever voted out a prospective president. His election was therefore assured.

Three of the other candidates were sitting council members and it would be surprising to see them lose. . Of them, Rex Alwaris was a star performer. If anyone had an issue to be sorted out at NICPA they had to just talk to Rex and he would get it done within the next forty-eight hours. His office had a secretariat dealing exclusively with NICPA matters. There was no way a region would vote him out.

Another was Joe Mathew, a low-key operator not given to swagger. In fact, he drove a ten-year-old car that had run 200,000 kilometers and was in no hurry to change it. Great at technical work, personable, and clean in his dealings, he was certain to sail through. Docking him would be an insult to the electorate, not to him!

The other sitting council member was Anand Prakash. He once organized a Committee meeting in Hyderabad because a friend's son was getting married there. Anand liberally distributed work to fellow professionals. Nobody complained because it was a win-win situation. Mahi felt that if Anand lost, it would be an upset.

All the sitting council members were certain to get re-elected. Where did that leave Mahi?

Mahi had a gut feeling that the fifth slot would go to Mullick Arjun. The state he hailed from had a large posse of CAs. Yet in the outgoing Council, the state had gone unrepresented. This time, a group of professionals was campaigning for Arjun on one plank: that he belonged to the state and hence must be voted in. While in public people denounced that strategy, in private most CAs agreed with the campaign and would hence vote in large numbers for Mullick Arjun.

That left only one seat, and seven candidates fighting for it. It would be a close call.

No one from the fairer sex had ever been elected to the National Council. Mahi's hunch was that women would vote for Rima Roy, the soft-spoken, well-mannered lady.

Reuben Patnaik had missed the bus three years ago by a whisker and had the sympathy wave floating around him. J Sabharwal belonged to the Big Six. Shyam Kumar was a rising star. Mahi felt he was a dangerous floater. Vikas Gupte and Prasad Rao could be considered lightweights, but you never know!

December 13 and 14 came and went peacefully. Three days later, it was time for the count. Within two hours of the counting, the voting percentage was declared. About 45 percent of the electorate had cast its vote. This meant that only 14,000 people had cast their franchise. It was the lowest turnout in history. It was a bad omen for Mike Mahi.

Polling agents flew to New Delhi to be present for the counting. The counting was manual, not electronic. David and Mike stayed away from the capital.

With 14,000 casting their votes, the "Quota" under the system of the transferable vote was 2,000. You had to get 2,000 "first preference votes" or "transferred next preference votes" to make it to the council.

At the end of the first round of counting, when all the first preference votes had been counted, the news wasn't good for Mike Mahi. He stood a distant eighth with just 1100 votes. As expected, the sitting vice president, Baruarkar, had cracked the quota. He received 2,400 votes, 400 more than the quota!

The second round of counting brought in some cheer to the Mahi camp.

Baruarkar was now president-elect. His first preference votes were now available for transfer. Of the 2,400 first preferences polled by him, 2,000 voters had given second preference votes to others. Mike Mahi got a stunning 800. Each of these votes carried a value of 800/2000 namely "votes above the quota divided by second preference votes cast". Thus, the transfer of 400 votes to Mahi gave him a value of 160 votes. Mike Mahi moved into the sixth slot, and Rex inched marginally ahead of Anand Prakash.

At the end of the second round of counting, since no one had obtained the 2000-votes quota, the lowest ranked Vikas Gupte (100 votes) got voted out. For the third round of counting, Gupte's next preference votes were transferred at full value. The rule was that surplus votes (i.e. winner's extra votes) got transferred proportionately, and loser's votes (i.e. the eliminated candidate) got transferred wholly.

At the end of the third round, Mahi was out of the top six. It was a sobering feeling. Anand Prakash was back at the top of the list with a slender lead. At 10 p.m., the election observers decided to call it a night.

Mike Mahi spent a sleepless night, wondering how his fate would turn in the next twenty-four hours!

At 7 a.m. the following day, the counting recommenced. In the fourth round, among others, J Sabharwal, the towering giant of the accounting profession bowed out. By evening when the fifth round was done and dusted Anand Prakash had been selected.

The sixth and last round could turn out to be like Russian roulette.

The clock struck 10 p.m. on the second day. The polling officer asked the candidates whether he could continue or wait until 7 a.m. tomorrow. The officer made it clear that the law allowed the opening even past 10 p.m. if all the surviving candidates agreed. Their respective polling agents made frantic calls to the candidates. The consensus was to get the darn thing completed then and there. After a roller-coaster ride, Mike Mahi made the cut.

The final result read: Shekhar Baruarkar, Anand Prakash, Mike Mahi, Rex Alwaris, Rima Roy and Joe Mathew. It was champagne time at the office of Mike, Mahi and Associates.

The hangover would begin later.

36. The Call from 7 RCR

By the year 2008, there was hardly anyone in the industry who did not know Mike Mahi. He was an authority on accounting and on the economy. Any audit firm that had a problem or an accounting issue came to him for help. He made sure that he didn't take their work away. He would never forget that day many years ago when a fellow professional had robbed him of his client.

The CII, the ASSOCHAM, the AIMA and almost every top institution chased him to speak in their forums and seminars. He was being seen and heard in different parts of the country and was quoted in high places. Mike Mahi had sort of 'arrived' though he always thought it was 'work-in-progress.'

ooo

The call came on his unlisted private line, a number known only to a select few.

"Mike Mahi?" said the husky voice.

"Speaking." He couldn't place the voice.

"Good morning, Sir. This is a call from 7 RCR. The Prime Minister wants to speak to you. He will be with you in thirty seconds. I am his secretary."

Mahi was speechless. The Prime Minister's Office was calling him? He scrambled to grab a pencil and tore a piece of paper from the scratch pad, ready to take notes. "Cool. Cool," he told himself as he sipped from a glass of chilled water.

The next moment, the PM was on the line. "Morning, Mahi. I have heard a lot about you."

"Thank you, Sir. It's a pleasure to speak to you." His voice sounded brisk and professional, without a trace of anxiety. But his heart thundered in his chest, and he was worried it could be heard through the phone.

"I know you are a busy man. I will come straight to the point. The government is contemplating a major initiative. We need a better capture of information, and one of the suggestions made by our consultants was to move over from single to double entry system of accounting."

"It's an idea whose time has come," said Mahi. Those were the exact words the Prime Minister had famously used many years ago when he was the country's Finance Minister and had opened up the economy. Mahi could sense the venerable gentleman smile.

"The cabinet secretary will speak to you today and organize a meeting with the finance minister and the latter will brief you. I wanted to speak to you personally to tell you about the importance of this initiative and of my own keenness. People say you are the right man for the job. Mike Mahi, India needs you."

Despite years of experience, Mahi was still exhilarated. He would give anything to dance around his office. But when he opened his mouth, he was as cool as ever. "Sir, I will not disappoint you. I will wait for the cabinet secretary's call."

"Thank you Mahi, and convey my wishes to Tanya."

"Ouch! The government had done its homework," felt Mahi.

"Thank you, Sir."

ooo

The local government bodies were currently operating on a system of single entry. This was defective since the accounting information it captured was incomplete. While the rest of the world had moved to the more professional double entry system of bookkeeping several summers ago, the Indian government stood rooted in time, married to single entry. It was time to change, time for a divorce.

"They are waiting for you, both the finance minister and the cabinet secretary," said the lady at the reception. She must have been in her late forties. "Why don't they promote them and keep younger women at the front desk?" thought Mahi.

"Just a moment Sir," she told Mahi and then spoke into the intercom to someone. As she escorted Mahi to the minister's chamber, she made small talk. "Sir, I am moving out next fortnight on a promotion."

"Oh my God. Did she just read my mind?" Mahi fumbled for words and said, "Wow, hearty congrats. I am sure you will enjoy your new job."

In the anteroom, the minister's personal secretary met them. He waved his thumb in the direction of the minister's room.

Mahi knocked at the glass-paneled door, saw the "Don't pull" sign in time, pushed the door and walked in. The minister stood to greet him. Mahi blinked. Although he had seen him several times on national television, he hadn't realized the minister was over six feet tall. Clad in a starched, white dhoti and full-sleeved Arrow shirt, he extended his hand to give Mahi a firm handshake.

The other man, also well-dressed, probably in his early fifties, with a physique that showed he needed to hit the treadmill more regularly, threw a warm smile. He was the Cabinet Secretary.

"I read your profile last night. I liked it. The Prime Minister thinks highly of you," said the Finance Minister. "We are looking for an accounting firm to study our present system and suggest how to transition to double entry. The firm will have to prepare an accounting manual, and train employees in the government bodies to convert the books into double entry. You will have to station guides who will coach the employees until the transition is effected."

It was one of the most ambitious projects the government had ever embarked on.

"The Prime Minister feels an external expert with his feet firmly planted on the ground would be the ideal person to execute this project. And he thinks you are the right man," said the Minister.

"We need a proposal from your firm," said the Cabinet Secretary.

"I first need to gauge the volume of work, the manpower we need, the duration of time it will take, the challenges involved, both technical and people related."

"Hey, you are an experienced hand. Your firm must have handled many such assignments."

"Sir, no Indian firm is likely to have hands-on experience in this because single entry accounting disappeared forty years ago. No corporate, no partnership firm, no sole-trader uses single-entry accounting."

The secretary let out a whistle. "You mean we are operating in the Stone Age? Why didn't anyone tell us about it?" He was asking no one in particular.

The Finance Minister was adjusting his dhoti, and sipping a cup of hot filter coffee. The coffee had a distinct aroma. Mahi wasn't a coffee buff but as the Finance Minister was ordering for the three of them, he didn't say he preferred tea. Some years ago he had read an article by Tejas Arya where the journalist said that the rich, the famous, and the powerful always drank coffee. Tea was for the commoner.

"I suggest that Mahi prepare a rough two-pager on how he will go about this and some indications of the manpower cost. You can give him the coverage we contemplated for the first month. At the end of the month, Mahi can come out with his full-scale proposal."

"Fine. What say you, Mahi?" The Cabinet Secretary rose from his seat for the first time and pulled up the zip of his pants. He had apparently forgotten about it.

"Perfect."

As he stood up to leave, the Finance Minister told Mahi, "We are not tendering for this engagement. That's against the standard practice. The boss is so smitten by you, and God knows why, that he has spoken to the Leader of the Opposition. The Opposition has agreed not to make a song and dance out of it, so make sure you deliver well."

"Sure, Sir."

ooo

As he drove away from the Finance Minister's office, Mahi was hardly concentrating on the road. This assignment, when it came through, would easily be the single largest billing of all time for his firm. More importantly, it would be a huge learning experience. It would surely catapult the firm into the Top Ten. Why, it might even place the firm at number seven, just below the Big Six. A ghost of an idea was beginning to form in Mahi's mind.

Screech! He hit the brakes hard as a pedestrian crossed the road. Thank goodness he had not been hurt! The pedestrian cursed him. Not a good omen.

An emergency meeting of Mike, Mahi & Associate's Apex Council was called the same evening. It didn't matter in which corner of India the members were; they had to drop everything to be available at the headquarters at 8 p.m. The Council consisted of six partners and handled major policy initiatives. It generally met twice a year. The last meeting had been held only twenty days ago.

ooo

"Sorry to pull you from work at such short notice and at such an odd hour. The Prime Minister spoke to me last evening, and I met the Finance Minister this morning."

Clap. Clap. "Yes, yes, we know," said the head of international operations. "The two-pager you faxed was quite clear. If we can pull this one off, it would be wonderful Mahi. Let's discuss the next steps."

"What are the next steps?" Mahi asked.

The Council began talking, people voicing opinion and dissent. There were ifs and buts flying across the room, and Mahi felt the temperature rising. He sat there, trying to catch every word that was being said.

"It's a once-in-a-lifetime project, but do we have the bandwidth to execute it? We have never worked on something like this before."

"You don't get to work on a once in a lifetime project a second time. We need to grab this with both hands. Doesn't matter if we don't have the manpower. We will advertise and find them."

"We can use our networked firms. We can bring in international experts to help us. We can even ask other firms we are not networked with, if we so desire."

"No, no, no, we can't do that. They would rip off our margin by a mile. Why should we share anything with them?"

"How will this affect our other engagements? Do we have the time to execute this? Or will it take place at the cost of our existing clients? Will interacting with the bureaucracy be a challenge?"

And so the discussion went on and on, well into the night. Mahi watched it from the sidelines, in silence, not giving his views. Dinner was served in the conference room.

The head of international operations turned to him. "What's your view Mahi?"

Everyone fell silent.

"Let's do it this way. We will accept the first month's engagement. In that time, let's try and understand how it works. Once we learn the ropes, we can draw up the proposal in terms of team and time. We will then have the NICPA execute this even as our firm takes some kind of a lead role," said Mahi.

"What? That's hogwash. Absolute nonsense. Why should we do that? If NICPA bills the government, we lose the top line. Our billing will be on NICPA. Not only will the number be smaller, we won't have the government on our client list. This won't work."

"Look at it this way. By passing on to NICPA, we achieve many advantages. We will have easy access to all accounting firms operating across India. They will be keen to work with us. We will end up having the best brains working along with us," said Mahi.

A senior partner jumped in. "God forbid something go wrong. And if it does, our firm will be insulated from attack. In a sense, it's insurance for us. If things go okay, given Mahi's new-found equation with the government, we will get the credit for spearheading the initiative.

"But with NICPA we may not have much say in team formation and execution. Hierarchical issues will crop up. A group consisting of too many first among equals won't work. I am not sure if Mahi can work with NICPA, which works like the government.

"By passing this to NICPA we will win the admiration of our fellow professionals. It's never been done before. We won't be charged with using our position in the Council to bag a professional contract."

"Come on, that's unfair. We did not scout. It fell into our lap because of Mahi's skills."

"The government may refuse the NICPA angle."

"Why should we lose professionally merely because Mahi is a council member? We don't take advantage of his position. Similarly, we should not embrace a disadvantage."

"Let's see when that happens."

As the night slowly slipped into day, Mahi said, "We can debate this endlessly. I think this matter is too important to go through without a vote unless there is unanimity amongst us. Let's put it to 'split vote' if you guys agree."

The split vote was an idea Mahi had conceived several summers ago to take care of contentious issues. You could vote 'Yes' or 'No' or 'Maybe'. If you said 'Yes' it meant you were assigning 100 points for the issue. If you said 'No', you were awarding 0 points. If you said 'Maybe' you needed to say how much for 'Yes' and how much for 'No'. So someone could vote 60:40 meaning 60 points for go ahead and 40 points for no-go. This was Mahi's way of providing weights for votes.

The six wise men voted. The votes were counted and the decision announced. Mahi neither smiled nor frowned.

ooo

At 8 a.m. the following day, he updated Uncle Krishna on the developments.

"Mike, I am thrilled the Prime Minister has placed so much faith in you. You should not let him down."

"Thank you, Uncle. What do you say about our decision?"

"Don't you think it's too late to ask my view? It isn't going to change the decision. Right?"

"I respect your view."

"Well, I am happy you guys decided. There are always two sides. If you give the business to NICPA, some would say you are benevolent; others would say you lack confidence. At the same time, you can't be faulted for taking the work into your firm though it might make a few go green with envy.

"I would vote 70:30 for retaining the work with the firm."

ooo

A few weeks later, after intense work at the government, Mike, Mahi & Associates presented a plan. The government accepted it fully. The following week *New Delhi Times* carried a front-page breaking story:

Government makes bold to step into double entry

Mike Mahi to lead the engagement

The accounting fraternity agreed that Mike Mahi had finally arrived, in his own right. There was the inevitable bitterness about how he had used his position to bag an assignment. At the corridors of power at NICPA, the murmur turned into a tornado waiting to break out. But no newspaper bothered about it because the Prime Minister was an upright man. That was when NICPA's President went public with the letter he had received from Mike Mahi some fifty days ago, brief and to the point.

Dear Mr. President:

Two days ago, the Prime Minister called to tell me about his plan to transition government bodies to double entry bookkeeping. For me, it was an unprecedented situation. Last morning I met with the Finance Minister and the Cabinet Secretary to discuss the modus operandi. I believe that NICPA, given its abundant talent in accounting research and the large army of accounting professionals in this country, should rightfully spearhead this initiative. I will do the initial assessment and once the engagement is ready, NICPA should execute it.

Regards,

Mike Mahi

37. 2-3-6-5-0-0-9-8

"Two, three, six, five, double zero, nine, eight," screamed the newspaper headline. And below it, the by-line: Tejas Arya.

As Mike Mahi began to read, his blood started to boil and beads of perspiration dropped from his forehead. When he finished, he wasn't too sure whom he should be angry with: Tejas Arya for not having taken him into confidence, or the wolves at NICPA. Seething, he clenched his fingers into a fist, banged it on the table, and immediately grimaced in pain.

His first thought was that the title referred to NICPA's telephone number and that Tejas was merely complaining about nobody picking up calls. He himself had experienced it. But in his very first sentence, Arya made it clear: "No folks, this is not a telephone number." So, it was far more serious than that. Arya came straight to the point: "It's the marks scored in eight papers by a student during the Final exam." Mahi caught his breath as he read the next line. "Is it possible that a person who was a top-10 ranker four years ago at NICPA's Level 1 exam and who had done commendably well in Level 2 score so low?" Then came the charges, one after the other, in the straight, simple, signature style of Arya.

The full text read:

"Two, three, six, five, double zero, nine, eight"

By: Tejas Arya

23650098. No folks, this is not someone's telephone number. Read again: 2, 3, 6, 5, 0, 0, 9, and 8. These are the marks scored in eight papers by a student who appeared for NICPA's Final level exam.

For a moment, let's assume that the marks are right. Why does NICPA entertain such dimwits? How did this person manage to pass two levels of NICPA to reach the final? Well, that's because he's academically bright; yes bright as in bright, no puns intended.

This lad obtained NICPA's 8th rank in the Level 1 exam and scored a creditable 65 percent in its Level 2. He (I shall not divulge his name) tells me he wrote to the Institute asking them to re-check his papers but hasn't received a reply. He tried calling them multiple times on the telephone but received evasive responses.

His call records show that he is telling the truth. I have seen his e-mail account. The forensic expert in my office confirms the mails have been received and read. But the gods at NICPA didn't heed his prayer.

His father is a friend of mine. By the way, he didn't come to me for making this matter public. When I casually asked about his son's progress in the course, he told me about his trauma. I have great respect for NICPA. I know it handles large volumes of students and does a comprehensive job. But it has to be sensitive to the feelings of the students who are at a very impressionable age. They need empathy. More important, NICPA has to be seen to be sensitive.

My friend Mike Mahi (we went to the same college and interned at the same accounting firm) is on the Board of NICPA and is an honorable man. I could have written or spoken directly to him, but I thought we must be open and transparent about this.

'23650098' is fine if it's right; if it's wrong, let's right the wrong. In either case, let the candidate know his fate. Even now it's not too late. Let's not stand on ego.

The photograph of NICPA's headquarters, a file picture of a handsome Mike Mahi waving after his electoral victory, a shot of a NICPA center with hundreds of students taking the exam and the contentious mark sheet with the name and roll number blacked out ran across the well laid Tejas Arya article. The write up was in a different font, making it scream from the first page of the newspaper.

Mahi was at NICPA headquarters when he read it. “Unbelievable,” he said to himself. It wasn’t the marks that stunned him; students did slack off or find the heat in the final too strong. “How did the morons let this reach the media when they had it in them to sort it out?” He gulped a glass of water to make sure he didn’t go berserk.

ooo

“Madam, could you come to Room 616 immediately?”

“No, Sir. I am preparing the text for the Vice President’s speech. He has to deliver it on the day after and he wanted me to complete it today,” said the lady.

“Madam, the matter is serious. The speech writing can wait. In any case, the Vice President’s speech never exceeds five minutes.” His voice was still soft.

“Sorry Sir, I can’t come now. Vice President’s work takes precedence.”

“Madam, I repeat, this is serious. If you want I will explain my reasons to the vice president later. In any case, I need only 20 minutes of your time.” The temperature indicator on the air-conditioner, which was showing 24 degrees, rose to 27.

“Sorry, Sir,” and she slammed the phone down.

Mike Mahi pulled open the door of Room 616, on the sixth floor, allowing it to slam back as he raced down the stairs, taking them two steps at a time. A guy in light blue pants and a dark blue shirt, balancing mugs of coffee on a tray, stood transfixed at the sight. No one had ever seen Mahi in a rage.

Mahi reached Madam’s desk and threw the newspaper down on its surface. “Have you seen this? You think a vice-president’s thanks giving speech at a Chamber function takes precedence over this? Are you out of your mind? Do you know what serious damage this has caused to us?”

“Sir, you can’t talk to me like that.”

He stared at her, his face growing redder by the second, his muscles tightening in his jaw. "Don't tell me what I can talk and what I can't. Shift your bottom out of the messy chair you are sitting on, and in the next hour get to the Controller's Office and pick out the answer scripts for this candidate. Get me the complete mail trail this student has with NICPA. Don't stand there like a fool. Speak to the Front Office and get the records of the conversations with the student. Our media cell will be meeting me in an hour. I'll need all this by then. I want to throw the material at Tejas Arya at a press conference this evening and prove him wrong."

"Sir, but it can't be done that quickly."

Mahi glared at her. She could feel the heat. "I don't care what the hell you say. I want action. If you don't get it by that time, you can find yourself another job." Nobody had seen an angry Mahi before.

An hour later, Madam turned up at Room 616, shivering in fright. As Mahi went through the 30 mails that the candidate had sent her on her official mail id and noticed she had not replied to any one of them, he lost his cool. "Do you really lack shame? How could you have sat on this? What was your provocation? Did you want money? Doesn't the Institute pay you a salary every month?"

Then he listened to the taped conversation.

It was incredible. "Yeah, we will see. Yes, yes we will check it. Give us time." On the other side: "Madam, my exam is coming closer. I need to know about this performance." This side: "Yes, I understand. I will do it. Don't think yours is the only case I attend to." Slam.

Mahi's plan of throwing the evidence at Tejas went up in smoke. He should have known it. Tejas would never have taken up an issue unless he was damn sure. And here the evidence was dancing before his eyes.

Four hours later, once he'd put the whole Institute on the job, it came to light that the student's roll number was 23650098 and this had been mistakenly entered as his marks. It was another matter that the candidate had failed five of the eight subjects. Mahi called Tejas personally and explained the situation. He also told him punitive action would be taken and requested the matter be closed.

The following morning, Tuesday, a letter went from the NICPA to the candidate informing him of his revised marks, which did not change the exam results.

On Wednesday evening, Madam tendered her resignation. It was the first time in history that someone in NICPA had been pushed to go. Mahi's stock went up.

On Thursday morning, a Tejas Arya article screamed across *New Delhi Times*, "Mike Mahi cracks the whip. NICPA staff sacked. Student's marks restored."

Mahi sighed. "These fellows are incorrigible."

38. Mahi Runs for the Presidency

Towards the end of his fourth year at the National Council, 2010, Mahi decided to run for the presidency.

At NICPA, presidency was a two-year stint. The Electoral College consisted of the office bearers of the various branches across the country, the elected members of the seven regional councils and the fifty elected representatives of the National Council. Each branch had on an average six office bearers and each region averaged fifteen elected members. With a hundred branches, the Electoral College had 755 members.

All votes were not equally valuable. Some votes were worth more. The vote of a branch office bearer counted for one, the elected Regional Council Member counted for four and of the National Council Member counted for seven. So the value of the votes of the branches was 600, those in the region were 420 and that at the National level 350. The total: 1370 votes. To win outright you had to get 686 votes.

It wasn't going to be easy. History wasn't on Mahi's side. No one had ever won the presidency with just three years of experience on the National Council. Worse still, every president had first been a branch office bearer, and then a regional council member before becoming a member of the national council. Mahi had side-stepped the first two to reach the national council.

There were four possible candidates for the presidency, including Mahi. One of these was Dr. Saurav Moraes, a one-time Sheriff of Bombay and an upright and honest man. If Moraes ran for the presidency, he would win hands down. Someone contesting against him was unthinkable. No one would forgive NICPA if Dr. Moraes lost! Moraes hadn't yet officially declared his candidature.

A second candidate was S P Ray. People said he had enough power to even fix a tribunal bench hearing. He could organize governmental transfers if the price was right. Of course, there was no proof for any of these. Mahi had interacted with Ray and thought that these were inspired charges.

The frontrunner was Neha Kulkarni. A partner in one of the large sized firms of the variety with whom Mike Mahi competed, she was a thoroughbred professional. Rumor had it that she could scan a ten-page report in a couple of minutes and point out all that was wrong. She commanded an unbelievable following. Mahi felt gender voting was possible especially if a top office was at stake. It would be politically right to see a woman as the president.

Mike Mahi felt that if people voted according to their conscience he stood a chance, but it was not necessary everyone would vote so. Voting loyalties could shift overnight; pledged votes would change by the hour.

Those were the circumstances in which Mike Mahi threw his hat into the presidency ring with a fair chance. It was then that from out of nowhere the first crisis hit.

Mahi received a copy of a nasty four-page e-mail full of litany. It had been mass circulated. It named no one in particular but left no one in any doubt as to who the target was. The aggressor was hiding behind an anonymous e-mail id. When the target didn't respond, the assailants became bolder and more reckless with their versions of the truth. A quarter-page advertisement appeared in the country's leading newspaper, *New Delhi Times,* asking six hard questions.

Question 1: Who do you want to represent you? Do you want an auditor and a gentleman; or do you want someone who knows the ropes?

Question 2: Do you want a person with huge academic accomplishments or someone with proven ability at getting things done in the places that matter?

Question 3: Do you know that if you open the cupboards of any successful man you will find several skeletons within?

Question 4: Want to select a man who has spent two nights in prison? Or would you prefer someone who grew up in a 12ft x10ft room?

Question 5: Want to pick a guy who has amassed wealth in the industry and not someone who has toiled in the profession?

Question 6: Do you want a president whose familial antecedents are suspect? "Should the private life of a public man not be open to scrutiny?"

It closed with a teaser. "We expect a reply from the target." It was clear as daylight that Dr. Saurav Moraes was the target.

Tejas Arya refused to divulge the source of the advertisement, claiming customer confidentiality. The money had been received in cash and no forwarding addresses had been given—that was the stand the newspaper office took. The ad appeared every day for a week.

Who was behind the ad? Was it a big business house or was it a big accounting firm, or worse still, was it a contestant? The nation needed to know. Someone suggested that Dr. Moraes get on television and take a Q&A session with an anchor. After all, the advertisement had been carried in *New Delhi Times*, India's top newspaper.

Tejas Arya invited Dr. Moraes to the *Talking Heads* program, a one-on-one interview. Dr. Moraes politely refused.

Dr. Moraes had been both hurt and shocked. How could this person have known some of the most private details of his life? Someone had betrayed his trust. If this was how the battle lines would be drawn, he wasn't going to go to war. He let it be discreetly known that he was not interested in running.

With that, the advertisements stopped.

OOO

One week later, Mike Mahi inked an agreement with S P Ray. The details of the accord would forever be kept a secret.

"This would amount to me selling my soul," Mahi told the other party.

"It doesn't matter. You wouldn't be the first presidential candidate to do it. You will also surely not be the last presidential candidate to do it."

A day before the elections S. P. Ray, dropped out. He had kept his part of the deal.

Mike Mahi won. It was a landslide victory. He pocketed 1010 points. No one had ever won by such a margin.

"President Mike Mahi," the words sounded sweet and good.

Mahi threw a big party, attended by all council members, almost all office bearers, most of Mahi's clients, staff and his close friends. It would put his firm back by several lakhs.

Both Uncle Krishna and his first client, Dr. D'Souza, were there, beaming at his success. Tanya was by his side at this moment of crowning glory. Tejas Arya was conspicuous by his absence.

That evening, Mahi remembered his days at school. How he had played marbles, how he had maintained an account of the marbles bought, earned, lost, lent, and collected. He remembered how he had walked to school and how he had studied with difficulty at home. He recalled his days in college, of how he got into it courtesy a hockey match. He remembered the last night in college, the missed award. He recalled his days as an intern, the rush to the airport and his role as a running boy to get a cheque signed. He remembered his exam results.

He remembered his first days in his office, waiting for clients to walk in. The phone would ring just once and he would speak into it, "Mike, Mahi & Associates."

Today, he had offices in every state capital in India, besides Washington DC, Ottawa and Sydney. And now he was president at NICPA. He had surely come a long way, but the road ahead was longer still.

He was justifiably proud of his profession. No other profession would have entrusted its highest office to the son of a colliery worker. He hadn't even turned forty. The next day, the newspapers reported that Mike Mahi had invited S.P. Ray to be his second in command. Mahi had kept his part of the deal.

39. The President Acts

Mike Mahi lost no time in delivering on the promises contained in his manifesto. It wasn't easy.

He first turned his attention to examination reforms.

Nishant Seth, one of India's best academicians, was invited to re-engineer the exam process. Mahi gave him a free hand. "Form a team. Interview anyone you want. You have unfettered access to any record at NICPA. But at the end of thirty days, come out with a report. Then implement it. Take a fat fee for the effort."

Mahi's colleagues were aghast at the terms, especially the last one. You don't pay a fat fee at NICPA. Most things are pro bono. Mahi would have none of it. "We can afford it," was his refrain. "And we must make it worth his while."

"What's the guarantee he will come out with an acceptable solution?"

"There is no guarantee. Life does not offer guarantees and warranties. It merely presents us with possibilities and opportunities," said the young president.

At NICPA, you don't form a committee without NICPA Council Members on it.

"How can the Council go unrepresented on this committee?" asked a Member.

"Please tell me why we need representation. After all, it is our committee. Plus I don't want anyone breathing down Nishant's neck."

"But that's how things are done at NICPA." Someone threw the precedence book at him. His predecessors had warned him about the precedence rule. The bureaucracy always did that. Mahi wanted to close this once and for all.

"Well, that's precisely why we don't want NICPA to be on this Committee. We don't want an *"it-was-always-done-like-this"* member in a re-engineering committee. Plus, if it has never been done this way in the past, let's create a precedent now."

Mahi remembered the very same remark he had made many years ago at the office of the National Registry of Companies.

The Council voted for the reengineering plan after humming and hawing for 30 minutes. Thus began Nishant Seth's tryst with NICPA.

For twenty-nine days, Seth and his team visited various zones of the NICPA, met up with past presidents, spoke to academicians, industry leaders, students and officers at the Institute. It was twenty-nine days of punishing work, eighteen hours a day. On the thirtieth day, Nishant Seth came out with changes that NICPA would find both hard to accept and difficult to resist.

The Draft Report was circulated to the Council Members the same day with a rider stating that one week later, the Council would meet to finalize the outcome of the report. The NICPA Secretary e-mailed everyone, asking them to come prepared, as there would be no adjournments.

The meeting began at 8 a.m. sharp. Seth began his presentation after a small preliminary by Mike Mahi. Neatly attired in a tie that matched his shirt, Seth let the blazer pass.

"NICPA should hive off its Examinations Department (ED)," screamed the PowerPoint. Seth had come straight to the point. There was a ripple of 'oohs' and 'aahs'. More murmurs could be heard from the audience.

"The ED should function under a Controller appointed by a three-man search committee consisting of the president, the vice president, and an eminent academician."

"Would that academician be Seth?"

Seth continued without batting an eyelid. "The Controller will be an independent authority and will hold a three-year term. No office bearer or employee of NICPA will be eligible for this position."

"What would independent authority mean?" shot a member from Jupiter.

"He would report only to the President. No one else will have access to him."

"What?"

"He would report only to the President. No one else will have access to him."

The Council fell silent. Mahi looked around as if he expected pandemonium to break out.

"I suggest the Controller report to the President only administratively."

"The Controller will form his own team, identify examiners and evaluators. The ED will be a separate profit center and will be under the audit of a different set of auditors. This will ensure complete autonomy."

"Why? Is there no autonomy now?"

"Well, Caesar's wife should be above suspicion."

After a lot of heckling and bawling, the proposition was accepted by voice vote.

"There will be four exams in a year," said Seth getting on to his second big- bang suggestion; March, June, September, and December. The slide on the PPT deck carried only seven words.

The NICPA was already reeling from the pressure of the examination system. Paper setting, guideline answers, evaluation of tens of thousands of papers was taking its toll.

"Why?" asked a member.

"While the number of exams will change, the number of students taking the exams will not. This is because a candidate will not be allowed to take consecutive exams. This will bring down the load factor on NICPA and also improve the quality of valuations."

There was heated debate, lots of deliberation and finally Seth's recommendation was accepted. At every stage, Mahi gave people the opportunity to express their views, but somewhere down the line, he would go a hundred percent with Seth's recommendation.

The NICPA ran exams at three Levels. Level 1 was always in the multiple-choice mode. Each paper would have 120 questions with four answers given. Every student would get the same 120 questions. Seth suggested that the questions should not appear in the same sequence. The sequence of the answers too should be changed for every candidate such that no two persons got the same paper, even though it was the same 120 questions. They would be sorted in different orders both in terms of questions and answers!

The Council voted for it with enthusiasm.

More reforms came in for evaluation. If a question paper consisted of six questions, three examiners would mark two questions each. Mahi recalled the old jibe of students: "If one teacher cannot teach eight subjects, how do you expect one student to master eight subjects?" Now Seth was suggesting that every chapter needed an expert!

Seth's most controversial suggestion was that valued answer books should be returned to the student.

"Impossible. We will open up a Pandora's box."

"This will introduce transparency."

"Transparency at what cost?"

"It would bring about greater accountability amongst the evaluators."

The arguments went back and forth, back and forth, but in the end they weren't able to bell the cat. Neither Seth nor Mahi could push it through.

Mahi said, "We can debate this till the cows come home. We have assigned the work to a set of professionals to whom we have paid a fancy price. Why lose precious time over it? Let's go with it."

The Council would have none of it. Graciously, Mahi let it slip, making it clear that they would come back to it next year.

Seth quickly thought of an alternative. "The candidates could be allowed to see their answer book and return it immediately."

"This will create a mad rush."

"Not necessarily. Let's keep the fee stiff. And no one other than the candidate will be allowed to inspect the papers. If we are not forward thinking, we will one day be pushed into doing this by the courts."

There was a vote. And it went through by a wafer-thin majority.

Next, Seth wanted revaluation. NICPA now allowed only retotaling and valuing of those questions that had by mistake not been evaluated by the examiners. If a candidate had been awarded 1 mark out of 10, right or wrong, the answer would not be evaluated again.

"What if the new evaluator downgrades the marks?"

"The student should be willing to take the risk."

"What if the valuation by the second examiner throws up a big difference?"

"In that case we should go to a third examiner. His decision will then be final. Of course, he will not be told that he is the third examiner."

The argument went on for some time. Finally, the proposal was cleared and a stiff fee fixed.

More exciting changes were brought in. They agreed to upload guideline answers to the examination questions on the very day of the examination.

Mahi worked hard to push the idea that CAs take a compulsory test in a chosen subject every five years, and the continuation of their membership would hinge on their performance in that test. The crowd refused. He then made it optional.

At the end of fourteen hours of non-stop deliberation, Mahi came out of the meeting a happy President.

OOO

As president he brought about more dramatic changes. He travelled extensively across the world to sign agreements with fellow institutes globally that would among others provide reciprocity in examinations, in award of charters and in work. Extensive training Sessions were conducted to ensure that CAs stayed current in both technical knowledge and in people related skills. Centers of Excellence sprung up across the country. NICPA buildings across the country were standardized in how they looked. India emerged as a leader in standard setting. The government turned to the Institute for support in preparing the national budget. Matters that had major implications on the economy were run past the NICPA. The Institute emerged as a partner in nation building in the true sense.

Mahi brought a sense of direction and purpose to the profession corporatizing it like no other president had done before. Those two years of his presidency he lived at the NICPA headquarters. In 2012 when his two-year term ended, he ensured that the rules were amended so that future presidents had a three-year term. He believed such a timeframe was needed to implement large vision. He remembered how a corporate leader had once said, "a CEO needs 10-years to firm up and execute a shared vision." As he got off the top slot Mike Mahi could proudly claim that he had made a difference to the lives of people in a blot-less stay at the top.

40. Alka's Mantras

Alka Varma had joined Hunt & Smith in 1984 as Audit Senior in its Transaction Advisory Department. Her job was to compute numbers and file monotonous forms. Sad. She was green with envy whenever she thought of her batch-mates who were now in the corporate sector with fat salaries while she was comparatively drawing peanuts. Worse still, they had loads of time on hand. Her heart sank every time she heard stories of them watching movies, their nights out, and their experiments with cuisines and vacations. On the other hand, Alka sat every day at her desk until the last bar in the town closed.

Slowly the fourteen-hour schedule at the Terminal no longer scared her. She got used to it. The 'Terminal' was the name of H&S headquarters.

Big firms offered you a stage to rub shoulders with the best brains in the business. Twenty CAs in 2,000 square feet were as hazardous as a group of stand-up comedians trying to outwit each other. You either made your presence felt or let yourself be fooled. This pushed Alka to work harder. She stayed up late and woke up early.

The hierarchy was steep with seven levels. If you were a CA, you were absorbed as Audit Senior. One year of grinding was enough to get you promoted as Assistant Audit Manager. One more year of doing every dirty job was sufficient to get you promoted as a Manager. After a three-year stint, the Manager could become a Senior Manager. Three years later, he could become a Director. Two years as director and presto, he could reach the top, a Partner.

From CA to partnership was ten long years.

Sometime in 1995, Alka got promoted as a Partner. One of the first things she did was to correct what she thought was a wrong practice being adopted by Hunt & Smith.

The firm poached clients and practiced it to a fine art. It offered to do audits at throwaway prices with the sole intention of upstaging the competitor. Later, once firmly entrenched in, it would jack up its price substantially.

There were rumors that the firm withheld audit qualifications in exchange for a promise of a group company's audit. No one knew whether this was true, but people argued that there could be no smoke without fire.

Alka thought poaching was wrong. She agreed the market was competitive, but she was dead against snatching another man's bread. "If I am given no choice, but to fill my stomach that way, I would prefer going hungry," she once remarked publicly.

The opportunity to change this presented itself on Day 3 of her elevation as a partner. At H&S, the partner had the power to accept or reject a client. Once a partner refused a client and recorded his reason for it, it would be very difficult for another partner to take him in. If he had to do so, it would have to go through an elaborate process and no one liked going through that.

That day, a client of a medium-sized company walked into Alka's office saying he wanted H&S to do their tax audit.

After some small talk, Alka Varma got into professional conversation mode.

"Are your accounts audited by another professional accounting firm?"

"Yes, Madam."

"Well, I don't want to know who they are and why you are planning a switch, but we cannot take up the assignment unless a partner of the other firm calls me and says I can go ahead with it."

"You can write to the firm, inform them that your firm has been offered the assignment, and you can ask them whether they have any objection to your handling the work. I guess your Institute's Code suggests that."

"But we don't work that way. We would prefer you to tell your auditor and we would expect them to call us or write to us saying it is okay for us to take up the work."

"But nobody works that way."

"But we are not a nobody."

The prospective client left promising to revert after discussion with his current auditor.

Meanwhile Alka wrote to the other firm indicating the client had approached them for audit. She didn't put the usual question of "Do you have any objections to our taking up the assignment?" Instead she just wrote about how she had politely turned them away. The auditor had replied thanking Alka. He then held a heart-to-heart meeting with the unhappy client and managed to pull him back.

Alka lost out on a new customer but won over a professional colleague.

This became her practice and slowly she began to pick goodwill amongst fellow professionals. Over time, she discouraged walk-ins. H&S only accepted high-profile clients or those who came with referrals.

She brought about other changes as well.

She took the unusual step of engaging former employees of the Tax Department. In a sense, the idea wasn't original. Although this was a standard practice among other firms, Alka institutionalized it. She took in lots of Tax officers and built a team around them! They were jocularly referred to as ex-service men.

Sanjay Banerjee was one such person. He had retired as Commissioner and was looking forward to a comfortable retired life playing with his grandchildren, tending the garden and cooking along with his wife. He had an enormous repertoire of knowledge and network. Alka Varma met and spoke to him about her vision for Hunt & Smith and urged him to lead the initiative.

Alka could be very persuasive whenever she chose to be, and she succeeded in winning over Sanjay Banerjee.

He was asked to assemble a team and mentor it. His mandate was to look at every tax case that came to H&S from the prism of the Tax Department. Towards that his team had to dissect all reported cases into three heads: One, those that favored the Revenue; two, those that favored the Assessee; and three, those that fell in the gray chasm, open to interpretation. It was the third category that brought in the money.

Banerjee's team would be the sparring partner. They would play Tax Department even as the H&S team would prepare the counter. This gave H&S the necessary practice. It was an idea Alka had borrowed from a Mike Mahi presentation. Alka commercialized it by making it workable and professional.

If "no-poach" was Mantra No. 1 and "Tax Department Role Play" was Mantra No. 2, Mantra No. 3 was to make the documentation picture perfect. Everything from the moment a client walked in with a requirement to the time he walked out with his need fulfilled was documented.

Individual clients were handled with care and respect. Despite being a large organization and dealing with customers who came in with giant sized egos (they were managing directors and CEOs), Alka was able to maintain professionalism. Return filing was a massive business area and was done strictly on a first-come first-serve basis. If it would take four days to do it, so be it. If the client pushed that it be done in forty-eight hours, they would be politely told that there were others in the queue.

Alka told her team members that while they should work hard for the client they should not lose sleep over the client's headache. There was no point in pushing up your blood pressure for the sake of the client.

Once H&S said ninety-six hours, it meant ninety-six hours. In the event of a delay by H&S and a penalty becoming payable, H&S would work it out with the Tax Department. Sometimes if an arrangement could not be worked out, H&S itself would cough up the penalty. People worked like an assembly line. Clients understood and respected the system and over time began to like it.

The fourth mantra was how Alka handled speed money.

In the Tax Department, most things came with a price. You could call it corruption. You could call it speed money. Alka recognized that this was okay with her so long as her firm did not get its hands personally soiled.

It worked like this. On most issues, H&S was clear about the correct legal position. The client would be informed if the legal status was against him. In such a situation, Alka wouldn't fight the case against the Department and would ask the client to pay up the legal dues or settle with it.

If the client still wanted to fight, Alka would refer him to a fellow tax professional outside the firm. She didn't like taking money for jam and didn't believe in spending professional time on losing causes.

Where the client wanted to settle, she would set up a meeting between the client and the Tax Officer. H&S would never get into the picture. There was no need for her to take a cut in a direct deal between the client and the Tax Officer..

Alka socialized heavily with the top brass of the Tax Department. Many of them were her bridge-playing buddies at the Cosmopolitan Club and she played golf with others. Quick discussions did take place at the bridge table or on the golf course.

Mantra No. 5 was that no client was unimportant. It didn't matter if the client paid Rs 500 or Rs 500,000. While the firm had the liberty to refuse a Rs 500 client, once it accepted him, it had to service him with the completeness with which it would maintain a customer who paid Rs 500,000.

She believed one happy client brought another.

41. Mahi in Blunder-land

In 2004, Mahi decided to go international.

He opened up his operations in four cities to begin with, namely Dubai, Los Angeles, Perth and Ottawa. It was based on the networking model he had pioneered in India. The decision was not exactly backed by any significant strategy.

An Indian with an entrepreneurial streak led the operations in each of the four cities. Each had been handpicked by Mahi and given the mandate to grow the firm to a certain size in three years' time. Size was defined in terms of turnover, headcount, client count, and profits.

Stationed in various cities, the Head would have unlimited powers. They could meet up and bring in clients, decide what engagements to take and what to drop, recruit people, and run the organization on a given budget. They were offered salaries significantly above market rates plus an attractive bonus package linked to the value of the business brought in. Mahi brought them processes, mentoring, knowledge bank and the occasional meetings from India. He was constantly in touch with them.

Each of these firms was a separate legal entity in their respective countries but called themselves "Networked with Mike, Mahi & Associates". A local firm was roped in as a business partner and strategic investor for each of these branches. This was a major risk, but Mahi had always been a risk taker.

Mahi's vision was successful, and business picked up everywhere. Professional work started to flow in: audit, tax, consulting, and compliance. The business heads exceeded their targets in just three years. Each of them had set different targets. Ottawa had set the goal in terms of turnover, and Los Angeles in terms of profits. Perth's target was to increase the number of clients, and Dubai took on itself to make its presence felt among the top ten firms in the region. All of them achieved their targets by a long mile.

With immense success comes the danger of betrayal and that was what happened.

One bright summer morning, the Ottawa head walked away with the entire business, hand-in-glove with the local partner. He took the business to one of the global Big Six, joining them as a partner. Mahi was shaken. Someone leaving an organization to join a competitor is one thing. But walking away with everything the organization had built – client, machines, employees, processes, etc., -- is another. He couldn't come to terms with it for a long time. He had after all, handpicked him to share his dream! What hurt Mahi more was that only fifteen days ago, Mahi had been in Ottawa and they had planned further growth. They had talked about opening a branch in the US!

The break up was messy. There wasn't even a phone call or a personal visit to explain the desertion. A simple e-mail had been sent to Mahi that they were now no longer part of the network. Mahi hadn't drawn up a formal legal arrangement because he believed in trust and maintained that legal battles could sap your energy. Mahi tried to reach out, but was cut off.

For Mahi, for yet another time in his life, the world came to a halt.

But Mahi would not be Mahi if he did not shake himself out of the crisis. He got a grip on himself and soon went into damage control mode. He called Perth, then Los Angeles and finally Dubai to brief them on the developments. He could have told them all the good things that he had done for them and implored them to stay on. He knew better.

"I am saying this to you because I want you to hear it from me; also because I was told by Ottawa that you guys would follow suit and I told him that you would never do it."

Los Angeles, Perth, and Dubai did not go the Ottawa way.

Ottawa taught Mahi an important lesson. Legal arrangements, even if they were arrangements of convenience, not tenable in a court of law, needed to be put down in writing. He told Doc, "Next time I do a deal without a written arrangement, just whisper the word 'Ottawa' in my ears."

In the next five years he added six international branches: Copenhagen, London, Lagos, Johannesburg, Egypt, Auckland and Washington DC. He now had one in every continent.

42. No Action, Only Talk

Kaleem had been with Mike Mahi for over ten years now.

Kaleem's mother, an elderly lady, worked as a domestic help in the same apartment complex in which Mahi lived. She knew Mahi by sight and knew that he ran a business. Ten years ago she had brought Kaleem to Mahi and asked Mahi whether he could give the boy a job.

Mahi was astounded. The boy looked all of eleven years and Mahi had strong views on child labor. Plus, boys that age would be taken for a ride in his office. The lady had come across similar situations before and said, "My son is fifteen. He has just passed his Class X." For good measure she added, "He doesn't want to study further."

When Mahi had said, "Mark-sheet," Kaleem's mother had proudly pulled a sheet that she had safely tucked inside her sari and Mahi could see that the boy had scraped through the exam.

"Smart lady, worldly-wise," thought Mahi.

Mahi took an instant liking to the boy. He fixed him up with a car mechanic so that Kaleem could learn the tricks of the automotive trade. Kaleem was quick on the uptake. He learned to clean, repair, drive, replace worn out parts, and all that. Two years later, he knew everything that anyone needed to know about a car. He knew the working of every car model, inside out, better than the guys who had designed the car, better than an automobile engineer!

Mahi then took Kaleem out of the mechanic's shop and asked him to drive his car. When he wasn't driving, Kaleem would work as the office help. He used his time productively and did not indulge in small talk. He quietly learned to operate the computer, could type with all his ten fingers in the classic mode of a typist, something that the others in the office, apart from Mike Mahi, couldn't do!

Mahi liked people who showed the virtues of the workplace: discipline, hard work, ambition, and perseverance. Kaleem displayed all of these in good measure. On the road, he never jumped lanes, never broke signals, never overtook on the wrong side, never swore and never drove rashly. If someone in traffic snarled at him, he would smile back. He would grin when anyone in the office lobbed verbal abuse at him.

Mahi trusted Kaleem no end. He let him go to the bank to deposit his personal cheques and draw tens of thousands of rupees. He let him do small errands as well. Mahi sometimes asked him to stay back in his house when he traveled on business or when he holidayed.

Kaleem never wasted his food. When someone had quizzed him on it, he had responded, "In a country where millions go without food, it makes no sense to waste it." He had picked it from Mahi who at restaurants never ordered more than he could finish. In the rare cases that he did, he packed the leftover food and took it home.

Like anyone of his social status, Kaleem had a limited wardrobe. Like anyone of his social status, he desired to hit the big time. Slowly his wardrobe changed. He began to develop a liking for the good things in life. He bought himself a couple of expensive jeans. He picked up pricey T-Shirts. When someone pointed this out to Mahi, he dismissed it, "Young boys like to dress well." He bought a fancy mobile. He visited a gym and worked hard to get a 'six-pack' ab. He began eating lunch at a nearby restaurant. Mike Mahi paid him well but not so handsomely that he could afford all these.

One day, Kaleem asked Doc, "Doc, do you own Hindustan Lever stock?" Doc paused and looked at him. "Nope."

"Purchase it Doc; it's a good buy." Doc put down his pen. He didn't know Kaleem had an interest in the stock market. Even the interns at the office were greenhorns in the capital market.

Kaleem, on the other hand, was making a recommendation. Before Doc could respond, he said, "If you have Telco, sell it."

"So, who told you HLL is good?" Doc asked, only half in jest.

"A bird told me, and I bought 400 recently at Rs.180 each." Even as Doc was hit by the lingo, Kaleem remarked, "The scrip is bottoming out. It will soon make a short rally." It was not just English, he had picked up the technical language as well. Doc couldn't believe his ears.

Doc did some quick math. At 180 a share, 400 shares cost Rs 72,000. It was an obscene sum for someone who lived so modestly and earned Rs 3,000 a month. The purchase was the equivalent of two years' salary. Doc kept the analysis to himself. He didn't ask him, "Where did you get all that money?"

"Have you made any money on the market?"

Kaleem replied confidently, "About two lakhs, Doc. I intend to make a million."

ooo

Mike, Mahi & Associates engaged a bookkeeper to maintain its accounts. An elderly man who had retired from government service, he displayed extraordinary work ethics. They called him Anna. Was it the Tamil word for elder brother or was it a proper name? No one knew for certain. When the firm began using technology for its accounting, Anna took to it like fish would to water.

His books of accounts were always up to date. He never left office without updating both the cashbook and the bankbook, without tallying cash balance and without preparing a draft trial balance. He readily gave any information that was requested. He was meticulous, almost to a fault. He would chase the bank for the bank statement on the last day of every month and complete the bank reconciliation as soon as he received the statement. Anna was efficiency personified. He rarely used a calculator.

He could add numbers up to three digits simultaneously. "After all he had worked during the days of the adding machine," as one of the interns would say, tongue firmly in cheek.

Mahi had recruited Anna in 2003. He had grown sick of hiring young boys for office accounting. They never showed the discipline expected of accountants. They were too flashy, too casual, and too lackadaisical. That was when someone suggested he pick a retired accountant. Mahi wasn't sure whether such an arrangement would work. But it worked flawlessly, and Mahi had no reason to complain about Anna except for the fact that he was too clinical to be real.

And then it happened.

Mahi always had a few blank cheques, some crossed and some uncrossed, signed and kept for an emergency, which he left with Anna. These were to be used when Mahi traveled. Anna would keep these cheques in his drawer. For a man of Anna's carefulness, it was surprising that he never locked drawers. He never thought anything could get lost in his office as there was enormous positive energy flowing there. Anna believed in what his grandfather had once told him: "You leave your money on the street; if your money was well earned in the first place it wouldn't get lost."

It was the 1st of August. Anna obtained Mahi's personal bank statement in the morning and began reconciling it with the books of accounts in the afternoon. Suddenly, he dropped the pencil and held his head with both hands, sweating. Three cheques had been debited that reduced Mahi's balance by 500,000. None of these cheques appeared in Mahi's books. Worse still, none of the payees were known. The cheque numbers did not appear in the bank statement. Anna called up the bank for the details and the banker supplied him with the cheque numbers. None of these matched with the cheque-book serial that Anna held to. He asked the manager for a copy of the cheques. They wanted a request letter from Mahi. Anna couldn't tell Mahi the reason why he was asking for a photocopy of the cheque.

He hence somehow prevailed on the banker to do away with the request letter. The manager obliged, as he had known Anna for a long time. The first thing that Anna did on getting the cheques was to see whether Mahi had signed it. Of course he had. There it was, the beautiful signature of Mahi, on each one of the three cheques. It wasn't forged.

How could this be? Anna didn't remember writing the cheque. Someone else had written it.

His eyes widened and he put his hands on his head again as it struck him.

Anna rushed to look into the record. There it was: a list of six blank cheques. The three cheque numbers matched with the three blank bearer cheques. He rushed to see the stock of blank cheques. Five of them were missing! His head was reeling. He called up the banker and enquired after the fate of the other two. His worst suspicions were confirmed when the manager told him those two cheques too had been cashed that morning, totaling Rs 425,000. This took the total value to Rs 925,000.

The matter could no longer be held back from Mahi. Bad news needed to be delivered fast, and in person. Anna met Mahi and briefed him on the situation.

Mahi called a meeting with Anna and Doc.

"We must inform the bank of the forgery," said Doc.

"But it isn't a forgery," said Anna.

"Doc, speak to the teller and ask him if he remembers who drew the money."

"But it's a wild shot as the teller sees hundreds of people a day. How would he remember who cashed that particular cheque?"

Anna called the teller. After brief pleasantries, the cashier said, "I had a conversation with the guy. He was new. I didn't ask him his name, but I can identify him if I see him."

It had to be a new guy. No one from Mike Mahi's office would be foolish enough to walk into the bank and draw that amount. But the planning indicated it was an inside job. Who could it be?

Doc was adamant that the police be called in.

Mahi felt otherwise. "It would lower the morale. Everyone will be a suspect. The police aren't known to be pleasant."

Doc remarked, "Well, we need to explain this to our team members. There is no choice. We can't let the guy go scot-free. We have to nail him."

"I cannot believe it is one of us. More than identifying and getting to know who the Judas is, the very idea of doubting our team is heart-wrenching."

"Mahi, you cannot be so weak."

"Call it whatever you like Doc, it hurts. If someone in this office needed the money and needed it without my knowledge, so be it. I do not want to find him."

"So what do you intend to do?"

"Well, we will right the wrong. No more blank cheques. Spread the word through the grapevine that this has happened and that we know who the culprit is."

Two weeks later Anna resigned, claiming moral responsibility. Mike Mahi would have none of it, but Anna refused to budge.

Kaleem continued to buy stocks.

Three days later, New Delhi Times carried a story title, **"Fraud at former NICPA President's office."**

ooo

One morning, six months after the deceit had been noticed, the 68-year-old Anna failed to wake up. His wife, Sneha, called up the only person the family knew, Mike Mahi. The big man was at their place within twenty minutes, Tanya in tow. The 62-year-old

Sneha's white hair was disheveled; her sari was crumpled and her red eyes indicated that she had been crying for a long time.

She walked up to Mahi and said, "He had been wanting to meet you for the last few weeks. He left behind an envelope, which he desperately wanted to pass on to you. Here it is. Please go through it at your convenience."

Sneha left his side and started talking to Tanya and the other visitors. Mahi went to another room and slit open the envelope. There, in Anna's handwriting, was a note of the train of events leading to the embezzlement of money at Mahi's office. Mahi was shocked. Yet, he could not bring himself to dislike the man who was his father's age. The note had an apology. Mahi closed his eyes as tears began to roll out.

When Anna's will was read, it was discovered that he had bequeathed Mahi a sum that was exactly equal to the sum that had been embezzled.

PART 4: FALLING DOWN
2013–2015

43. Stocks Crash

YEAR: 2014

DATE: June 23

Monday 09:55 a.m.

When trading opened at 09:55 a.m., the markets crashed. Hindustan Bank led the fall, hurtling downwards.

Hindustan Bank was India's star stock. It was the most actively traded, the most liquid, the most highly priced, and the most in demand stock. It had closed at Rs 24,000 the previous evening and had opened this morning, 12 percent down, at Rs 21,000

Other stocks were sucked up in the reverse frenzy. It was a free fall, a "fire-sale". With buyers drying up on the Hindustan counter, more sellers joined the queue, pushing the price down further. Unfortunately, there were no circuit breakers as the bank was in the derivative segment. Stocks on cash segment had circuit breakers, which meant that on a particular day if a stock changed by eight percent either way, trading would be stopped for an hour to let tempers cool. Stocks on the derivative segment weren't subject to circuit breakers.

10:30 a.m.

By now, thirty-five minutes after the opening bell, Hindustan Bank had fallen a full 20 percent to Rs 19,200. Mahi punched 59 on his remote control to check out *New Delhi Times* and the analysts were screaming about only three stocks: Hindustan Bank, Hindustan Bank, and Hindustan Bank. Mahi was not surprised because he knew news channels thrived on bad news.

"Where will it be by closing hours?" asked the anchor. "All bets are off," said an all-knowing analyst. It was the same analyst who some months ago when asked, "Which way is the Sensex headed this week?" had remarked, "It might go up or come down." The anchor had responded saying, "Cool." Apparently the noisy anchor didn't know stocks could move sideways.

There were vague discussions of whether Mahi would be called in by the police or the Anti-Corruption Bureau for questioning and possible arrest.

12:00 noon

By noon, there were serpentine queues outside various branches of Hindustan Bank. Every branch opened at 8 a.m. One branch did not, because one of the two men who held the key hadn't turned up. Someone remarked, "Hey, the branch has pulled down shutters." The news spread like wildfire.

People started lining up, demanding their money back. On any given day, a bank holds about six percent of the total deposit in liquid cash for payment. There was a mad rush at the ATM counters. Hindustan Bank did a commendable job in putting out large posters saying it would honor all its commitments.

On Dalal Street, fear is contagious. With all sorts of rumors about Hindustan Bank floating about, the stock continued to take a beating. On television, an analyst said, "Someone influential has to speak to the stock exchange to have the market closed for the day. If that is not possible, we should at least halt the trade in Hindustan Bank."

2:00 p.m.

A special edition went on air to debate the crisis. Mahi didn't have lunch. His rage killed all his hunger.

The channel invited everyone who was anyone on banking to speak on the panel. Mahi, now at his farm resort, sat on the edge of his sofa, wiping his forehead and running his fingers through his hair. He helplessly watched pompous souls babbling outrageous nothings.

One of the experts was saying, "If all the relevant adjustments are made, Hindustan Bank's EPS will fall by half. Given the bad accounting, investor trust will come down and this will pull the PE multiple down by 20 percent."

EPS stands for earnings per share. It is arrived at by dividing the bank's after-tax profits by the number of equity shares. This is a critical number on the Street. The PE multiple stands for price earnings multiple. The ratio of market price per share to EPS is the PE multiple.

The anchor asked, "So you are saying the stock will fall by 60 percent?"

"Yes, the stock has fallen by 30 percent. It has another 30 percent to fall before fresh buyers come in."

On the panel, there was just one person who seemed to be talking sense, but his views were submerged by the din the others, including the anchor, were creating. There was a passing reference to the fact that Mahi held a million plus shares in Hindustan Bank and whether the Insider Trading Act could be invoked.

3:00 p.m.

By now, the stock had fallen to Rs 18,000. By closing hours, it had hit 14,400; a full 40 percent down. The anchor, this time a woman, was at her screechy worst. "This is unbelievable. An express train has rammed into a bullock cart. Who will pick up the debris?"

Mike Mahi had significant holdings in Hindustan Bank. While accumulating the stock, he had listened to a 72-year-old lady who had recommended that he leverage 1:1 to buy more. He had done that. Now the lady was on the telephone. "This is time for bargain hunting, Mahi. Buy as much as you can," she said. Mahi nodded, his eyes drooping and brain shutting off. He lost his balance on the sofa. He knew he couldn't take in anymore. He switched off the television, dragged himself upstairs, hit the bed and fell asleep with the phone still dangling from his hand.

10:00 p.m.

The crash was making waves. Google reported that Hindustan Bank had received the maximum number of hits ever on any single day. It was the most searched term on the Internet. Mike Mahi refused to meet the media.

YEAR: 2014

DATE: June 24

Tuesday

The following day, the pink papers had only one theme: Hindustan Bank. *New Delhi Times,* both the paper and the channel, had only one item on the news, Hindustan Bank. They ripped both the bank and Mike Mahi. Stories of corruption were tumbling out of the cupboard. There were reports of loans advanced for a price, kickbacks given to each party, as well as an unofficial price list! X percent to the head of operations, Y percent to the credit analyst and Z percent to the loan officer.

It was scandalous. Mahi didn't believe one jot of it. It was yellow journalism at its worst. "Sensational tabloid garbage," he told Doc. Yes, loans had gone sticky but that was an error of judgment, and not corruption. If there was a miscarriage of reporting, it was this.

The scribe called it "The ugly truth." To give the devil its due, the guy had an engaging writing style that was entertaining as well. He was a man Mahi quickly learned to hate. He was clearly grandstanding but the public was buying into his analysis. That's the incredible power of the press.

The media tried to meet Mahi, but Rupa shielded the poster boy of the accounting profession. "He is in a meeting," was what she told those who called non-stop.

Mahi stayed at the farmhouse for a second day in a row. He lost his appetite and sat before the television screen to see what they said next. He was red with rage that Tejas Arya, now the CEO of the paper and the channel, was not reining his men in. Suddenly he wondered if all these charges were true, if his firm had missed it while doing the audit. This is what the fear of the unknown does to people.

YEAR: 2014
DATE: June 25
Wednesday

On day three, even as the media looked for Mike Mahi, he stayed underground. "What's the point?" he argued. "You have already passed your judgment." He was right. On days one and two, it had been trial by media. The box item that had appeared on page 1 on day one and the one that appeared today told its own tale.

Rupa continued to ward off the vultures.

"Mike is in a meeting. You can call him later," was the standard reply. This was very different from the response that was given in normal times. "Mike is in a meeting. He will call you in twenty minutes." There were 710 unread messages on his mobile, 315 on WhatsApp and 140 missed calls. He ignored them. He didn't open his e-mail.

He wasn't keen to offer his version of the truth because he felt it would not be heard in the noise. His friends suggested that he allow things to cool down for a few days and then go on national television with his point of view.

Those few days were free publicity for the firm but as his National Partners would later say, "We could have done without it." Apparently, someone in the know was singing a mixture of truths, half-truths, and naked untruths. The media was buying it with a straight face because it was peppered with salacious gossip.

The contagious effect continued to hit other stocks. Across the board, banking, real estate, and technology stocks went for a toss. The argument was that if a highly-respected, rich in corporate-governance, Hindustan Bank could play it coarse, what was the guarantee others wouldn't have? This was the single largest crash in Indian stock market history. Newspapers were quick to report the Monday as Manic Monday and the Tuesday as Tsunami Tuesday. Wednesday came to be called Black Wednesday.

On Thursday, the *New Delhi Times* carried an interestingly-titled boxed item. The correspondent wrote, "The following is a preliminary list of the dead and the injured in the stock crash." There he chronicled who had lost how much.

ooo

A story put out in the papers had the signs of catastrophe. It was an old case that had happened a year-and-a-half ago. Yes, Mahi was privy to it.

One day, a person whom he later came to know as Aditya Ganguly, a middle-aged failed photographer, walked into the bank with a loan request. A few hours later, he signed the necessary papers and walked out with a loan of Rs 100,000. It was express service. Given his declared income, the bank should never have advanced money to Ganguly. But the collateral, a fixed deposit placed with a different bank, was too good to let go. As events subsequently revealed, Ganguly wasn't the real borrower; he was a surrogate.

ARE Private Limited, a little known real estate company, was not eligible to borrow money from any bank because of a national policy of not lending money for a land purchase. Property loans, yes; land loans, no. You could argue with the law, the law could be asinine, but then it was the law. Like many daredevil entrepreneurs, Rattan Sharma, who ran ARE, had found a way to beat the rule.

Sharma looped around 2,000 people like Ganguly. His men helped Ganguly and his ilk borrow Rs 100,000 each from the bank. These men wouldn't actually walk into the bank hand-in-hand, but they would help the Ganguly- types get the right documents and tell them whom to meet and when and where.

A not-so-straight loan officer, Vir Chadha, was in their rolls, picking up 1 percent of the total loan amount. His job was to process the loan within two hours. Since the loan was covered by reasonable collateral, the risk was minimal.

This loan was repayable in 24 equal monthly installments. The lending rate would range between 8 percent and 13 percent, depending on the collateral. ARE took the 100,000 from Ganguly and promised to pay him Rs 6,000 per month for the entire duration of the loan. Ganguly planned to use the money to repay the installment and the balance would be his. It was an exceptional deal. An inflow of Rs 144,000 over two years for an outflow of Rs 100,000 translated into a return of 38 percent per annum. The borrowing rate was at most 13 percent.

With 2,000 such people having been roped in, the money collected was a cool Rs 20 crore. At a one percent unofficial commission, Chadha pocketed Rs 20,00,000, which was about two years' salary!

Five months later, the volcano erupted. Aditya Ganguly defaulted because ARE failed to pay him his sixth installment. Within days, Rattan Sharma's office pulled down the shutters. Most of the people he had used were like Ganguly, people without resources and who didn't create a ruckus because they didn't know whom to go to.

Aditya Ganguly and three others moved a lawyer to fight their case against Rattan Sharma. The lawyer suggested they also sue Hindustan Bank. Ganguly pointed to Vir Chadha as the rogue officer. The lawyer argued in Court that Hindustan Bank could not demand the money from his clients because the Bank was privy to the fraud. He claimed that the bank was in fact routing the loan to Rattan Sharma's ARE Private Limited through a number of small borrowers.

It was an ingenious argument.

The bank argued that it was Ganguly's signature that was on the loan papers and that therefore it was not a loan to ARE.

Even while the court hearing was on, Hindustan Bank did an internal inquiry and found Chadha guilty. Since his action hadn't cost the bank much in terms of cash flow, he was just asked to resign. And then they did the unthinkable. The bank went into an out-of-court settlement with Aditya Ganguly and three others for a sum of Rs 144,000 apiece!

On the fourth day, a boxed item appeared in the *New Delhi Times* recalling the fall of Rattan Sharma, a story that no one had heard, and speculating that Hindustan Bank could have had a role in it. Mahi knew that this was turning logic on its head; but in moments of madness, logic has no place. The newspaper report also carried a broad hint that some settlements had been made; that the firm's auditors were aware of the deal and they hadn't explicitly reported it to the shareholders.

There was also a suggestion that others like Ganguly should now file a class- action suit. Mike Mahi knew that this thing could spin into a major catastrophe.

He tried to reach Tejas Arya but to no avail. The celebrated anchor seemed to have vanished from the face of the earth.

44. Insider Trading

Mike Mahi had never been shy of publicity. While others called advertising a vulgar show of one-upmanship, Mahi regarded it as a natural way to grow. In fact, he assiduously cultivated journalists during his "rising star" days to get good press. "While good press is always welcome," he once told Doc, "no press is better than bad press." That statement was now coming home to roost.

For four full days, Mike Mahi and Hindustan Bank occupied the front page in national newspapers. The two continued to hog prime time television. In its characteristic style of mixing fact with fiction, the media was turning shrill and nasty.

But there was no word yet from the man whose views everyone trusted, the country's most respected journalist, Tejas Arya. Amidst the noise and the cacophony, people who did not understand the sequence of events and its myriad legal implications wanted to know what Arya had to say. They also were eager to know whether Mike Mahi had played it straight. Mahi was an icon. A vote of approbation from Tejas would act as a vote of confidence.

The award-winning journalist had simply gone underground. It was unbelievable, considering this was the biggest financial scandal to hit the country, greater than Haridas Mundhra, larger than Harshad Mehta, and possibly as big as Satyam.

Then on Day 6, the familiar face reappeared. Tejas Arya wrote a story that spelled double trouble for Mike Mahi. It was a piece that offered no views, no opinions; it was a crass statement of facts. No fancy headlines. No hunky dory talk. It was just facts and simple facts.

Mike Mahi read it with a mixture of anger and helplessness.

Mike Mahi makes it Big

Tejas Arya

Thirty months ago, Mike, Mahi & Associates conducted a due diligence for the takeover of a FOREX broking business.

The assignment was done on behalf of Business Finance Majors International Ltd (BFMI). Co-owned by two aggressive young entrepreneurs, this company harbored dreams a zillion times larger than the money it had. BFMI wanted to grow the inorganic way, acquiring organizations, quick and fast. To fund it, they resorted to several innovations like raising high-yield bonds, promising deferred payments and in some exceptional cases offering equity stake.

Mike Mahi received the entire consulting fee as stock options. The stock was trading at Rs 210 a share at the time of the offer. The firm offered 100,000 shares at Rs 10 apiece, exercisable after a vesting period of two years. The value of the fee was Rs 20,000,000, Mike Mahi bagged this assignment ahead of the global major Hunt & Smith, which had quoted 25 percent more; all cash, payable upfront.

For BFMI, having the due diligence done by Mike Mahi was an act of inspiration. The charismatic public accountant runs one of India's best homegrown firms and thus far there has been no whiff of scandal in their work.. BFMI was able to get them to do top work without paying a pie from their pocket. The payment would come either in full or in part or more than in full from the marketplace. For sure, there would be a dilution of equity but the number of shares issued would just add 2 percent to the total capital of the company.

The company wasn't playing with the books. In the best traditions of financial reporting, they expensed the full value of the option in line with the Black-Scholes Model of valuation. As the gap between the exercise price and the market price on the grant date was enormous, the value under the model approximated towards the market price on the grant date. That was fine with the company so long as it did not call for cash obligations.

Eighteen months later, a year ago, BFMI took over the forex broking business on the strength of Mike Mahi's valuation and due diligence report. That, plus a series of other out-of-the-box acquisitions put the stock on a one-way street: upwards. It raced from Rs 210 to Rs 510 and six months ago, on the first possible date of exercise by Mike Mahi, it touched Rs 710.

Mike, Mahi & Associates lost no time exercising the option and immediately sold the stock. The firm made a profit of Rs 50,000,000 on the deal. They reported it on their tax return and paid tax on the transaction.

Every sentence was correct. But Mahi wondered why it had to be carried now, and what was the context? Apparently they wanted to write anything about him that would make readers lap up the paper.

Under other circumstances, Arya's story might have even created a halo around Mike Mahi. The world loves a financial whiz. But these weren't ordinary circumstances. Other newspapers and television channels picked on the Arya story with unusual alacrity. Headline writers were having a field day.

"Is Mike Mahi guilty of insider trading?"

"Audit Big Boss has feet of clay?"

Analysts on television were sharply divided in their views. Each was quick with his opinion.

"This is insider trading." In the market language, insider trading is an act of purchase or sale of a stock by a person having access to price sensitive information, which is not available to others, because of a position he holds in the company and who profits by that act.

"No, it is not. A valuation report does not constitute price sensitive information. How would Mahi know that the company would go ahead with the purchase?"

"This is payment contingent on the result. It violates professional ethics."

"How is it payment contingent on the result? There is no result in a valuation report. This is like getting paid Rs 200 lakhs and then investing the money in the market."

Finally, there were some supporters for the beleaguered Mahi.

But the biggest salvo, the most frightening of all, came from a senior journalist on the panel. He remarked, "This is a Tejas Arya story. Tejas doesn't do matter-of-fact stories. For sure, there is something deeper. He is testing waters before he comes out with finer details."

ooo

While there was no follow-up story from Tejas Arya, it started to pour elsewhere. More stories began appearing with each passing day. None of them was flattering to Mike Mahi. A pink paper led the charge in reporting that Tanya Roy had pocketed close to a crore on a derivative transaction.

"Three years ago," it said, "Tanya Roy, psychologist, and Mike Mahi's wife, bought a put option on 30,000 shares of National Housing Ltd (NHL), India's second largest housing finance company, at an exercise price of Rs 650."

It then went on to explain what a put option was.

"That option gave Tanya the right to sell NHL stocks on or before 30th May at the exercise price of Rs 650. A put buyer would exercise an option if the market price fell below the exercise price. In effect, it would mean that she could buy the shares at the prevailing market price and sell it at Rs 650."

Finally, it stated what happened on 30th May.

"On the expiry date, the stock had crashed to Rs 350. Tanya exercised her option and pocketed the difference of Rs 300 per share on the 30,000 shares leading to a profit of Rs 90 lakhs."

"Well, what was illegal about it?" wondered Mahi. The story went on to explain just that.

"Now that's a perfectly legal transaction. But what is raising eyebrows is the size of the kill. What should go against Mike Mahi is that during the three-month period when Tanya Roy held the put option, NHL had reported its most disastrous year in history. A company that had reported bumper profits for ten years was now declaring losses."

The report offered some value judgment. "The company announced that it was cleaning up its balance sheet and hence the need for the spate of provisioning in the books and the fat loss."

Lest someone did not catch the insinuation, the author wrote, "Mike, Mahi & Associates were the newly (repeat newly) appointed external auditors of the company for that year and it was Mike Mahi himself who had signed the accounts."

The charge, as Mahi could read in between the lines, was that he was privy to price-sensitive information, which he used to make a crore. This was a never-ending nightmare. The litany of fresh charges continued, day after day. He just wanted to disappear – from the city, from the country, somewhere far away from all the chaos.

Suddenly, these unpopular stories were coming out into the open. The sheen around the bank, and around the man, was getting stripped away and it looked very naked. The heat was on. Rumors were flying thick and fast.

- "There is an arrest warrant against Mike Mahi."
- "Bank's loan officer is running for cover."
- "The CBI could zero in on Tanya Roy anytime."
- "The Tax Department is going to seal Mike Mahi's office."
- "NICPA has received a complaint against Mahi and the complainant is seeking disciplinary action."

There were no confirmations.

Would they face a malpractice suit? If so, how big could it be? What would happen if someone initiated a class action? Would the consumer court award huge damages just for the sake of publicity? For the first time in his life, Mike Mahi felt scared. For the first time, it occurred to him that he might lose everything he had earned.

That moment he decided he would meet the media.

45. Tejas Calls

YEAR: 2014

DATE: June 27

Seated in his glass-paneled corner office on the 24th floor of Express Towers, Mike Mahi reflected on the week that had gone by. He ran and reran, at least a hundred times, every single moment since that fateful night when Alka Varma had walked into his office. From being very close to stitching up an international affiliation that would have taken his firm to pole position, he was now fighting to save his personal integrity.

It was then that he saw a number flashing on his mobile screen. Mahi stared at the incoming call, unsure of whether to pick it up or not. Beads of perspiration were trickling down. It was an international number, a UK number to be precise. Who could it be? Well, come what may, this call had to be taken. He did not have a choice.

"Hello."

"Hi, Mahi. This is Tejas. I understand you have been trying to reach me over the past few days. Sorry, couldn't return the call. I am in England accompanying the Prime Minister on his European tour."

"Wow. That's good to hear."

"So boss, how are you? How's everything?"

Only a journalist could ask such questions while he knew fully well that someone was in a pothole sixty feet deep. Mahi checked himself, "I am fine. What about you?"

"Perfect. Tell me what can I do for you?"

Stupid fellow creates the mess and asks what can I do for you. "You see… you see… I am sure you know what your channel and your newspaper have been saying for the past few days." There was a slight edge to his voice.

"Yes, Mahi, I do. Hindustan Bank is the biggest news. At last, we have evidence against India's largest bank, which was always rumored to be a rogue bank and whose principal shareholding pattern was always suspect. We cannot stay silent."

"No, no, no. I am not suggesting you should. It's your prerogative. Truth, no matter how bitter, must come out. But I think both the paper and the television are needlessly dragging our firm into this mess."

"Well Mahi, the accounting profession has often gotten away with its sins. My sense is that the sins of the past are coming to haunt it. I am not too sure if your firm is suffering collateral damage. There are many who think your firm's role is suspect though most people believe, me included, that you are personally pure. I think the cost is direct. You don't get ignored when financial irregularities tumble out of the cupboard of a top bank audited by a firm of your standing."

Mahi was surprised at the directness of the attack.

He heard Tejas say, "But I do agree the personal pitch at you is a tad unfair."

Jesus H Christ, this man was now talking like a saint!

"This publicity is doing us a lot of harm. I don't want to argue with you, but on a different day our firm would have defended itself. Even now, we can and will, but fights take time and our global plans are going to be badly hurt."

"I agree. I promised you we would break this only after your meeting the US team. I am really sorry about this. We got information that another network was whiffing this news, and so we had to break it first. Personally, I wasn't aware until I saw it on television. You know, our organization is run on professional lines. They can take calls on the move. They don't have to wait for my clearance. I hope you believe me."

Goddamn, fool. What an apology-and-a-half.

Biting his little finger and swallowing his pride, Mahi asked, "Can you think of a way out?"

There was a long silence at the other end.

"You there?"

"Yes, Mahi. I was digesting what you said. I don't think you can buy our silence. Yes, the media is news-hungry. Our owners will be happy to receive regular advertisements and big ticket sponsoring by your firm or by your firm's clients, but I think this is not the time. We have a survival instinct. If we are seen going soft, we will be finished."

Mahi saw the door opening and Rupa's head appeared through the gap. It disappeared the moment she saw him frantically waving her away.

"I never meant that. I am sure you don't imagine we would ever suggest something like that."

"I believe you. Our friendship goes back a long way. But not everyone would believe you."

Mahi let the barb go. It always hurt him when someone insinuated Mike, Mahi & Associates worked like any other Indian business.

"We can move the courts."

"Yes, Mahi you can. But trust me, given the current mood, it won't help. You will needlessly let the public focus its attention entirely on you. The media will gang up on you. Whatever sympathy anyone in the Fourth Estate has for you will evaporate once you sue one of us. That's how our breed works."

Mahi didn't respond.

"You've one option though. I understand you intend to meet the media soon. The heat is on your firm because of your high profile stature. Tell them you did not sign the financial statements of Hindustan Bank."

"Good God! That information is already in the public domain. Don't tell me no one is aware of it. By the way, I don't believe I will ever say, either in public or in private, that a partner signed the report. They can't become the fall guys. If the heat is on me, so be it. You guys will move on to something else a few days from now."

"Mahi, let me give you some free, unsolicited but well-intentioned advice. This scandal is the biggest since Enron, if not bigger. Remember, we are in 2014, not 2001. Today, if you are not careful, an Arthur Anderson can happen to your firm. You will be hurt more than the partners of AA. Those guys grew up in their firm. AA was their parent and parents depart ahead of the kids. But you built yours. *Mike, Mahi & Associates* is your child. Parents can't handle the trauma of their child dying in front of their eyes. So please don't make the mistake of underestimating the gravity of the situation. Go out there and save your firm."

"You don't realize, Tejas. The Big Six will come together if they find the media is playing up without cause."

"I would like to believe so; but Mahi, that's not how it's going to happen. I know your profession far better than you do. Your guys are spineless. Many crooks in your profession would like to see you fall. You, despite your experience and exposure, are still naïve and good. You are still the marbles boy."

Mahi didn't interrupt. He wasn't sure what would be coming up next.

"You think the media is getting its story by doing investigative journalism? Fat chance. The CA firms are leaking. Worse still, there is a mole in your firm."

The Coke in Mahi's hand spilled over onto his trousers. "Impossible."

"Give me a day and I will get you the name. Thanks, Mahi."

"Tell me now."

"No. Not on the phone. Thanks, Mahi."

Mahi's heart was racing. With blood shot eyes, Mahi stared at the handset. Jesus Christ. Who was the Judas?

ooo

True to his word, Tejas called the following day.

"Mahi, I have the name. Someone will reach you in fifteen minutes and give you a cover. Receive it personally. Open the cover and the slip inside will carry the name."

"You are sure of the source?"

"Never been surer."

Fifteen minutes later, the cover arrived. Mahi tore it open clumsily. He had no time for a paper knife. Out popped a sheet on which was written: "See door can see!" Had they slipped him the wrong sheet? Then came the Eureka moment. Yes, a secret code. He ran the code through anagram software without luck. "What if See, See stood for C and C?" he asked himself. Yup, yup. He tried the software again. No luck. He scribbled the letters in a circle and stared.

The words danced in front of his eyes. His heart sank.

He grabbed the phone to speak to Tejas.

"Impossible. Can't be. It's not true. You picked the wrong man. I've known him for twenty years. I have given him everything a man could want. You have got it wrong. It cannot be CRANCO DOC."

Tejas could understand Mahi's agony. "Well, Mahi tell him 'Operation Door' and watch him respond."

Mahi threw the phone away and stormed to Doc's cubicle. His right hand was shaking as if he had Parkinson's. He had only one aim: refrain from breaking the jackass's nose.

"You are fired. Stat." His voice was unusually calm.

"What? What are you saying?" Doc's eyes widened.

"I said you are fired." Mahi was still calm.

"You, you cannot throw me out like that. We built this firm together. At least tell me the reason. I have the right to know."

"Treason, Operation Door."

Doc slid down, knowing his game was up. His body was rattling the chair.

"Look Mahi. I did not sell any state secrets. It was harmless information, which I shared in good faith. We cannot afford another crisis right now in the middle of a larger crisis. My departure will send the wrong signal to the media. The firm will be in a bigger crisis."

"I said, 'clear out'. I don't even want to know why you did this."

Mahi just stood there, his eyes following Doc as he stumbled out of the door, without a glance, without a goodbye. A twenty-year association was gone in twenty seconds. Emptiness engulfed Mahi, and he felt completely drained of all energy. First Muscles, then Anna, and now Doc. It was 'MAD'.

46. Mahi meets the Media

It would be his first interaction with the outside world after news of the Hindustan Bank skullduggery had come into the open.

Tanya advised him against it. His partners felt it would be better to give the Press a written statement. The NICPA took a "we are watching the situation" position. His close friends felt that taking on the hostile media might not be such a great idea. Only Uncle Krishna sided with him.

Against everyone's advice, and banking on his personal charisma, and Uncle Krishna's words, Mike Mahi decided to meet the Press.

He walked in smiling, oozing confidence. This surprised the media who were expecting to see a forlorn, defeated man. Those seeing him for the first time couldn't help liking him. In person, he looked far more attractive than he did in his photographs. Charm personified, he had an answer to every question on Hindustan Bank. He assured them there had been no shenanigans that he knew of and that at worst there could have been routine errors of business judgment.

Suddenly an unknown journalist, with a sneer on his face, said, "I am from the Associated Press. Mike, what do you have to say about the activities of your wife, Tanya Mahi?"

Mahi instantly disliked him. He couldn't exactly say why.

"Tanya Mahi is not my wife."

The room fell silent.

As the audience grappled with the weight of his statement, Mahi said, "My wife's name is Tanya Roy."

"Oh. What's the difference?"

"To journalists who don't have the desire to verify facts, there is no difference."

That was Mahi's first mistake. There was no need to take potshots at the media. At this time, Mahi needed friends, not enemies. A seasoned Mahi had fallen into the oldest trap. You don't take on journalists as a community without paying a steep price for it.

"Okay. How do you account for the Rs 90 lakhs that your wife made on a derivative transaction?" The journalist was aggressive.

"I don't have to account for it. She will account for it as short-term capital gain."

Laughter broke out. Mahi hadn't lost his sense of humor. But some weren't amused.

"That's fine. What do you say about her buying a put option at the most opportune time?" asked a senior journalist with a long white beard.

"She seems to have received excellent investment advice."

The rookie was back. "The charge, Mike Mahi, is that it was you who gave her that piece of investment advice."

"I could not have. I hardly get to meet her, given the kind of demands that my job makes of me."

"But surely you go back home to sleep."

"That will do. Any other questions please," said Mahi, realizing it wasn't turning out to be a walk in the park. It was his second mistake. He should have taken the question.

The next day, the Associated Press carried the banner headline, **"Tanya Roy pillow talks her way to a crore?"** Everything else was lost under that sensational headline.

Forty eight hours after the pillow talk story, a television channel made a direct charge of insider-trading against Mike Mahi.

"One of India's most dynamic public accountants has a lot of answering to do," the anchor said. "We now have documentary evidence that may finally nail him. It does not have to do with Hindustan Bank, but if the Anti-Corruption Bureau digs deep it may come out with evidence in the Hindustan Bank case as well." The anchor spoke on, unmindful of falling off the thin line into defamation.

It was followed by a brief recap of Mahi's career chart. Anyone tuning into the news would have thought that Mahi had been arrested. A voice in the background was saying, "Mike Mahi has had a meteoric race to the top. From a 12x10 feet office to the presidency and running one of the best networked public accounting firms…"

"Crap," said Mahi to himself. "They say I raced to the top. Do they know of the hours and hours of struggle that I put in to reach the top? Do they know how hard I worked? How lonely the path was?"

Now the anchor was saying, "On various dates over the last year, Mike Mahi bought and profited immensely from three stocks. Each time, the purchases were made six days before a piece of price sensitive information became available to the public. In one case, he had sold extensively and after his last sale the stock had crashed."

The co-anchor, a charming lady who never spoke above a whisper, took over. "In all three instances there are adequate indications that he might have been guilty of insider trading. One of his international partners was on the Board of those companies."

Oh God. Now they were dragging his partners into the muck. His extended firm was home to a hundred partners.

This was followed by a voice-over from a reporter who claimed the channel had the relevant contract notes and bank statements, and that the evidence of insider trading was clinching.

Mahi's heart stopped beating for a moment. He was shocked. He ran his hands through his hair. They weren't naming the stock. This innuendo journalism was getting on his nerves. Beads of sweat appeared on his brow, and he felt he was breathing more heavily. Under all the smooth talk at the press meet, he had been afraid. Now he was losing hope. That was very unlike Mahi. Something inside told him that he had to fight. It was a battle between fear and hope.

A couple of days later, Rupa met with Dina at the office and asked about futures and options.

"Rupa, why this new found interest in the stock market?"

"Dina, in these troubled times it is criminal negligence not to read the morning's paper."

With that, Mahi's Executive Assistant tossed the day's copy of the *New Delhi Times* at Dina Iyengar. There on page 1 was Tejas Arya's story titled **"Insider Trading in Hindustan Bank"** with Mike Mahi smiling from it. Dina's heart stopped as she raced through the writing.

Hindustan Bank may have looked the other way in what could turn out to be one of the biggest cases of insider trading.

A year ago, the bank had informed the market regulators, the Securities and Exchange Board of India (SEBI) that they were offloading a 15 percent stake in their hugely profitable subsidiary DB Broking. Documentary evidence now suggests that people and parties close to the Bank traded in the F&O market, possibly with prior knowledge of the bank's plan to sell.

These insiders may have made up to Rs 500 crore by going short on DB Broking in the futures market.

This was vintage Arya. No frills. No breast-beating. It was a straight narration of facts. Dina wondered what was coming next.

Because Hindustan Bank was offloading stake in DB Broking, the latter's shares were expected to fall. The insiders built huge short positions in DB Broking futures. Consequently, the price in the cash market started falling and DB Broking fell by close to Rs 100."

Then Arya slipped into a sideshow.

We must understand that "shorting" futures are different from buying a put option although both have the same objective, namely to sell on a future date. Under a put, the buyer has the right, and not the obligation, to sell. If the share price falls, the put buyer exercises his right and makes a profit. If it does not fall, he simply lets the option lapse and loses only the premium that he paid to buy the put.

In contrast, a sale in the futures market carries an obligation to sell. So if the price falls he gains; if it rises he loses. He would make a killing if the price fell but would be killed if the price went up. The quantum of loss is higher than in the case of put option. It is hence necessary for those who build short positions to be certain that prices would fall."

"Neat explanation," thought Dina. Now the conclusions were coming.

"The huge short position in the futures market triggered the fall in price in the cash market. The subsequent announcement of the 15 percent offloading by Hindustan Bank and the actual offloading built traction and accelerated *the fall. This ensured that the prices stayed low and helped the short sellers amass profits when the futures expired."*

The last sentence was the most crucial.

"There is no evidence, no evidence, to suggest that Mike Mahi was one amongst those who sold short."

Just then, the phone rang. Mahi was on the line.

"Rupa, speak to our lawyer. Ask him to file a defamation case against *New Delhi Times*."

"But it's a Tejas Arya article."

"Precisely so. He is a hot name and people will believe him."

"Mahi, let's speak to him. I know using your photo was bad. I know people will think that you were involved. The case won't stick because of the last sentence. And he is your friend."

"He is 'my foot.' Call Tejas and tell him we are filing a case today."

OOO

The following morning, the ACB turned up at Mike Mahi's residence for questioning. The investigative agencies quickly went about their task and a week later, announced that they sought to arraign Mike Mahi. The son of a colliery worker, who had punched beyond his weight to become the President of NICPA, was to be arrested. The NICPA was saved the blushes as Mike Mahi's lawyers had sought and gotten anticipatory bail, even as they worked towards a quick settlement. No President of NICPA, present or past, had ever been arrested. That position would stay unsullied for the moment.

47. Dramatis Personae

The whole of India, and the accounting profession in particular, waited expectantly for *The State vs. Mike Mahi* to open for hearing in the court.

In the normal course of events, the Disciplinary Committee of NICPA would hear the case first. If Mahi lost, he could appeal to a higher court.

Mahi argued that whatever be the Committee's verdict, people would suspect him because he was a former President. If he were acquitted, people would say his proximity to NICPA helped. If charge-sheeted, he would, in any case, knock at the doors of the High Court. He therefore wanted to dispense with appearing before the Committee and move the High Court directly.

A three-member bench, headed by Judge M. Scott, agreed with Mahi's argument. Immediately, the media went to town claiming Mahi was receiving preferential treatment. Had they known some of the behind-the-scene deals he had struck with the Prosecution, they would have screamed murder.

The Prosecution and the Defense had, at Mahi's behest, agreed before the judges that neither party would move a higher court. They also agreed to file documents in advance, and not seek adjournments. There would be forty-five minutes of opening arguments on either side, three or four days of examining witnesses and closing arguments would be for a maximum of fifteen minutes each. In all, the case would close in five days flat. All of this was a break from the time-honored ways courts functioned in the country.

Thus, on a cloudy Monday morning, the case of *State vs. Mike Mahi* came up for hearing with the express understanding that the judgment would be delivered next Monday evening.

Forty-eight hours earlier, on Saturday, a dramatic event had unfolded. The Anti-Corruption Bureau (ACB) arrested Judge M. Scott on bribery charges. Based on a tip-off, the ACB intercepted Scott's speeding Jaguar at King's Circle, in the wee hours of the morning. They recovered Rs 10 lakh from the car. A CCTV grab at Express Towers, the opulent business center that housed the headquarters of Mike, Mahi & Associates, showed an aide of the judge coming out of an elevator with a brown parcel identical to the one found in the car. This held the cash.

ACB sleuths took Scott to an undisclosed location to question him. Meanwhile, police teams conducted simultaneous searches at Mahi's residence and offices across India. The police came up with nothing. Scott was produced before the special court for ACB cases and remanded to police custody. As the media openly speculated about Mike Mahi's role in the bribery scandal, Judge M. Scott maintained a stoic silence.

The trial opened to unprecedented media attention. It was the first time a former President of NICPA was in the dock. This man was no ordinary former President; he was a national icon. Many disliked his guts but to a majority, he was a hero. After all, no son of a colliery worker had ever risen so high in the profession.

OOO

KASHYAP WORAIYUR was a huge man. More than six feet tall, he weighed 120 kg. Gregarious and outgoing, he had taken to law like a fish to water. Completing his prizefighter's build was his razor sharp mind, which could weigh options with remarkable ease. In 2011, *Time* magazine named him as amongst the world's 50 most influential law officers. In 2013, *Business Today* honored him with "Lawyer of the Year" award.

Born to mixed-caste parents, the pipe-smoking Kashyap grew up in Bombay, studied at Yale Law School, and for five years worked with US attorneys Latham, Moore and Cooley. Thereafter, KW, as he was called, returned to India and along with his English friend, Stanislaus Smith, set up a law firm, Kashyap Woraiyur & Stanislaus Smith (KWSS).

The two men worked long hours and employed a team of aggressive attorneys. KW had no compunctions about whom he represented. He once defended a reputed tobacco manufacturing company, months after his own daughter, a chain smoker, had died of lung cancer. Over the next fifteen years, KWSS raced to pole position. Then, one evening, Woraiyur received an invitation from the national government to take up the position of the Principal Prosecuting Attorney (PPA). The PPA's office provides enormous prestige, extraordinary work and little money. Tejas Arya once wrote, "Wolves worked there for peanuts."

The pay did not bother KW. As a lawyer, he had earned staggering sums, which would last generations. The power, which came with prosecuting the high and the mighty, gave him his daily dose of adrenaline. Under him, the PPA hanged terrorists, benched politicians on corruption charges and jailed business czars guilty of corporate frauds. In the five years KW had been in office, he had lost only two cases.

It was this man, with an impeccable conviction record, who would prosecute Mike Mahi on behalf of the State.

In contrast, Ramnath Parkar was puny. At 5'1", he weighed 44 kilograms. It included his platform shoes, thick spectacles, silken tie, and heavy blazer. In appearance, he resembled a mouse; in work, he was a tiger. He would expect his juniors to pick case laws at the drop of a hat. If they didn't come up with it fast, he screamed, "Dumbo. Dumbo. What the hell are you still doing?"

He walked into courtrooms with a carefree attitude but behind the calm exterior, a storm brewed. While his assistants scurried to find citations, he hardly used them. Instead he told stories and drew parallels to the case on hand, to win over judges. "Citations are test match stuff and stories are juicy T-20s" he quipped. His clients ranged from ministers to mass murderers. He counted amongst his friends both the country's Home Minister as also the nation's most wanted terrorist. Parkar could converse in Marathi, Hindi, French, Bengali, and Malayalam, but always spoke in halting English.

It was to this man with an encyclopedic knowledge that Mike Mahi turned to for help, as his defense attorney.

ooo

The New High Court in Mumbai where the case was to be heard is a large building, designed by an internationally-acclaimed team of architects. Between the main courtroom and the multiple smaller courts, is a magnificent lobby with amazing tapestry. Classy paintings cover the walls of each courtroom. It is one of the most beautiful Courts in India: spacious and luxuriously furnished with a well-equipped library, a sprawling swimming pool, a state-of-the-art fitness center and a swanky food court.

Hours before the trial opened, Room 17 was a sea of humanity. This was where the case would be heard. It could accommodate 750 people and was fully air-conditioned with state-of-the-art video conferencing facilities. The room was jam-packed; more people sat in adjoining rooms and still more stood in the corridors. The proceedings would be beamed live to Rooms 13 to 16, implying that about 3,000 could watch. For the first time, seats in the courtroom were officially sold. The Director General of Police had come to oversee arrangements. OB vans swarmed the place.

There wasn't an inch of space in the parking lot, and the cops had given up on controlling the haphazard cars.

A battle between Kashyap Woraiyur and Ramnath Parkar was guaranteed to generate fireworks.

The clock struck ten.

48. Day One in the Court: Opening Statement

The bailiff, dressed in spotless white kurta-pajama and a red pugree, stood up. "All rise; the court is now in session. Judge Dr. Rakesh Rao is presiding. He is accompanied by Judge Anand Mahajan and Judge Sheila Nair Talwar." Then he said, "Please be seated."

The bald, bespectacled, heavy set, 55-years-old Judge Dr. Rao was born into a successful family. His courtroom was amongst the quickest in India, disposing of at least 100 cases a month. He drew extreme reactions. Some called him brilliant, while others called him a maverick.

It was this no-nonsense judge, who would sit on judgment over Mike Mahi.

Rao said, "Happy morning. I am about to start the case of the *State vs. Mike Mahi.* Are both sides ready?"

"Ready for the People, Your Honor."

"Ready for the Defense, Your Honor."

KW stood up, adjusted his blazer, and made his opening statement.

"Good morning, ladies and gentlemen. My name is Kashyap Woraiyur. I am the country's Principal Prosecuting Attorney and I shall lead the prosecution in this case."

Not a soul moved. Pin drop silence.

"My lordships. You're here to look at evidence in the trial of Mike Mahi who is being charged with multiple acts of omission and commission that lower the dignity of the accounting profession and which lead to a huge loss to the shareholders of Hindustan Bank."

His voice now dropped to a whisper.

"We have three baskets of charges.

"The first relates to professional incompetence. Yes, professional incompetence. We will get an expert witness to testify to how Mike Mahi's firm, and by implication Mike Mahi, slept while loans were given with inadequate security."

"A succinct summary of what the newspapers have been carrying for the last few days," thought Mahi.

"The second relates to insider trading. We will provide you with evidence to show Mahi held a million shares in the bank. We will also show how his wife Tanya Roy traded in those shares by using price-sensitive information that had not yet become available to the public, even while he was auditing the bank."

These too had been aired in the newspapers and television channels earlier.

"The third relates to professional misconduct. The evidence will show that against every canon of professional propriety, Mike Mahi drew fees contingent to result and his wife pocketed close to a crore on a derivative transaction. The evidence we present will prove the defendant is guilty as charged."

Having neatly summarized the issues, KW stepped into anticipating what the defense would come up with.

"The Defense will either tell you Mahi committed no crime or that the law is wrong. They will present to you a man who was so busy that he delegated all his work to colleagues who let him down. They will talk to you about his meteoric rise from a slum-dog accountant to super-stardom and about how he is a role model to the profession.

For God's sake, don't buy it. Justice doesn't care whether Mike Mahi delegated or not. Justice doesn't care whether the law is right or not. It is of no consequence what position Mike Mahi holds today. Like every Indian, I love the law. I studied law and live by it. In the next three days I will show you that Mike Mahi broke the law and broke it wantonly. He broke our trust in him and therefore, it's our job to make him pay for it. Thank you."

He had spoken with clarity and authority and finished the opening statement in 35 minutes flat.

OOO

The Defense Attorney rose from his seat, took a sip of water, and said:

"Good morning, your lordships. I am Ramnath Parkar, attorney for the accused, Mike Mahi. The prosecution took ten minutes less time than what was allotted to it to make the opening statement. With your permission, I would like to add it to the time allotted to me."

"Objection," screamed Kashyap.

"Overruled," said the Judge.

Pleased with himself, Parkar began: "The Prosecution leveled three charges. These are not charges at the professional accountant. These are charges against Mike Mahi, the individual. I mean, had it been anyone else, they would not have even considered these. But because this is Mike Mahi, because this is the poster boy of the accounting profession, and because they want to make an example of him, they have brought those charges."

Parkar had the court's attention while Woraiyur stifled a yawn.

"The first charge relates to professional negligence, the second to insider trading and the last to professional misconduct. All are serious offenses and let me tell you, with all the authority in my command, that Mike Mahi committed none of these. He unequivocally pleads 'Not guilty'.

"Your honor, let's understand this man whose credibility the prosecution wants to tear apart. Your lordships, Mahi was born amidst poverty and was not privy even to the smallest of luxuries. His father was a colliery worker, and Mahi walked four kilometers to school. It was his extraordinary ability to play hockey, not his school marks, which took him to St. Anne's, before he landed up for his internship with Hunt & Smith, one of the big six public accounting firms. He gave up the opportunity to play for India, because it clashed with his CA exams. That's the sort of dedication he brings in to the profession.

"His rise in the profession is nothing short of spectacular. He is a man of substance and integrity, and became NICPA's president. Till date, there has not been a single charge against him, either in public or in private life. Why, he hasn't even been charged for a traffic offense. Sir, it is this man the prosecution is charging with grave crimes, blowing things out of proportion.

"Your honor, please remind the prosecution that it must not just prove, but prove beyond all reasonable doubt that Mahi is guilty as charged. If you return a verdict of guilty even when there is an iota of doubt, it would be grave injustice to Mahi and to the CA profession."

Judge Anand Mahajan was showing slight signs of restlessness.

Parkar continued. "Please don't take my word that Mahi is NOT GUILTY of professional negligence. We will place before you expert witnesses, some of whom fiercely compete with Mahi for clients and fees. These are people, who from a business perspective, would like Mahi to fall. But they will all say they would have done exactly what Mahi did in his audit. These men are the best in the business. So, if the best would not have done differently, then what Mahi did was the best. You cannot implicate a man for that.

"Your lordships, the prosecution will rely on small firms who have no idea of how large audits are done. When the prosecution presents its witnesses, please ask them whether they are in the same league as Mahi. Please ask them whether they would have done things differently. We will also show you that the ACL software Mahi used for sampling is globally recognized and there is enough documentary evidence to prove Mahi did what he claimed he did. Not just that your lordships, sampling is a legally accepted standard auditing practice.

"As to the matter of insider trading, your honor, we will demand of the prosecution to provide at least one document, just one document, to prove Mahi bought the shares he is accused of having bought. You will see the Prosecution hum and haw. On our part, we will bring to the witness box men of integrity who will testify Tanya Roy was competent enough to make investments and had retained professional advisors.

"Your lordships, in the matter of professional misconduct we will ask you to dump the charge in its entirety, because what Mahi did was within the best traditions of professionalism. He did not, I repeat, did not pick fees contingent to result. Such a charge is based on a flawed understanding of fee and of results.

"Please ignore the biased media reporting. Journalists often write without being aware of all the details. You see, they are always in tearing hurry. Based on facts we will present before you, your lordships must return a verdict of not guilty. To return any other verdict would amount to a travesty of justice. Judge a man by what he did, not by the position he holds. Mahi is a man of trust and he did not break our trust in any way. Thank you."

There was a small round of applause as Parkar sat down after a forty-minute oration.

49. Day One in the Court: Arguments

The Prosecutor called Mike Mahi to take the box reserved for the Accused. The popular accountant, fully aware of the history that surrounded the occasion, head held high, took four brisk steps to the box.

The preliminaries were quickly done with. Then began a barrage of questions.

"What's your name?" The voice was just above a whisper.

"I am Mike Mahi."

"I didn't want to know who you are. I wanted your name." The decibel level was a shade up.

A surprised Mahi said, "My name is Mike Mahi."

"Nonsense. You are lying. Just the way you lied in your audit reports." Woraiyur could be heard in the next room, even if he didn't hold a mike.

"I don't lie." Mahi was quiet and dignified.

"Okay Sir, then tell this court the name you were born with."

"Well, no one is born with a name."

Many in the audience laughed. Justice Sheila Talwar suppressed a smile.

"Silence. Silence. Both counsel and the accused shall not resort to verbal gymnastics."

"Oh, is it? Pray tell, are you or are you not Muthukumar Mahalingam?"

After what appeared an eternity, although only ten seconds had elapsed, Mahi responded, "Well, yes and no."

"Vintage auditor. Can't make up his mind. Just like he couldn't make up his mind when he audited Hindustan Bank." The sarcasm was dripping.

Woraiyur then looked at the judges and thundered, "Your honor, this man is a pathological liar. You cannot take his words at face value. I don't think I should ask any more questions to Muthukumar Mahalingam."

The audience was shocked. Why was Mike Mahi calling himself Mike Mahi if his name was Muthukumar Mahalingam? Was he, like KW was insinuating, a liar ?

Parkar rose from his seat with deliberate slowness. This was news to him. He used a tissue to wipe non-existent sweat from his forehead, and turning towards Mike Mahi, smiled and asked, "Did you ever change your name with a gazette notification?"

"No, Sir."

"Does your school leaving certificate show your name as Mike Mahi?"

"Yes, Sir."

"What does your graduation certificate show?"

"Mike Mahi, Sir."

"Your CA certificate?"

"Mike Mahi, Sir."

"What does the birth certificate indicate?"

"The certificate doesn't spell out a name. It simply says, 'baby boy'."

"Will you be able to tell this Court what the learned lawyer means when he says you lied?"

"I wouldn't know, but there is something that happened years ago. When I was three years old and went to school for admission, the Principal asked me my name. My mother lovingly calls me Mykku (short for 'my Kumar') and I told the Principal this, which he apparently understood as Mike. My dad said 'Good Mahi' (short for Mahalingam), and the principal wrote the name as Mike Mahi. Thus the name stuck: at home, in school, in college, in CA and everywhere…" said Mahi.

"...Until this moment, when Woraiyur did some extensive, useless research to cull out a long-forgotten, hardly-remembered, never-used name," said Parkar.

OOO

KW introduced the prosecution's first expert witness, Shomenath Shome.

Dressed in oversized safari suit, a fashionable wear of the late 1980s, Shome struggled out of the chair. His large shock of silver hair disturbed his vision, his recently-operated knee was very unhelpful, and he walked less than briskly, aided by the cane he tapped on the new wooden floor.

"How long have you been practicing, Mr. Shome?"

"Fifty years."

"You are familiar with the audit of receivables, I suppose."

"Yes, Sir. Every auditor my age is an expert. We have done dozens of such audits."

"If you were to audit sales or receivables, how many transactions would you verify?"

"We would verify all of them."

"All? You mean you wouldn't do a test check?"

"No, Sir. With the arrival of applications like the spreadsheet, it is possible to write formulae and macros to test all the transactions."

"Even if there are 40,000 transactions?"

"Even if there are 40,000 transactions."

"Can you explain please?"

"Sure. Suppose we have to verify Value Added Tax (VAT) computations, we transfer data to the excel sheet, write a formula for VAT calculation, write another to compare it with the VAT value already arrived at, and then mark the differences."

"That's for VAT. What about collaterals?"

"We can write the value of the loan and the value of the collateral and run a formula to test its adequacy."

"Your honor. You may take note of this point. Shome, thank you."

Turning to Ramnath Parkar, with the gesture of a man who has just won a major skirmish, Woraiyur said, "Your witness, please."

Parkar had scorn written all over his face. He stared at Shome as though he were the accused and asked: "Mr. Shome, you are a CA in practice?"

"Yes, Sir."

"How big is your firm, relative to that of Mike Mahi's?"

"I wouldn't know the size of Mahi's firm."

"Okay, I will help you. He has offices in every Indian state capital, 28 of them to be precise. He is present in fifteen countries, spanning four continents. He is professionally connected in some form or the other to 160 of the BT 500 companies. There are 1200 CAs working with him."

"That's pretty big, Sir. We are nowhere close."

"Yet you pass judgment on him."

"No, I didn't pass judgment on him. I merely said we audit 100 percent."

"You say collaterals' adequacy can be verified using spreadsheets? Right?"

"That's what I said."

"Do you know Mike Mahi is a champion of MS Office?"

"No, Sir, I didn't know that."

"Well, let me tell you he is. If there were a way by which the adequacy of collaterals could be verified through Excel, Mike Mahi's firm would have done it. Please also remember it's important that the value you enter into a sheet be correct."

Shome mumbled something that no one could hear. He had a tired look that came from many years of auditing books.

"Do you know that Mike Mahi is widely regarded as an expert in auditing?"

"After hearing he tested only 150 transactions out of 40,000, I wouldn't think so."

"How do you know he tested only 150 transactions?"

"It is in the papers. Every bit of what Mahi did in the Hindustan Bank audit is with the media."

"By the way, have you ever audited 40,000 transactions in a single audit?"

"No, Sir."

"Thank you. That's all. You may resume your seat."

"Hold on, hold on" said Woraiyur. "Please stay in the Witness box."

OOO

KW turned to Mahi. In his rich baritone voice he asked, "Can you tell this court how you went about auditing the loan transactions and why you found nothing amiss?"

"We worked on a scientifically-chosen sample. We populated the spreadsheet with data and wrote a formula to flag up under-valuation. Unfortunately, the sample didn't raise any suspicions."

"Did you verify each of the 40,000 customers who had taken a loan?"

"We verified each of the customers on the sample. We did not verify each of the 40,000 customers."

"Why? Will you tell the honorable court why you did not verify all of them?" Woraiyur's voice boomed. "Did you not think it was your duty to do so?"

Mahi kept his cool, despite the provocation. "That's because each account would take at least half an hour to audit. You see, documents need to be verified. Loan processes need to be checked. For 40,000 accounts, it would take 20,000 man-hours. At ten hours per day, it's about 2,000 man-days. Even if we put ten people to work on it, it would take 200 days while we get only 30 to audit."

"Oh I see. Who asks you to audit in thirty days? This isn't a crash course. You could have taken your time." Woraiyur exploded clocking 7.1 on the Richter scale!

Keeping his voice flat, Mahi said, "The profession doesn't work that way. For one, there is the cost. With a minimum charge card of Rs 1,500 per hour, this would cost the bank Rs 300 lakhs just to do this work."

"Wow. The profession doesn't work that way. Silly profession." KW was speaking to himself, but the whisper was audible. Then in a sharper tone asked, "So how many records did you select?"

"The audit software picks up how many customers to audit. When there are 40,000 customers, at 99 percent confidence level and 5 percent margin of error, we need to audit only 500 records. If these records do not throw up a red flag, we leave it; otherwise we increase the size of the sample."

"Oh, good. It means you audit sketchily, right?" He paused before saying, "And you didn't see a red flag in the 500 records audited?"

"Our team didn't notice a red flag in the 500 records audited. Incidentally, in the first half of the year, the joint auditors had selected a different set of 500 records and that didn't throw up red flags either."

"Mr. Mahi, you will answer only the questions I ask. Don't give us your views," said Woraiyur, unhappy at Mahi's reference to a fellow auditor.

"How did you select these 500 records? Did you pick whatever you liked? Or was there some other statistical hogwash used?"

Mahi ignored the jibe. The lawyer was simply rephrasing the same question each time.

"We do random sampling. We break the population into sub-categories, like large, medium and small customers. Within that we further split into parts: like high, medium and low values. We apply random sampling separately on each of these categories. That way we ensure the final sample is representative. The software selects the accounts based on random number tables. It's called stratified random sampling." He remembered his chat with Antony Patnaik on Prostar many years ago.

"This is absolute hogwash, your Honor. I don't buy any of what he says. I am done with him for now. I would like you to record that his firm audited only 1.25 percent of the accounts and passed judgment overall 100 percent."

With glee in his eyes, he said, "Shome sahib, thank you for your time, and for showing how sketchily these biggies work."

Ramnath Parkar said he had no counters. "We want to bring in our star witness."

ooo

"Your honor, I would like to call Alka Varma as witness for the Defense."

"Please go ahead."

As she stepped forward, few men in the audience smiled at her. She looked good even at fifty and the strands of gray made her that much more fashionable. The aroma of success could be smelt.

"Would you tell the Court your qualifications?" asked Parkar.

"I am a Chartered Accountant in practice. I specialize in fraud detection. I am a partner in Hunt & Smith, a Big Six public accounting firm."

"Where is the firm located?"

"Our corporate office in India is in Mumbai, but our offices dot the world. Internationally, we are headquartered in Geneva."

"How big is your firm?"

"We are pretty big. In fact, we are ranked No. 2 globally, based on a study done by a Chennai based research-house."

"That would place you well ahead of Mike Mahi & Associates?"

"Despite their size and scale, and with due apologies to Mike, we are miles ahead, both in India and globally."

"So you are well qualified to assess Mahi's work?"

"We do peer reviews of firms substantially bigger than Mike, Mahi & Associates. Such reviews are mandated under law and are intended to assess whether the firm reviewed carried out the best practices of the profession."

"How well do you know Mike Mahi?"

"Reasonably well. He is a distinguished colleague. He has been our President. Many look up to him as a role model."

"How would you rate his auditing skills?"

"First rate."

"You are saying this despite the fact that you are in competition with his firm."

"Yes, Sir."

Turning to KW, Parkar said, "You may cross examine."

XXX

"Alka Varma, you heard Mike Mahi. Don't tell me this is how auditing is carried out."

"Yes, Sir. This is how auditing is carried out. In fact, I am impressed he sought 99 percent confidence levels. Many of us would be fine with 95 percent while doing an external audit."

Still trying to find a hole, Woraiyur retorted, "So you get away with doing half work?"

"It depends on how you wish to see things Mr. Public Prosecutor." Alka's patience was wearing thin. "When a lawyer handles a case, he takes a brief from the junior; he doesn't read loads of paper. When a customer buys rice, he dips into the bowl and checks a few grains of rice for quality. You don't dip into it time and again to find out if every granule is fine. In the same way, we pick a sample and audit."

Woraiyur was scratching his head. It was an ominous sign.

Alka was still talking. "When a psephologist makes a prediction based on exit polls, he takes a small sample, extrapolates, and invariably comes out with the right result. In fact, the larger the population, the smaller the percentage selected."

Woraiyur threw up his hands. "Wow. I was always of the view that psephology was astrology. Now you suggest even audit is like that."

There were smiles all around.

"Are you saying that because he was your protégé at Hunt & Smith?"

"True, he interned at Hunt & Smith, but I never knew him then."

"So Mike Mahi is in no way to blame?"

"No, because the law as also standard auditing practices permit sampling. Yes, if he picked his sample in the wrong way."

50. Case continues... Driver's drive

At 2 p.m., Mahi entered the court premises, trying to dry the few droplets of water, which wet his blazer from the sudden drizzle. Unpredictable weather! Like unpredictable lawyers and unpredictable judges.

He jogged with cameras following him, and journalists screaming, "Sir, this is such an important case. You are the accused. How can you afford to be late?"

Mahi turned a deaf ear to them and went straight inside. Moments later, the judges made an appearance. The proceedings began in the next few minutes even as Mahi took the stand. Woraiyur appeared happy as he ruffled through the documents.

Waving his index finger at Mike Mahi, as though addressing a criminal, Woraiyur asked, "Did you or did you not loan your driver Rs 20 lakhs?" The lawyer had come straight to a point, without any preliminaries. Mahi took twenty seconds to digest the question. Parkar was flipping through a magazine and looked up in surprise. He hadn't known about the loan. Like he hadn't known about Muthukumar Mahalingam.

"Yes, I did. I gave him money because he wanted to buy a house," Mahi said matter-of-factly. "I paid him through a crossed account payee cheque. It is receipted and accounted for in my tax return."

"I am sure it would be receipted. After all, you aren't a certified accountant for nothing. By the way, please answer only my questions. We don't want any supplementary information."

The judge frowned. He disliked taunts. He wanted court scenes to be handled with grace, more so when they involved suave men.

"Are you telling the truth, the whole truth, and nothing but the truth in the manner you promised?" asked Woraiyur.

"Yes, I am telling the truth, the whole truth, and nothing but the truth. And I told you several times, I don't lie."

"Did you lend him another Rs 10 lakh in cash?"

Mahi was silent for a while, as though trying to remember. "I don't remember. If I or my office gave it to him, it must be accounted for and reflected in the tax return."

"Did you visit his house for house warming?" A few laughs were heard, but soon stifled.

Mahi turned to Ramnath Parkar. The lawyer continued to flip through a magazine. Mahi said, "He never invited me."

"Is it not surprising that he didn't invite a principal lender for a house warming?" Worayiur's voice hinted deep sarcasm. People smiled. The lawyer was providing good entertainment!

"Perhaps he thought I was a banker. We don't invite the HDFC manager when we do a house warming function, do we?" Mahi served up a rare smile and quickly regretted it.

"Maybe. But you are no HDFC manager. You are his employer. He should have invited you." Woraiyur was sounding like a well-known television journalist who berated his guests.

"Well, he didn't invite me. I don't mind it."

"Are you aware he didn't invite even your wife?" There were giggles from the crowd.

"Order, order. Mr. Public Prosecutor, can you get to the point?"

"Perhaps he didn't want us to see his house. Maybe it is somewhere in a village," said Mahi, encouraged by the Judge's admonition.

"Well, what if I told you he didn't build a house at all?" Woraiyur was waving a pen at Mahi's face. Mahi ducked.

Taken aback by the question, Mahi said, "It means he didn't complete the house, which is perhaps why he did not invite us."

The crowd roared.

"Order, order!"

"Mike Mahi, are you naive or are you acting naive?" The lawyer had him on the mat. "I mean a certain Mrs. Sana Ahmed, who happens to be the wife of Mr. Kaleem Ahmed, a guy who is on your payroll as a driver bought shares in Hindustan Bank; and the payment was Rs 25 lakhs."

A pin dropped somewhere. It sounded like a bomb. It was now clear Woraiyur would be leading up to a significant charge. There had been no inkling of this in the papers and on the news channels.

Mahi's heart plummeted into his stomach. He stared at Woraiyur for a moment. Pulling himself together, he said, "What do you expect me to do? Counter-check his every activity?" He was surprised he was taking the fight to the lawyer's camp.

"Well, I am telling you, you routed your stock purchases through Kaleem." Woraiyur had an evil smile on his face as he turned to face the judges.

Mahi turned to Ramnath Parkar, half expecting the lawyer to jump to his defense. But the man was still busy leafing through a magazine. "You expect me to route the transactions through my driver? I hope you are not out of your mind."

"Mind your language." Woraiyur's coat swished as he turned. His volume had increased.

"You make stupid, third rate charges. Back them up with proof."

"Don't teach me the law. For your information, circumstantial evidence will do. There is no need to prove beyond all reasonable doubt."

Parkar had lifted his eyes from the magazine. "Mr. Woraiyur, the court will take that call."

Woraiyur slammed his fist on the table. "Yes, the court will take the call. And once I prove it to them, they will call for Mahi's head."

51. Day Two and Insider Trading

As the big hand of the magnificent antique clock touched six, and the small one rested between eight and nine, Judge Dr. Rakesh Rao, Judge Anand Mahajan and Judge Sheila Nair Talwar walked in together. Mike Mahi was already seated, one leg crossed over the other, and eyes closed as though in deep meditation. He wore a faded Levis blue jeans and a sparkling white t-shirt. A Mont Blanc pen was slotted in the shirt pocket. A journalist noticed that Mahi wore an expensive pair of Adidas shoes.

As the crowd stood in a show of respect, Mahi glanced at the female judge. She had large lustrous eyes and for the second day in a row, the sight of the 48-year-old Sheila Talwar, draped in a silk sari, made him gasp for breath. A slim necklace adorned her neck.

A former actress with a high intellect, she was the youngest woman to ever become a high court judge. She didn't "couch" her way to the chambers. Talwar graduated in history, because she loved stories of the past, and later went to law school after her movie career hit a roadblock.

Widely respected and admired for her no-nonsense approach, Talwar would be an important cog in the judicial wheel. Parkar had found out that in case of a split verdict, she was on the side of the majority judgment. She had the mojo to swing judges her way. She turned towards Mahi, and the accountant shifted his eyes away.

Ramnath Parkar sat, his legs stretched, his court-mandated white-and-white attire crumpled, his body making an angle of 75 degrees to the chair. "What does he do with all the money he earns?" wondered Talwar. Woraiyur, looking fresh and smelling of fragrance, was conversing with his juniors. Talwar saw he wore an antique Rolex. The rooms were overflowing. If anything, more people had checked in today compared to yesterday.

The TV channels had gone to town with their screaming headlines of Day 1.

"Colliery worker's son in the dock."

"NICPA past president wasn't born with a silver spoon."

The story of his hockey exploits, including of how he sacrificed national duty to become a CA, was discussed on a third channel. Mahi treated television with disdain. He called it the "picture book for people with an IQ of minus 2". He searched for Tejas Arya, but the star anchor was nowhere in sight. For him to sit out of the story of the decade was surprising.

The morning papers had been more nuanced. "Mahi looked good," said one analyst. "Alka Varma's expert testimony is extremely favorable to Mahi," noted another. There was shock that a seasoned lawyer like Woraiyur had picked Shome as his star witness. In equal measure, there was surprise at the quantum of checking. "Inadequate," was the near unanimous verdict, at the ground level, whatever the technical experts might say.

ooo

Mahi's mind drifted into the past. He had built his equity stake in Hindustan Bank stock by stock. The company had 10,000 lakh shares. At a face value of Rs 10 a share, it was Rs 1,000 crore of capital.

One day, the price fell by a whopping 20 percent when a global banking scandal broke. A large bank had been robbed of a billion dollars. Mahi ordered his broker to unload the war chest to buy Hindustan Bank. Another day, when the RBI governor announced a massive rate hike, the share price fell by 7 percent. Mahi bought more shares on the spot.

On the day his firm received the letter of appointment as external auditor of the bank, Mahi had ten thousand shares. It gave him a 0.001 percent in the company. The shares were bought at an average price of Rs 570. That day, Hindustan Bank's share price stood at Rs 3,750. So his wealth in Hindustan Bank was

Rs 3.75 crore. On his total portfolio of Rs 25 crore, this represented 15 percent of his holding.

Mahi handed over all the shares to a Certified Financial Planner (CFP) and asked him to build a discretionary portfolio. A discretionary portfolio meant that the portfolio manager had the absolute right to buy or sell whatever shares he wished, without seeking Mahi's approval. Mahi did not think it necessary to sell the shares because he genuinely felt that, with an independent portfolio manager in charge, the stocks were outside his control.

In theory, Mahi and the manager were to meet every quarter to review the portfolio. In practice, no such thing happened. The manager would send Mahi a quarterly dashboard. It would contain profit from capital gains, profit from dividends, the value of holdings, the cost of holdings, and unrealized appreciation. Mahi also got a sector-wise breakup, but not a stock-wise breakup. He was a 'big picture' kind of guy.

Busy with his work, Mahi never gave these reports a second glance, sure that his money was in safe hands. It was a mistake, which he would come to regret one day. The day was today, the second day of the hearing.

ooo

Mahi heard his name being called, and that broke the reverie. The Prosecutor wanted him to take the Accused's box.

Woraiyur said, "You have been sworn in. There is no need to swear you in again. Understood? You are on oath."

"I am always on oath." Laughter ensued and Judge Dr. Rao had difficulty restoring order.

"Let's see." Woraiyur was at his sarcastic worst.

"Did you hold shares in Hindustan Bank?"

"Yes, I did."

"Do you now hold shares in Hindustan Bank?"

The judge intervened: "These matters can be easily verified with documents. Why do you want to go through an elaborate process?"

"My lord, I want to show this court Mahi's penchant to take himself too seriously and self-righteously."

"Mahi, you may answer," said Judge Rao.

"Well, yes and no."

"Wow. Come on, auditor. Don't tell me you can't make up your mind. Yes or no? It can't be both."

The audience sat shocked. How could Mahi be and not be a shareholder at the same time?

Ramnath Parkar bristled up and rose to his full height. "Can you explain? This court trusts you."

Woraiyur was on his feet. "Objection. The attorney cannot speak on behalf of the court. He can only speak for himself."

"Sustained."

"Okay Mahi, give us the facts as you know them. I trust you."

"I had shares in Hindustan Bank at the time of my appointment. I made them over to a portfolio manager, and I remember suggesting they be sold. I now understand this has not been done."

Woraiyur waved a document even as he said. "That's another lie. Here's an affidavit from his CFP saying no such instruction was ever given."

Parkar said, "It's the auditor's word against the CFP's. By the way, if you want, haul up the portfolio manager. Why didn't he sell the shares?"

Woraiyur screamed, "So Parkar, you agree that it's wrong to hold shares in the client company?" Turning to the judges, he said, "You may note the confession, my lordships. Also the confirmation that he holds the shares even today."

Parkar stopped in his tracks. He was ashen-faced. How could he commit such a faux pas? Shaken, he turned to Mahi only to find his client red with rage. Parkar stumbled to his chair and plopped down. Drops of perspiration dripped out. Despite his suave facade, he wiped his sweaty forehead with his shirtsleeve.

Mahi's hopes sank. "Bloody inefficient fool! How could this lawyer who charged a bomb be so careless? Should he not be roasted alive?"

He asked himself for the umpteenth time, "Why oh why did I not sell those shares? Why did I ever ask this CFP to do it for me? Damn it, when he gave the reports, why didn't I check them? Why was I so lackadaisical? " He shuddered to think of what would happen if the judges didn't agree with his arguments.

Now after Parkar's thoughtless remark, the nightmare returned to haunt him.

ooo

When the court resumed after recess, Rohit Appana, Mahi's wealth manager, was sworn in as witness for the Prosecution.

Now in his mid-thirties, fair, and a shade plump, he wore a pinstriped suit that went well with his profession and gave him the air of solidity judges love to see in a witness. It wouldn't have been the same if he had come in dark brown trouser and a red jacket, his standard attire at the social club. Mahi recalled how a mutual friend had referred him and while Mahi and Rohit had not quite hit it off, there was no friction. He did a decent job and Mahi recognized the value of his service.

"Do you handle the portfolio of Mike Mahi?" began Woraiyur.

"Yes, I do. I have been handling it ever since he became the auditor of Hindustan Bank."

"Did you like advising him?"

"While engaging me, he told he was too busy to look after his monetary affairs. I like such people. After all, it brings me my money."

"Any idea how many shares Tanya Roy holds?"

Parkar was on his feet in a trice. "Objection. We don't even know who Tanya Roy is. We don't know why the Witness would be privy to the shares Tanya holds."

"Sustained."

Woraiyur was annoyed. "Okay, if the counsel wants to play it that way, it's fine with me." He then asked Appana, "Do you also advise Mahi's wife, Tanya Roy?"

"Yes, I do."

"How many shares does she hold in Hindustan Bank?"

"One lakh shares."

"What? Come again." Woraiyur was faking his surprise. Anyone familiar with court scenes knew witnesses are asked well-rehearsed questions.

"Ten thousand shares at an average price of Rs 2,100."

"You mean over the last three years while Mahi audited the Bank, his wife accumulated ten thousand shares at an average price of Rs 2,100? Have I understood this right?"

"Yes, Sir. In the last three years, while Mike, Mahi & Associates audited Hindustan Bank, with Mike as its signing partner, his wife Tanya Roy bought shares in Hindustan Bank at an average cost of Rs 2,100."

"Your witness," said Woraiyur, quite satisfied with the progress.

Parkar wanted to make amends for his earlier foolishness. Without any preliminaries he asked, "Are you saying Tanya Roy bought those shares all by herself?"

"Yes Sir, it was her money. No Sir, she bought them through a broker."

"I didn't mean that. I wanted to know if she made the investment all by herself or if she received advice to make the purchase."

Rohit turned left, he turned right, and with a straight face said, "On most occasions, I advised her to buy."

"You advised her knowing full well her husband was the bank's external auditor."

"No, you are wrong. Then I did not realize Mahi was the bank's external auditor."

Parkar saw an opening and jumped in. "Don't lie. What kind of an investment analyst are you who doesn't even see who the signing firm is?"

"I don't need to see every document. I don't need to read annual reports." Appana was trying to save his skin, trying to build a protective umbrella should an ethics issue arise in the CFP Institute with respect to his conduct.

"On one occasion I sold them for her when she indicated prices were likely to fall, and it would be good for us to pick shares. I have no way of knowing how she arrived at the conclusion. On another occasion, Doc advised me to buy."

"So she didn't take the investment decision by herself?"

"No Sir."

"Thank you, Mr. Appana. I just have one piece of advice. Next time around, answer only the questions that are addressed to you."

OOO

Woraiyur indicated he wanted to examine Mike Mahi again. Parkar reluctantly agreed.

"Are you aware your father has 1,000 shares in Hindustan Bank? Are you aware he bought them a year ago?"

Only this morning, both Parkar and Mahi had come to know of it. Senior had called up Mahi to ask him if it was okay after he had heard the story about the driver on television. Initially, Mahi was angry at what his dad had done, but when the reality began to sink in, he was touched by his father's gesture. Parkar had suggested a certain strategy if the Prosecution came out with the charge, though they were rather certain that the Prosecution would never stumble on it.

"So what? If you have the money, you too can buy," Mahi told Woraiyur.

"Ha, I am aware of that. You know no person can be appointed as auditor of a company if he or his close relatives own shares in the company. There cannot be a closer relative than a father."

"I was not aware that my father owned shares. How do you expect me to keep track of it? He lives 400 kilometers away and I don't peek into his financial affairs."

"Mike Mahi, how does a man who all his life spent time in a colliery, buy 1,000 shares? Where did the money come from? Did you divert your money to help him buy?"

The reference to a colliery worker was fair and genuine but in the surcharged atmosphere it was the wrong word to use. In a different situation, even KW might have regretted his words, but not today.

"Excuse me, have you gone crazy? Do you think I would be foolish enough to do that?" It was uncharacteristic of Mahi to use such language. There was a razor-like edge to his voice.

KW knew he had his victim on the ropes. He needed a knockout punch to put him on the mat. In a cold voice he said, "Sorry, but it's you who's gone crazy after being caught out."

Mahi asked for water and drank it. It soothed his nerves. "Even if he did, he lost money on the transaction given the rate at which you say he bought it."

"Your mother bought 500 shares. Not too sure if she can even sign."

"How does it bother you?"

"It bothers me because she could not have had the money without you loaning it to her. She was your front, your proxy." KW knew Mahi was referring to the signature part, but the seasoned attorney turned it to his advantage by diverting attention to the purchase part.

"Mr. Prosecutor, I have no time to for this kind of money."

"Oh okay, I didn't know you loot."

By end of the day, the Prosecution had shown that Mahi, his wife, his parents and his relatives held shares in Hindustan Bank. Parkar argued that Senior had bought shares thinking them to be a wonderful buy because Mahi audited the company. The Prosecutor showed a line of family members, close and distant, who had bought shares in Hindustan Bank at various points in time, and had either profited or lost from their act. Parkar argued that they were adults and could do what they wished.

It was 5:55 p.m., five more minutes to go for the long hoot. Mahi had lost the battle of perceptions. Unless Parkar could come out with some legal pyrotechnics tomorrow, the case was lost.

It was then that the super cat, Woraiyur, overplayed his hand.

He was saying, "So Mahi, you agree that holding shares in the company you audit is bad in the eyes of the law."

For a moment, Mahi turned to Parkar. The wily fox butted in. "I will prove that holding shares is legal."

There was bedlam in the court. KW rose to his full height, angry at being tricked. "My Lord, questions to the accused should be answered by the defendant, not by his lawyer."

"My apologies, your honor," said a grinning Parkar. He had already made his point. Mentally, he patted himself on the back for making amends for yesterday's blunder.

He saw Talwar smile.

The judges ordered that closing arguments commence.

KW stood up, and enjoying the limelight, said: "Your honor, we believe we have made our case impregnable. Mike Mahi may have been president of NICPA, he may have enjoyed an immaculate reputation, but in the instant case he is painfully guilty. You heard Shome, with fifty years of practical experience behind him, confirm that, since technology facilitates it, he would have audited every transaction. On the other charge, we have shown you how Mahi, his wife and his parents held shares, some of which were bought during his tenure as auditor, and how they profited therefrom. This is a breach of trust. Finally, Mahi pocketed money on derivative transactions that amount to drawing fees contingent on result. Your lordships, please don't treat him with kid gloves. Treat him like any other individual. Make an example of him. Return a verdict of guilty on all three counts. That's all, your honor."

He had taken just four minutes to make his neat summation.

Ramnath Parkar rose, swept a glance at the jam-packed courtroom, and addressed the judges: "KW is a star attorney. He is always spot-on. But this time he has been blind-sighted by the stature of Mike Mahi. Your honor, you must deliver judgments, not make examples of people. The very distinguished Alka Varma told this court so eloquently that Mahi in his audit went beyond the call of duty. If something goes wrong despite that, you then cannot hold him at fault. We have also read out to this court the law, which says that his or his relatives holding the kind of shares they held is not illegal and that no big financial benefits accrued. Not just that; Mahi disclosed his holdings to the Board. And finally my lordships, fee paid in the form of an "Option" is fee in kind and cannot be called a transaction 'contingent on result'. I have only one request. Please judge Mahi like you would judge anyone else. If anyone else would have been penalized for this, penalize Mahi. But if anyone else would have been spared, spare Mahi. That's all, my lord.

Justice Dr. Rakesh Rao adjourned the court for the day and announced that the judgment would be delivered on Monday.

52. Monday, Judgment Day

It was the fastest case hearing in Indian history. The arguments, on either side, had been heard in a mere five days. The judges sat over the weekend to write their judgment. Now, this Monday, Judge Sheila Nair Talwar was ready with the verdict. Outside, the security had been beefed up as the police made special arrangements. In all, 150 policemen were deployed at multiple entrance points and barricades were placed to control the crowd.

Room 17 was packed to overflowing. Unlike last week there were no giant screens outside, as the judges did not want a public spectacle. There was a graveyard like silence as everyone waited for the verdict. The Court Registrar reserved 30 percent of the seats for the media and 5 percent for Mahi. The rest were for anyone who could pay Rs 10,000 to buy a ticket.

Mahi waived off a major part of his quota. This was not a celebratory function to which you invited guests. This was the Day of Judgment.

Tanya Roy was present. So was Jia Sharma. Mahi had earlier shot down Tanya's request to bring Jia along for the hearing, because he felt her presence would affect the judges. And now, as she walked in wearing loose pants, a short top, stilettos, and an overtly-confident gait that made every male eye turn, Mahi knew he had been right. Eyes popped and jaws dropped.

Tejas Arya was personally present, as part of the media contingent. He sat far away from his wife. He smiled at Mahi, but no words were exchanged. A photographer took some shots. Uncle Krishna had come down from Ooty at Mahi's request. Prof Muscles had asked for an invitation and got it. David Kocher had arrived unannounced.

Doc sat in the gallery having bought a ticket on the gray market.

Mahi's mother refused to come and his dad was too shaken to turn up. They would watch the proceedings from their home. It was the first nationally-televised judgment. Later in the night they would learn that this had been the most-watched show since the arrival of private TV channels.

As each one of the grandfather clocks placed on the four walls of the courtroom chimed ten in unison, Judge Talwar began reading from her double-spaced manuscript, typed in Book Antiqua font, size 16. It made easy reading for the 48-year-old, even as she pushed the spectacles on to the bridge of her nose.

Elsewhere, in TV studios, the hacks were busy writing smashing headlines.

BREAKING NEWS: Justice Talwar begins reading the judgment.

"This is the biggest trial this century, involving as it does a high-ranking professional accountant. Neither the fact that Mike Mahi was President of NICPA nor that he started his life in a coal pit matters to this court. Justice is the same for all. Mahi is charged on three counts: professional incompetence, insider trading and professional misconduct. In respect of each of these charges, we arrived at a unanimous judgment," Talwar began.

At the Mahi home, the television screen popped up the breaking news.

BREAKING NEWS: It's a unanimous verdict. Blink, Blink.

"On professional competence, the primary question that arose was whether the audit methodology adopted by Mike, Mahi & Associates was appropriate in the context of the size of the bank's business and the nature of its operations. This court understands it is impossible to do a 100 percent verification of transactions. At the same time, the auditor cannot do test checks and absolve himself of blame."

In his home, Senior who had the television on mute, saw the breaking news. His heart sank.

BREAKING NEWS: Auditor cannot absolve himself of blame. Blink, Blink.

Mahi's heart skipped a beat. Was his career as an accounting professional coming to an end? An indictment here would mean the end of the road, sentencing or no sentencing. And indictment would mean there would not be a place in the world where he could hide his face.

"We have the word of an expert auditor, Alka Varma, that the practice adopted by Mike Mahi was above reproach and was far more scientific than one would normally use. We do not think Varma was covering for Mahi. You may not know, but last week we asked an independent firm to verify the working papers Mike Mahi had uploaded for us. The firm filed its report yesterday. The independent firm tells us the papers are in order. To us, it's a vote of confidence in Mike Mahi. We believe that a bunch of rogue transactions not getting selected is sheer accident. This court absolves Mahi of the charge of incompetence."

Mahi sat there with a straight face even as Justice Talwar adjusted the *pallu* of her sari, pushed her chair back, and turned in his direction. Mahi sensed a ghost of a smile. Did she also wink? After all, she had done him a favor by pronouncing him not guilty.

At home, his mom saw the breaking news. Senior explained to his wife the implications. Her heart jumped with joy.

BREAKING NEWS: Mahi cleared of professional incompetence charge. Blink, Blink.

After a pause, when she sipped in the cool apple juice, Justice Talwar continued reading the verdict.

"The second charge against Mahi is that he charged fees contingent on results. This is a matter between NICPA and him, and this court should have nothing to do with it. But because there was a tripartite agreement between the State, NICPA and Mahi to skip the disciplinary proceedings, and because this court was a party to the agreement, it is our moral obligation to pass a judgment so that the ends of justice are well served. "We saw the video clipping of the press meet, we perused documents and written arguments presented to us by the attorneys whose personal appearance we dispensed with. We have now arrived at our verdict."

Mahi closed his eyes and looked down at the floor. He believed he had lived his life with scrupulous honesty. One diktat by the judge and a reputation built over twenty years would be smoked out in twenty seconds. Were these judges gods?

He took a deep breath.

"Mike Mahi picked up shares in lieu of fees. That's the same as taking money and buying shares. There is no law that says he cannot invest in the company for which he consults. There is of course the little matter that through the consulting engagement he would become privy to information relating to the company, price sensitive or otherwise. The charge today is not one of insider trading. The charge today is whether he took fees contingent on results. We don't think he did it."

For the second time, Justice Talwar turned in his direction. For the second time she smiled at him, expecting him to return the smile. For the second time she felt she had done him a favor by pronouncing him not guilty.

Mahi let his breath out.

On the 24th floor in Express Towers, at the global headquarters of Mike Mahi & Associates, his colleagues did high-fives even as the channels blinked…

BREAKING NEWS: Mike Mahi cleared of professional misconduct.

BREAKING NEWS: Mahi absolved on two charges…

"We now step into the third and final charge. This is the one of shareholding and insider trading and is by far the most complicated. We need to segregate the issues and address it from multiple standpoints.

"First, were his holdings illegal? The answer is a clear 'No'. Every man has a right to buy shares in companies of his choice.

At worst, his appointment as auditor can be questioned. For long, until the year 2000, the law in India did not preclude a shareholder from being an auditor, except under very select conditions. Those conditions don't apply to the present case. Post 2000 also, the law allows an auditor to be a shareholder of Category B shares. These are shares which don't give their holder voting power. These non-voting shares are traded at a healthy discount to voting shares."

Turning her gaze to Rohit Appana, she said, "We inspected and Hindustan Bank confirmed that Mahi holds only Category B shares. We also learned that Mahi wrote to the Audit Committee, and a copy of that letter has been made available to us by the Defense Attorney and confirmed by the Prosecution, indicating he holds such shares and that he has asked his portfolio manager to sell them. He cannot be faulted on a legal basis. So long as a shareholder cannot in any way control the company, there should be no bar on his auditing the firm."

The judge took another sip from the glass of apple juice and said, "The right to hold or not to hold shares has nothing to do with insider trading. Ideally, charges of insider trading can fly when one trades in shares. Mahi has not bought any shares on his own account. His portfolio manager too did not trade on his account. There is however one purchase transaction in the name of Mahi in respect of voting shares. It is difficult to believe he would trade in 500 shares and that too in the last one year. We are prone to believe his account was hacked. We have asked the Prosecution to identify the hacker."

In the visitors' gallery, Cranco Doc winced.

"The purchase of shares by his driver is in a class apart. The prosecution has not advanced any evidence to show these shares were bought at Mahi's behest. The driver's testimony too bears this out. We cannot hold Mahi responsible for this. The prosecution was on a fishing expedition."

At home, Senior was excited by the turn of events but still had a premonition something might go wrong.

BREAKING NEWS: Mahi NOT GUILTY on shareholding charge. Blink. Blink.

"Second, the purchase of shares by his parents was bad in the eyes of the law. The question is, can you hold Mahi accountable for what his parents did, if he did not decide financial transactions for them? It's reasonable to believe his parents did not know they had broken the law. We don't think the shares his dad held (which were shares that entitled him to vote) provided any monetary benefit to Mahi."

Kashyap Woraiyur could not believe what he was hearing. How could this no-nonsense judge take such a lenient stand? Judge Sheila Nair Talwar delivered her punch in the very next line.

"However in the larger interest of justice, as a moral issue, Mahi should pay twice the value which his parents traded. It doesn't matter whether they incurred a loss or made a profit."

Hearing that, a part of Mahi died. He loved his parents dearly. They stayed in another part of India. He felt guilty for leaving them grow old alone. At his home, Senior closed his eyes and tears began trickling down.

BREAKING NEWS: Mahi loses moral game. Parents' holding wrong. Penalty imposed. Blink, Blink.

"I now come to the shares held by Tanya Roy. The shares held by her were non-voting shares. She hasn't broken any law. She is an independent professional with a right to make independent gains and losses. There is nothing that suggests insider trading.

"However, it would have been better if someone as close as a wife had not held these shares, even if permissible under law. This is clear from the fact that the law is now set to undergo a change in 2014.

"Tanya should not have traded in those stocks. It is hard to believe Mahi was unaware of it. It is best auditors and their wives don't trade in any security of the company they audit or consult. These come from a larger inner purpose, and not from legislation.

"In the interests of justice, the entire profits made by Tanya should be given to charity. This is not a reflection on Mike Mahi."

Tejas Arya walked out of the court, his nostrils flaring in anger. Reporters started texting the judgment.

Mahi continued to stare at the floor.

BREAKING NEWS: Tanya Roy shareholding. Mahi GUILTY… Blink, Blink

That's how the media plays it! Star reporters rushed out to the court grounds where OB vans were waiting for them to file their reports.

That night Tejas Arya made his increasingly rare appearance on national television. For full twenty minutes the soft-spoken, widely-respected journalist tore into Judge Sheila Nair Talwar, saying that the judge had committed manslaughter. "This is a legal case, not a moral issue. Every shred of evidence showed Mike Mahi was not guilty. We cannot hang a man based on our perceptions of morality. It's time we learned to treat law with respect and not deliver judgments to make an example of others," he thundered. "We must move a higher court, notwithstanding what Mahi's agreement was with NICPA," he said with a rare public show of anger. Our channel will take the lead.

That night Mike Mahi told Tanya Roy that he would step down from his firm as he had lost the moral authority to lead. His national partners quickly organized a meeting via the satellite to vote decisively in favor of Mahi's continuance dismissing the judgment as legalistic.

That night Mahi and Tanya drove down to his parents' house, some 400 kilometers away, reaching there in the wee hours of the following morning. There Tanya consoled her inconsolable parents-in-law telling them they should be proud of their son, that his stature had been vindicated by the courts and that the penalty was at best a technicality.

PART 5: LATER

53. Afterwards

YEAR: 2015

DATE: March 15

When he heard the news from Jia, Mahi's stomach lurched. He rushed out, opened the car, jumped into the driver's seat, and locked in the key, all in one motion. Tanya managed to get into the adjoining seat as Mahi pressed the accelerator, the speedometer zooming to 120 kilometers per hour as he raced on the highway in complete disbelief.

The street was jammed with cars. It took Mahi twenty-five minutes to reach the gate of Tejas Arya's residence. The usually shut massive iron gates were wide open. Mahi saw the security struggle to keep people at bay. Cameras flashed and reporters jabbered away, occasionally speaking to a few of the 3,000 plus people who had assembled there.

It was all over the media.

Early that morning, in Dubai, the 43-year old Tejas Arya had died in his sleep. A year or so ago doctors had diagnosed him with cardiomyopathy – deterioration of the heart muscles' ability to contract -- and had given him about three years to live.

In the afternoon, the shocked family had arranged for his body to be flown to India, amidst tight security and total secrecy. The news was revealed only after it reached India. The few hours when he went missing were reported as, "He is flying back to India for some urgent work." He had kept the information private.

At 5 p.m., at Arya's funeral, Uncle Krishna told Mike Mahi that Mahi's scholarship at college, covering hostel expenses and study fees, had been from the Tejas Arya Foundation.

"What?" The news shocked Mahi as much as Tejas's death. "But Coach Mukherjee told me I was the recipient of the TA scholarship."

"Well, TA stands for Tejas Arya."

Some 100 feet away, Tanya was talking to Jia Sharma. Mahi hadn't seen her until now. With a lump in his throat, he walked up to her. The stunning lady had aged overnight. Putting an arm around her shoulders, he said, "I have always liked Tejas. Circumstances, and my nature, never allowed me to show those emotions."

"I know."

"He never told me about his condition. Not that I could have helped much." Ouch! Tanya squeezed Mahi's shoulder hard to silence him.

At 6 p.m., Uncle Krishna told Mike Mahi that his recruitment to Hunt & Smith had been due in large part to a glowing recommendation from Shakti Arya, the powerful CEO of Coca Cola India. Mahi's mind had gone blank for a few seconds before it dawned on him that Shakti Arya was Tejas Arya's dad. The corporate honcho, himself a St. Anne's alumnus, was amongst the crowd watching Mahi's tantalizing hockey during the match between the alumni and the college students.

Over dinner, Uncle Krishna told Mike Mahi that Dr. D'Souza had been a long time family friend of the Aryas, and when he was looking for an auditor, Tejas recommended Mahi.

Tejas 10: Mahi 8

As he retired to bed, Uncle Krishna delivered the coup-de-grace. When the Finance Minister had asked Tejas Arya about Mike Mahi in the context of the government accounts, Arya had told him they couldn't have zeroed in on a better man.

Tejas 11: Mahi 8

And moments before the advocate dozed off, he told Mahi that it was Tejas Arya who had convinced Dr. Saurav Moraes not to contest the presidential election, suggesting that if he did, news not personally palatable to Moraes may get aired on television.

Tejas 12: Mahi 8

Mahi had always believed that life had been infinitely fairer to Tejas than it had been to him. He had once told Tanya, "Tejas raced up the escalator, I had to walk up the staircase on crutches."

Everything looked so different today. For the first time in his life Mike Mahi no longer felt that he was a young man. Something inside him had died.

54. A Matter of Ethics

A little boy was standing in front of the cash counter in a bookstore. Behind him stood Mike Mahi. That day, the computer system in the store had crashed and so invoices had to be made manually. The boy had picked a number of books and Mahi helped him place them on the billing counter.

The billing officer made out the invoice and handed it over to the boy.

The boy took one look at the paper and said, "Uncle, I think you have billed me one book short. I bought eleven books; you have billed me for only ten. I think *Summer Term at St. Clare's has not been billed*."

Mike Mahi watched the scene with interest.

The cashier took the books from the boy, counted them, then recounted them, and finally revised the invoice. The amount read Rs 1,570.

The boy took one look at the invoice and said, "Uncle, the invoice should read Rs 1,730, it reads Rs 1,570,". He didn't need a calculator.

Mahi's heart was pounding.

The surprised officer checked the books and then the invoice and then the books again. "Oh, so sorry. Thank you. I will correct it." He made out another invoice, destroying the old one.

The boy gave him Rs 2,000 and the man returned Rs 370. Mahi wondered what the kid would do next.

Turning to the cashier the boy said, "Uncle, I think you have paid me Rs 100 extra." So saying he handed over a hundred-rupee note. The cashier looked at him in shock and awe. "Oh. Thank you. Thank you." He then added, "You are such a sweet kid. Have this extra book."

Even as Mahi wondered which book the kid would choose, he heard him saying, "Oh, no, no. My mother asked me to buy six books. I have already bought ten. I cannot buy another. She will kill me."

"But this eleventh book is free. It's my gift to you," said the officer.

The boy gave him a big smile. "Oh I haven't done anything special," and asked with a childlike innocence, "have I?"

The cashier was speechless.

Mike Mahi's skin had goose pimples. Tapping the boy, he asked, "Have you come alone?"

"No, uncle. My grandpa is in the next shop."

"And what's your name?"

"Nikhil."

He escorted Nikhil to the door. "Nikhil, what game do you play?"

"Cricket."

"Batsman or bowler?"

"All-rounder."

"What's your highest score?"

"Hmmm…105. But actually 45."

"What do you mean?"

"You see, in one match I scored 105 but I was out when I was 45. I nicked the ball and the keeper took the catch. The umpire was quiet and I continued playing."

"Then what happened?"

"I told my mother about it. She said, 'When you remember your century you will remember not your century but your dishonesty. Never do that again!'"

"What's your mom's name Nikhil?"

"Jia Sharma."

To be doubly sure, Mahi asked, "And your dad's name?"

"Tejas Arya."

Mike Mahi couldn't sleep that night. A little boy had opened his eyes.

ooo

The following morning, as rains lashed the city, Mahi flipped through the newspaper sipping masala tea. His eyes scrolled through until he found this story.

A farmer under thirty-five years of age, who had debts worth Rs 20,000, had committed suicide because he could not settle the EMI. There was a long story about how he had borrowed at usurious rates, how his life had been reduced to shambles, how a young wife had aged beyond her years, how the little boys went to a corporation school that didn't have basic amenities and how the farmer, finally unable to bear the ruin and dishonor, took the step to end it all.

He took another sip and his eyes caught another report.

A businessman in his forties, who owed Rs 100 crore to a nationalized bank, had reinvented himself. He and his aggressive young wife were fighting a battle in the court against the bank. His sons continued their studies in a residential school located in a hill station, and the man had come to grips with life.

Where does that place a CA, practicing or in employment? Does he respond like the farmer or like the businessman?

How often have accounting firms acted as middlemen between the clients and the arms of government? How often had some padded numbers? His own firm had suggested a client settle with a Tax Officer rather than go up on Appeal despite having a strong case. The argument was that legal fees and other costs would be greater than the refund amount. How often were all-expense paid trips given out in return for favors? How often did manufacturers and service providers advertise knowing fully well that the advertisement was misleading? How did children like Nikhil, clearly knowing right from wrong, grow up and begin rationalizing all this?

Mahi couldn't focus much that day.

55. The Merger

In the end, it was a presentation by a B-School lad that made Mike Mahi think the unthinkable and do the undoable.

He had been invited to be on the jury of *Just an Idea* at Fiesta, the International Inter B-School Cultural Festival. Hosted by Global School of Management (GSM), it was the one place where management graduates from across the globe battled it out. Harvard, Stanford and Kellogs, you name it, and they were there.. Some came from engineering backgrounds and some were accounting professionals.

Had circumstances been different, Mike Mahi would have refused. But today, he needed every inch of good press. An invitation from GSM boosted Mahi's confidence that was going downhill at the moment.

Just an Idea was a contest where the prize would go to the speaker who presented the best un-implementable idea! The idea had to be smart and yet, for whatever reasons, un-implementable.

The e-mail to Mahi read, "You may get to hear some of the most outstanding ideas that are far ahead of time." Legend had it that the concept of the mobile phone had originated here many decades ago. They had called it SNOW (Single Number World Over). Mahi wasn't sure what he would gain from hearing wildcard ideas, but there was no harm in taking a chance.

More importantly, the break would do him good.

All sorts of ideas cropped up. Some were insanely loony. A lady talked about "Seating a man on the Sun." A young lad spoke of a Committee of Workers running a factory. Mahi yawned. Another one of the clean- cropped, blazer-wearing students asked, "How would it be if Coke and Pepsi merged first in India and later globally?" Mike Mahi almost leapt out of his chair.

The clean-cropped guy proceeded to answer his own question, looking quite pleased with himself. "If nothing else, their ad budgets would come down by half." With characteristic managerial ease, he went on to supply the numbers. "Suppose the two annually save Rs 1,000 crore because of the merger. Suppose this figure rises annually by five percent, courtesy inflation. Further, suppose the time value of money is fifteen percent. In that case, the value of the merger would be Rs 10,000 crore."

There were too many suppositions, but Mahi's mind was racing.

The second judge said, "But the customer will lose. The merger will kill competition, as the duo would have captured the whole market. How do you think this is good for the customer?"

Clean-Cropped had come well prepared. "That's precisely the point. It may create a monopoly, but it will not necessarily bring in the evils of monopoly. Overwhelming volumes will bring about economies of scale and drive the price down. It would help in staying motivated when you are the market."

The third judge asked, "Why aren't they merging? Surely, you aren't the only one with the smart idea?"

"Simple. Because there is no guarantee that they would click. Remember, all these years the two companies had referred to each other as 'Us' and 'Them'. It's not easy to suddenly become friends even when the monetary rewards are enormous."

Mahi remembered a story his client had told him about the antagonism between Coke and Pepsi. If a Coke employee were found sipping Pepsi anywhere in the world, he would be sacked, pronto. The hate was mutual.

The lad was giving the same example. "Under such 'mutual hostility, bruised sentiments and wild ego trips' there would be no meeting of minds."

"How do you know that?" asked the judge.

"My Dad is President, India Operations, PepsiCo."

A small idea was beginning to form in Mahi's mind. It was as outlandish as the merger between Coke and Pepsi and as impossible as the unification of India and Pakistan.

He remembered reading somewhere, "Every revolution was once a thought in one man's mind." He wasn't too sure whether it would work. First he had to convince himself. Then he would have to convince others.

Despite the fact that he was the founder, principal owner and force driver, it wouldn't be easy to achieve a merger between Hunt & Smith and Mike, Mahi & Associates; between the world's number two accounting firm and India's number seven. These were two firms who, on Indian soil at least, competed like hungry dogs for bones.

Everyone was likely to benefit. Hunt & Smith would straight away become global number one. Mike, Mahi & Associates would spin into a different orbit. The leap from number seven in India to number 1 globally would otherwise take ages, if it happened at all. This would immediately pitch Mahi to the global center stage. There was the flip side. Could he call the outfit his own? Would he be flying with borrowed feathers? Would it amount to selling his mother?

Mahi was too shrewd not to know that he might have to leave within a few years, if the merger did come about. It was probably possible to carve out a separate space for him, but history wasn't on his side. Merger and takeover history was replete with examples of how the original promoter always had to leave. Sabeer Bhatia of Hotmail and Raman Roy of Spectramind blinked on his mental radar.

The heart of the problem would be the contrasting working style and personality of the two organizations. Mahi was a hard taskmaster, but at the personal level he was incredibly warm. He never wore the warmth on his sleeve, but anyone who closely interacted with him knew it. He met everyone who joined the firm within three months of joining, be it an Associate Director or an Office Assistant. His firm had a generous mix of committed performers who shared the firm's values and star performers who put self before others.

Every organization had a mix of these types. At Mike Mahi, the ratio was 2:1. At the Big Six he believed it was 1:2.

Two, Mahi had instilled a few values in his firm. There was no bureaucracy, no hierarchy. Command and control was taboo. It was surprising in a firm of its size. It also had a flat structure, flexible designations, flexible working hours and flexible holidays. In contrast, at the Big Six, an employee had to wade through myriad layers before becoming a partner. The structure was important. Designations were pre-fixed and there were no compromises with them.

Three, at Mike Mahi, execution was swift with no protocol, no lengthy meetings and no bulky minutes. Detail and documentation were important, but results counted. They worked at the speed of the leopard. No certification ever took more than forty-eight hours to execute. This had little to do with the size of the firm. It had more to do with the culture.

This contrasting culture was something Mike Mahi had to ponder over before he could be 100 percent sure that it would work!

Four, his understanding of competition turned conventional wisdom on its head. He never wanted competition to end up in conflict. He would always say, "The purpose of the competition is not to kill the opponent." He often gave the example of car manufacture. "To make a car you need hundreds of components produced by thousands of firms. Without their help and support it just can't come off the assembly line."

He wasn't very sure whether the Big Six worked that way.

Five, Mike Mahi was a Warren Buffet acolyte. There were a lot of similarities. Buffet lived in the same house that he had bought fifty years ago. Mahi continued to live out of a 1400 square feet apartment. In 2006, Buffet took home an annual salary that was much less than what an HBS fresher would draw. Mahi's own salary was well below what other partners drew. The investment guru never interfered with a business's day-to-day affairs whenever he bought a controlling interest. Ditto with Mahi. He listed down the KRA and the compensation package of the principal executive and then gave them a free hand to run the business.

He wasn't sure if the Big Six would work that way.

Suddenly an even more loony idea struck him. Was it impossible?

After all, didn't a 55-year-old man gobble up a global major? He remembered, "In the monsoons he had walked through waist-high water to school because he didn't have enough money for a rickshaw," Tejas Arya had written about it. L N Mittal had taken over Arcelor, the world's number one steel company, and to Mike Mahi that story represented the arrival of India in the global M&A marketplace. Merger and Acquisition now stand for Mittal & Arcelor, he had told everyone within earshot!

Hadn't an iconic Indian businessman in his seventies taken over the British steel maker Corus to make Tata Steel a global powerhouse ? What excited him most was that, in true Tata style, the acquired company would run under its original name.

Just an Idea was coming to a close. Mahi had been in his own world for most of the debate. He was sure he had seen the winner. In a way, the idea wasn't preposterous and so was not eligible to win, but it had activated a train of thought in Mahi!

Clean-Cropped walked up to receive the prize from Mike Mahi. Mahi nearly dropped the prize when Clean-Cropped said, "I actually wanted to talk about the takeover of Hunt & Smith by Mike Mahi & Associates. But seeing you there on the jury I changed the script because I felt that you would think I am having a joke at your expense."

Mahi smiled. The idea had been seeded.

56. A View of Tomorrow

Dateline: Dec 31, 2020

Country: India.

Up there in the Victoria Hills is the seat of the world's foremost accounting firm – Hunt, Smith & Mike Mahi (HSMM). The queer comma between Mike and Mahi was gone. Now a multi-faceted, multi-disciplinary firm, it is at the cutting edge of knowledge. An apex body consisting of a star-studded board of trustees handles laying down the broad direction for the clutch of activities that it now has under its belt. These activities operate from a sprawling campus on the outskirts of India's key metropolis and the capitals of various states.

An apex body, an eight-member Board of Trustees -- consisting among others, a financial expert, a human resource star, a marketing czar, a management consultant, and a knowledge-dissemination specialist -- oversee the overall operations HSMM hasn't lost any of its old brand: it continues to be flexible enough to adjust quickly to changing market conditions, innovative enough to keep its products and services fresh, and dedicated enough to deliver maximum quality and customer service. It's a place that won't dwindle away in a hurry.

ooo

It is now a world full of opportunities.

Mike Mahi stepped into his office for the first time in months. It was buzzing with activity. He saw employees meeting clients, discussing laws, on calls, walking around, and sipping coffee. All these days he had kept in touch with his offices via phone and the mail.

His first assignment, back in the mid 1990s, had been done for the princely sum of Rs 40,000 per annum. Today, in the 21st

century, his firm wouldn't touch an assignment that wouldn't fetch less than Rs 500,000. Those that offered less were outsourced.

Today, his firm specialized in auditing, consulting, corporate finance, legal, research, information technology, international taxation, M&A advisory, BPO, fraud detection and corporate legal – each headed by a partner. Chartered accountants, MBAs, Engineers, and lawyers worked with him.

It has a global presence with offices in Sri Lanka, the Middle East, the Far East, Europe, Australia, USA and UK. House to over 30,000 trainees, 8,000 professionals, 2,500 non-professionals, 1;000 partners and an annual turnover of Rs 20,000 crore, HSMM is the most modern, most state of the art knowledge center of its kind.

From a humble beginning, Mike Mahi had finally, truly gone global! In the next one year he would formally walk into the sunset and begin a second innings elsewhere. Tanya Roy continued to be friends with Jia Sharma. .

Mike Mahi missed Tejas Arya.

THE END